McNALLY'S SECRET

McNALLY'S SECRET

LAWRENCE SANDERS

G. P. PUTNAM'S SONS
New York

G. P. Putnam's Sons
Publishers Since 1838
200 Madison Avenue
New York, NY 10016

Library of Congress Cataloging-in-Publication Data

Sanders, Lawrence, date
McNally's secret / Lawrence Sanders.
p.   cm.
ISBN 0–399–13675–4
I. Title.
PS3569.A5125M37 1992   91–9803CIP
813′.54——dc20

Printed in the United States of America
1   2   3   4   5   6   7   8   9   10

McNALLY'S SECRET

1

I poured a few drops of an '87 Mondavi Chardonnay into her navel and leaned down to slurp it out.

Jennifer's eyes closed and she purred. "Do you like that?" she breathed.

"Of course," I said. "Eighty-seven was an excellent year."

Her eyes popped open. "Stinker," she said. "Can't you ever be serious?"

"No," I said, "I cannot."

That, at least, was the truth. In my going-on thirty-seven years I had lived through dire warnings of nuclear catastrophe, global warming, ozone depletion, universal extinction via cholesterol, and the invasion of killer bees.

After a while my juices stopped their panicky surge and I realized I was bored with all these screeched predictions of Armageddon due next Tuesday. It hadn't happened yet, had it? The old world tottered along, and I was content to totter along with it. I am an amiable, sunnily tempered chap (and something of an ass, my father would undoubtedly add), and I see no need to concern myself with disasters that may never happen. The world is filled with kvetchers, and I have no desire to join the club.

I could have explained all this to Jennifer, but didn't. She might think I was serious about it, and I wasn't. I mean I wasn't even serious about not being serious, if you follow me.

So I took up where I had left off, and the next hour was a larky interlude of laughs and high-intensity moans. This was the first time we had bedded and, though I cannot speak for the lady, I know I was delighted; it was one of those rare sexual romps when realization exceeds expectation.

Part of my joy was due to pleased surprise. Jennifer Towley was almost as tall as I, and had impressed me as being a rather reserved, elegant, somewhat austere lady who dressed smartly but usually in black—and this is South Florida, where *everyone* favored pastels.

That was the clothed Jennifer. Stripped to the tawny buff and devoid of her gray contact lenses, she metamorphosed into an entirely different woman. What a jolly lady she turned out to be! Enthusiastic. Cooperative. Acrobatic. I felt a momentary pang of how I was deceiving her. But it was momentary.

Later, a bit after midnight, I regretfully dragged myself from her warm embrace and dressed. She rose and donned an enormous white terry robe that bore the crest of a Monte Carlo hotel.

"Thank you for a super evening," I said politely.

"The dinner was splendid," she said. "And the dessert even better. But wait; I have a gift for you."

I felt a perfect cad. Here I was deluding the poor girl, and she was about to give me a present. Perhaps a gold lighter or cashmere pullover—something expensive she could ill afford. I was shattered by shame.

But she brought me a packet of letters tied with a bit of ribbon. She had replaced her contacts, and gave me the full force of a direct, chilling stare. I glanced at the letters and knew immediately what they were: the reason for my duplicity.

"I believe these may be what you want," she said sternly.

I looked at her. "How long have you known?" I asked.

"I suspected you from the start," she said. "I don't ordinarily attract the attention of handsome, charming men my own age. Most of them are looking for teen-aged centerfolds. And then you claimed to be a tennis pro. Your game is good, but not *that* good. So tonight, while you were in the john, I went through your wallet."

"You didn't!"

"I did," she said firmly. "And discovered you are Archibald McNally, attorney-at-law."

"Not so," I said, shaking my head. "If you examine my business card closely, you'll see it says McNally and Son, Attorney-at-Law, not Attorneys-at-Law. Singular, not plural. My father, Prescott McNally, is the lawyer. I am not."

"Then what *are* you?"

"I am the Son, in charge of a department called Discreet Inquiries. It consists of me."

"But why *aren't* you an attorney?" she persisted.

11

"Because I was expelled from Yale Law for not being serious enough. During a concert by the New York Philharmonic I streaked across the stage, naked except for a Richard M. Nixon mask."

Then she laughed, and I knew everything was going to be all right.

"If you had asked for the letters at the beginning," she said, "I would have been happy to hand them over. The man is obviously demented. But I had no idea what your game was, and I was curious."

I sighed. "Our client, Clarence T. Frobisher, is a nice old gentleman, but not buttoned-up too tightly, as you've noticed. How did you meet him?"

"At a charity benefit. He seemed harmless enough. A bit vague perhaps, but nothing to scare a girl out of her wits. When I found out he was loaded, I thought of him as a potential customer for my antiques. We had a few dinners together—nothing more—and then I began to get these incredible letters from him. He loved me passionately, wanted to marry me, would give me as much money as I wanted if only I would let him nibble my beautiful pink toes. My toes may or may not be beautiful—that's in the eye of the beholder—but they are certainly not pink, as you well know."

I nodded. "Mr. Frobisher has a thing for toes. I must tell you, Jennifer, this is not the first time he has written to women much younger than he, offering to buy, or rent, their toes. In three other cases we have bought back his letters to prevent his being sued or exposed to publicity that would make him the giggle of Palm Beach. It is a pleasant shock to have one of his toe targets return his letters voluntarily. I thank you."

She looked at me thoughtfully. "If I hadn't given you the letters, or sold them back to you, would you have stolen them?"

"Probably," I said. "Now there is one final matter to discuss."

"Oh? And what might that be?"

"When may I see you again?" I asked.

Once more that cool, level gaze was aimed at me.

"I'll think about it," she said.

I drove home in my red Mazda Miata, one of the first in South Florida. As I headed eastward, I whistled the opening bars of Beethoven's Fifth. Or perhaps it was "Tiptoe Thru the Tulips." I wasn't sure and didn't much care. I was puffed with satisfaction: a job accomplished, a fine dinner and, most important, I had been intimate with a splendid woman.

I will not say I was smitten; that would be a bit much. My devotion to triviality as a way of life had taught me to automatically suspect and shun strong feelings. But still, I was intrigued by Ms. Jennifer Towley, no doubt about it. I wanted to see her again. Dine with her again. And then, I confess, the thought occurred to me that Clarence T. Frobisher may have had a perfectly reasonable and understandable fantasy. Forgive me.

We lived on A1A, right across the road from the Atlantic Ocean. Our manse was quite different from neighboring homes. They were mostly two-floor faux Spanish haciendas with red tile roofs; ours was a three-story faux

Tudor with mullioned windows and a leaky copper mansard roof.

It was no Mar-a-Lago, but we had five bedrooms, which were sufficient to accommodate the annual visit of my married sister from Tucson with her family. In addition, our five acres included a two-story, three-car garage. Our houseman and cook-housekeeper, a married couple of Scandinavian origin, occupied an apartment on the upper floor.

There was a small greenhouse where my mother cultivated six million varieties of begonias—or so it seemed. There was also a formal garden, a potting shed, a Victorian-styled gazebo, and a doghouse that had once sheltered our golden retriever. He had gone to the Great Kennel in the Sky, but his home remained.

There was no swimming pool.

Actually, I thought the McNally estate was rather pukka. The main building was boxy with awkward lines, but ivy covers a multitude of sins. The entire place projected moneyed ease—costly comfort without flash. The weathered buildings and ample grounds bespoke old family and old wealth. It was all a stage set, of course, but only I knew that.

I parked the Miata between my father's black Lexus LS-400 and my mother's old wood-bodied Ford station wagon. There were no lights burning in the servants' quarters and none on the upper floors of the main house. But the portico lamp was on, and I caught slivers of light coming from between the drawn drapes of my father's first-floor study.

I went directly there. The heavy oaken door was ajar,

and when I peeked in, I saw him comfortably ensconced in his favorite leather club chair, a port decanter and glass at his elbow. He was reading from a leather-bound volume, and I'd have bet it was Dickens. For years he had been digging through the entire oeuvre, and at the rate he was going, he'd be a Dear Departed before he got to *Bleak House.*

He looked up when I entered. "Good evening, Archy."

"Evening, father," I said, and tossed the tied packet onto his desk. "The Frobisher letters," I explained.

"Excellent," he said. "How much did they cost?"

"A dinner at Cafe L'Europe. The lady handed them over voluntarily. No charge."

"She *is* a lady," he said. "Will she accept a small gift in gratitude?"

"I suspect she will," I said. "She's a tennis nut, but her racquet looks like an old banjo. I think a new Spalding graphite would be appreciated."

He nodded. "Take care of it. You look bushed. A port?"

"Thank you, sir," I said gratefully, and poured myself a generous tot in a glass that matched his.

"Better sit down," he advised. "I have a new assignment for you, and it'll take some telling."

"It can't wait until tomorrow?"

"No," he said shortly, "it can't. It's not something I care to discuss in the office."

So I lounged limply in an armchair and crossed my legs. He cast a baleful look at my lavender socks but made no comment. He'd never persuade me to emulate him by wearing knee-high hose of black wool, wingtip brogues, and a vested suit of gray tropical worsted.

He sat a few moments in silence, and I knew he was considering what to say and how to say it. My father *always* thought long and carefully before speaking. It was a habit I was used to, but I can tell you it sometimes caused awkward moments with clients and acquaintances who feared the old man was woolgathering or had gone daft.

"Lady Cynthia Horowitz came to the office this evening," he said. "After you left."

"Good Lord!" I said. "Don't tell me the old bird is changing her will again?"

"Not today," he said with a faint smile. "She had something more urgent to discuss. She wouldn't come upstairs—because of the air conditioning, you know—so I had to go downstairs and sit in that antique Rolls of hers. Roomy enough, but stifling. She made her chauffeur take a stroll while we conferred in private. She was quite upset."

"And what's bothering her now?"

My father sighed and took a small sip of his port. "She alleges that an important part of her estate has vanished."

"Oh? Lost, strayed, or stolen?"

"She believes it was stolen. It was kept in a wall safe in her bedroom. It is no longer there."

"What exactly is it?"

"A block of four U.S. postage stamps."

I was amused. "And this was an important part of her estate?"

My father looked at me thoughtfully. "A similar block of four was recently auctioned at Christie's in New York for one million dollars."

I hastily took a gulp of wine. "Then I gather they're not the type of stamps one sticks on a letter to the IRS."

"Hardly. They are part of a sheet of one hundred 24-cent airmail stamps issued in 1918. The stamps are red with a blue biplane framed in the center. Due to a printing error, the plane was reproduced upside down on this particular sheet. Since the biplane pictured was popularly known as the Jenny, the misprinted stamp is famous in philatelic circles as the Inverted Jenny. Why are you laughing?"

"The lady I dined with tonight," I said, "the one who surrendered the Frobisher letters—apparently you don't recall, father, but her name is Jennifer Towley. I suppose some people might address her as Jenny."

He raised one eyebrow—a trick I've never been able to master. "And was she inverted?" he asked. Then, apparently fearing he had posed an imprudent question, he hurriedly continued: "In any event, Lady Horowitz doesn't wish to take the problem to the police."

I stared at him. "She thinks someone in her household might have snaffled the stamps?"

"I didn't ask her. That's your job."

"Why on earth didn't she keep them in her bank's vault? That's where she stores her furs in the summer."

"She kept them at home," my father explained patiently, "for the same reason she keeps her jewelry there. She enjoys wearing her diamonds, and she enjoyed showing the misprinted stamps to guests."

I groaned. "So everyone in Palm Beach knew she owned a block of Inverted Jennies?"

"Perhaps not *everyone,* but a great number of people certainly."

"Were they insured?"

"For a half-million. She has not yet filed a claim, hoping the stamps may be recovered. Since she desires no publicity whatsoever, this is obviously a task for the Discreet Inquiries Department. Archy, please get started on it tomorrow morning. Or rather, this morning."

I nodded.

"I suggest," he went on, "you begin by interviewing Lady Horowitz. She'll be able to provide more details of the purported theft."

"I'm not looking forward to that meeting," I said, and finished my port. "You know what people call her, don't you? Lady Horrorwitz."

My father gave me a wintry smile. "Few of us are what we seem," he said. "If we were, what a dull world this would be."

He went back to his Dickens, and I climbed the stairs to my third-floor suite: bedroom, sitting room, dressing room, bathroom. Smallish but snug. I showered, pulled on a pongee robe, and lighted a cigarette, only my third of the past twenty-four hours, for which I felt suitably virtuous.

I'm a rather scatterbrained bloke, and shortly after I joined my father's law firm and was given the responsibility for Discreet Inquiries, I thought it wise to start a private journal in which I might keep notes. That way, you see, I wouldn't forget items that, seemingly unimportant, might later prove significant. I tried to make daily entries, but on that particular night I merely sat staring at my diary and thinking of my father's comment: "Few of us are what we seem." That was certainly true of Prescott McNally.

My father's father, Frederick McNally, was not, as many believed, a wealthy member of the British landed gentry. Instead, *mirabile dictu,* my grandfather had been a gapping-trousered, bulb-nosed burlesque comic, billed on the Minsky circuit as Ready Freddy McNally. He never achieved stardom, but his skill with dialects and his raunchy trademark laugh, "Ah-oo-gah!", had earned him the reputation of being the funniest second banana in burley-cue.

In addition to his dexterity with pratfalls and seltzer bottles, plus his ability to leap like a startled gazelle when goosed onstage, Ready Freddy turned out to be a remarkably astute investor in real estate. During the Florida land boom of the 1920s, my grandfather purchased beachfront property (wonderfully inexpensive in those days) and lots bordering the canal that later became the Intracoastal Waterway.

By the time he retired from the world of greasepaint, he was moderately well-to-do, rich enough certainly to purchase a home in Miami and send his son, my father, off to Yale University to become a gentleman and eventually an attorney-at-law.

Shortly after Ready Freddy made his final exit, my paternal grandmother, a former showgirl, also passed from the stage. Whereupon my father sold the Miami home (at a handsome profit) and moved his family to Palm Beach.

He had been admitted to the Florida bar and knew exactly how he wanted to live. Had known, as a matter of fact, since his first days as a Yale undergraduate.

The world my father envisioned—and this was years before Ralph Lauren created a fashion empire from the same dream—was one of manor homes, croquet, polo, neatly trimmed gardens, a wine cellar, lots of chintz, worn leather and brass everywhere, silver-framed photographs of family members, and cucumber sandwiches at tea.

That was the life he deliberately and painstakingly created for himself and his family in Palm Beach. He was Lord of the Manor, and if this necessitated buying an antique marble fireplace and mantel from a London dealer and having it crated and shipped to Florida at horrendous expense, so be it. He believed in his dream, and he realized it beautifully and completely. Gentility? It was coming out our ears.

That made me not merely a son but a scion. (Lords of the Manor had heirs or scions.) And if I recognized my father's spurious life-style at an early age, that didn't prevent me from taking full advantage of the perks it offered.

I recalled a conversation with comrades at Yale Law before I was booted out. We were discussing how sons often followed in the footsteps of their fathers, not only adopting pop's vocation, but frequently his habits, hobbies, and vices.

"The apple never falls far from the tree," someone remarked sententiously.

To which someone else added, "And the turd never falls far from the bird."

I didn't wish to brood too deeply on how that latter aphorism might apply to me. But I want you to know that I was aware of what I considered my father's masquerade. And although I might regard it with lofty scorn, I was willing to profit from it. Perhaps I was as much an actor as my father.

I put all these heavy ruminations in a mental deep six and resolutely turned to making suitable entries in my daily journal. To accomplish this, I was forced to don reading glasses. Yes, at the tender age of thirty-six-plus, the peepers had shown evidence of bagging at the knees, and I needed the horn-rimmed cheaters for close-up work. Naturally I never wore them in public. One doesn't wish to wobble about resembling a nuclear physicist, does one?

I made notes regarding the recovery of the Clarence T. Frobisher letters. Then I jotted down what little I had learned from my father regarding the claimed theft of the Inverted Jenny stamps from the wall safe in the bedroom of Lady Cynthia Horowitz. I scrawled a reminder to phone Horowitz and set up an early appointment.

Then, staring at my diary, I made a final note that amazed me. It read as follows:

"Jennifer Towley!!!"

2

I overslept and by the time I trooped downstairs my father had already left for the office (we usually drove in together), and my mother was pottering about in the potting shed, which seemed logical. I learned all this from Olson, our houseman, who was seated in the kitchen smoking a pipe and working on a mug of black coffee to which he may or may not have added a dram of aquavit. He also told me his wife, Ursi, had taken the station wagon to seek fresh grouper for our dinner that night.

You would think, wouldn't you, that a man with the red corpuscles of the Vikings dancing through his veins would have a given name of Lars or Sven. But Olson's first name was Jamie, and it was not a diminutive of James; it was just Jamie. He was a wrinkled codger, about my father's age, and he and his wife had been with us as long as I could remember. They were childless and both seemed content to go on working at the Chez McNally for as long as they could get out of bed in the morning.

"Eggs?" he asked.

I shook my head. "Rye toast and coffee. I'm dieting."

He set to work in that slow, deliberate way of his. Both the Olsons were good chefs—good, not great—but neither would ever qualify for a fast-food joint. They didn't dawdle, they were just unbrisk.

"Jamie," I said, "do you know Kenneth? He drives for Lady Horowitz."

"I know him."

"What's his last name?"

"Bodin."

"What kind of a guy is he?"

"Big."

I sighed. Getting information from Olson isn't difficult, but it takes time.

"How long has he been with Horowitz—do you know?"

He paused a moment to think. "Mebbe five, six years."

"That sounds about right," I said. "A few years ago there was talk going around that he was more than just her chauffeur. You hear anything about that?"

"Uh-huh," Jamie said. He brought my breakfast and poured himself more coffee.

"You think there was anything to it?" I persisted.

"Mebbe *was*," he said. "Then. Not now."

His taciturnity didn't fool me; he enjoyed gossip as much as I did.

You must understand that Palm Beach is a gossiper's paradise. It is, in fact, the Gossip Capital of the World. In

Palm Beach everyone gossips eagerly and constantly. I mean we *relish* it.

"Is this Kenneth Bodin married?" I pressed on, slathering my toast with the mango jelly Jamie had thoughtfully set out.

"Nope."

"Girlfriend?"

"Mebbe."

"Anyone I might know?"

He slowly removed his cold pipe from his dentures and regarded me gravely. "She gives massages," he said.

"No kidding?" I said, interested. "Well, at the moment I'm not acquainted with any masseuses. She work in West Palm Beach?"

"Did," Olson said. "Till the cops closed her down."

"And what is she doing now?"

He was still staring at me. "This and that," he said.

"All right," I said hurriedly, "I get the picture. Ask around, will you, and see if you can find out her name and address."

He nodded.

I finished my breakfast and went into my father's study to use his directory and phone. The old man puts covers on his telephone directories. Other people do that, of course, but most use clear plastic. My father bound his directories in genuine leather. I mention this merely to illustrate how meticulous he was in his pursuit of gentility.

I looked up the number of Lady Cynthia Horowitz and dialed. Got the housekeeper, identified myself, and asked to speak to the mistress. Instead, as I knew would happen,

I was shunted to Consuela Garcia. She was Lady Cynthia's social secretary and general factotum.

I knew Consuela, who had come over from Havana during the Mariel boatlift. A few years previously she and I had a mad, passionate romance that lasted all of three weeks. Then she discovered that when it comes to wedding bells I am tone-deaf, and she gave me the broom. Fair enough. But we were still friends, I thought, although now when we met at parties and dances, we shook hands instead of sharing a smooch.

"Archy," she said, "how nice to hear from you."

"How are you, Connie?"

"Very well, thank you."

"I saw you out at Wellington last Saturday," I told her. "That was a very handsome lad you were with. Is he new?"

"Not really," she said, laughing. "He's been used. What can I do for you, Archy?"

"An audience with Lady C. Half-hour, an hour at the most."

"What's it about?"

"Charity subscription," I said, not knowing if Horowitz had told her of the disappearance of the Inverted Jennies. "We've simply *got* to do something to save the hard-nosed gerbils."

"The *what?*"

"Hard-nosed gerbils. Delightful little beasties, but they're dwindling, Connie, definitely dwindling."

"I don't know," she said doubtfully. "Everyone's been hitting on her lately to help save something or other."

"Give it a try," I urged.

She came back on the phone a few moments later. "If you can come over immediately," she said, sounding surprised, "Lady Cynthia will see you."

"Thank you, Connie," I said humbly. I can do humble.

The Miata is not a car whose door you open to enter. As with the old MG, you vault into the driver's seat as if you were mounting a charger. So I vaulted and headed northward on A1A. Lady Horowitz's estate was just up the road a piece, as they say in Florida, and traffic was mercifully light, so I could let my charger gallop.

As I drove I mentally reviewed what I knew about the woman I was about to interview.

Her full name was Lady Cynthia Kirschner Gomez Stanescu Smythe DuPey Horowitz. If she was not a clear winner in the Palm Beach marital sweepstakes, she was certainly one of the contenders. Around her swimming pool, in addition to Old Glory, she flew the six flags of her ex-husbands' native lands. Everyone said it was a sweet touch; the divorce settlements had left her a very wealthy woman indeed.

She had won her title from her last husband, Leopold Horowitz, who had been knighted for a lifetime of research on the mating habits of flying beetles. Unfortunately, a year after being honored, he had fallen to his death from a very tall tree in the Amazon while trying to net a pair of the elusive critters *in flagrante delicto.* His bereaved widow immediately flew to Paris to purchase a black dress (with pouffe) from Christian Lacroix.

Long before I met Lady Cynthia I had heard many people speak of her as a "great beauty." But when I was finally introduced, it was difficult to conceal my shock. It would be ungentlemanly to call a woman ugly. I shall say only that I found her excessively plain.

While not a crone, exactly, she had a long nose with a droopy tip and a narrow chin that jutted upward. Drooping nose and jutting chin did not touch, of course, but I had this dream that you might clamp a silver dollar vertically between nose and chin tips and, by flicking it with your forefinger, set it a-twirling. I could not understand how old age could so ravage the features of a "great beauty."

"Why, she must be over eighty," I remarked to my father.

"Nonsense," he said, rather stiffly. "She's a year younger than I."

I still could not comprehend the "great beauty" legend or how she had been able to snare so many husbands. The mystery was solved when a national tabloid (published in nearby Lantana, incidentally) printed a sensationalized article on Lady Cynthia and her myriad marriages and extracurricular affairs. The article was, as they say, profusely illustrated, and it provided the reason for her allure.

She had been born Cynthia DiLuca in Chicago, daughter of a butcher, and even at an early age it was observed that she had a face that would stop a Timex. But to make up for this, she was blessed with a body so voluptuous that her first published nude photos made every geezer in the world snap his braces.

During the 1940s and 1950s she posed for many photographers and artists. Her face was usually turned away, masked in shadow, or concealed beneath a gauze scarf.

One photographer even went so far as to graft a more attractive feminine head onto Cynthia's body, but viewers weren't deceived; her figure was as unique, universally recognized, and dearly beloved as a Coca-Cola bottle. Even the immortal Picasso painted her portrait, converting her divine form into a stack of shingles that was much admired.

Now, at the age of seventy-plus, she apparently retained the body that had electrified the world fifty years ago. She also retained more spleen than anyone, woman or man, had a right to possess. Her temper tantrums were legendary. She was notorious for a long list of peeves that included cigars, dogs, and men who wore pinky rings. But tops on her roster of grievances were air conditioning and direct sunlight—which made it difficult to understand why she had decided to spend her remaining years in South Florida.

All in all, she had the reputation of being a nasty old lady, short-tempered and, when provoked, foul-mouthed. But she was tolerated, even treasured, by Palm Beach society as a genuine "character." Part of her popularity was due to her generosity. She held wondrous parties and galas, and few rejected her invitations, mostly because they knew that one of the things she found unacceptable was dining at other people's homes or in public restaurants, and her guests would not be expected to return her hospitality.

She had an excellent reason for reclusive dining: She employed the best French chef in South Florida.

Having said all this, I must also add that Lady Cynthia Horowitz had never treated the McNally Family with anything less than charming civility. My mother, father, and I had dined with her privately several times, and she couldn't have been a more gracious hostess and fascinating raconteuse over postprandial brandies. You figure it out.

Her home looked like an antebellum southern plantation: Tara transplanted to Florida's Gold Coast. The only anachronisms in this idyllic scene were the high wall of coral blocks topped with razor wire surrounding the estate and a large patio and swimming pool area at the rear of the main house.

It was to poolside that the black housekeeper conducted me, and I was happy to see the ex-husbands' flags snapping merrily in the breeze. Lady C. was reclining on a chaise lounge in the shade of an umbrella table. Not only was she lying in the shade, but she was swaddled in a voluminous white flannel robe, wore white socks to protect feet and ankles, and long white gloves to shield wrists and hands from that old devil sun. And, of course, she wore a wide-brimmed panama straw hat that provided even deeper shadow for her face and neck.

There were two phones, cordless and cellular, in view as I approached. Horowitz was using the cellular and waved me to a nearby canvas director's chair while she continued her conversation. I could not help but overhear.

"No, no, and no," she was saying wrathfully. "Just forget it. I don't want to hear another word about it. Listen, sweetie, if I thought it was humanly possible, I'd tell you to go fuck yourself. Am I coming through loud and clear?"

She hung up and glared angrily at me through green-tinted sunglasses. "Have you met Mercedes Blair?" she demanded.

"I don't believe I've had the pleasure," I said.

"Believe me, lad," she said bitterly, "it's no pleasure. That woman is one of the great bubbleheads of Palm Beach. The last time I was in Cairo, I bought this absolutely divine ivory dildo. After I got back I made the mistake of showing it to Mercedes, not knowing she's one of these save-the-elephant people. Well, she turned positively livid, and ever since she's been busting my chops. She wants me to throw it away! Can you imagine? I just can't get it through her tiny, tiny brain that the elephant croaked centuries ago. That ivory dildo is ancient Egyptian, a beautiful antique, and besides, it's quite useful. But she keeps insisting I get rid of it. I'll never speak to that stupe again as long as I live."

Years ago I had come to the conclusion that life is strange. I decided then that the only way to hang on to one's sanity with a sweaty grasp is to acknowledge the incomprehensibility of life. Accept all—and just nod knowingly.

So I listened to this tale of the ivory dildo, nodded knowingly, and made sympathetic noises. Lady Cynthia finished her tirade, leaned down to pick up a tumbler alongside her chaise. It contained what I guessed to be her first gin-and-bitters of the day. She took a sip and visibly relaxed.

"Want a drink, lad?" she asked pleasantly.

"Not at the moment, thank you."

"That jazz you gave Connie about the hard-nosed gerbils—that was all bullshit. Right?"

"Right," I said.

"And you want to ask about my missing stamps. Prescott said you'd be looking into it. Ask away."

"Who knows about the disappearance of the Inverted Jennies?"

"Me, your father, you."

"You haven't told Consuela or anyone else on your staff?"

She shook her head. "Maybe one of them pinched the stamps," she said darkly.

"Maybe," I said. "Let's see . . . in addition to Connie, you've got a butler, housekeeper, two maids, chef, and chauffeur. Right?"

"Wrong," she said. "The butler and one of the maids quit about two weeks ago. Claimed they couldn't stand the summer in Florida. Idiots!"

"So that leaves a staff of five," I said. "Anyone else staying in the house?"

"My son Harry Smythe and his wife, Doris. Also my son Alan DuPey and his bride, Felice. They've only been married a month. And my daughter, Gina Stanescu. Also Angus Wolfson, an old friend. He's down from Boston for a couple of weeks. He's gay—but so what?"

"A full house," I commented. "They were all here when the stamps disappeared?"

She nodded.

"Who knew the combination to the wall safe besides you?"

"No one. But that doesn't matter. I never locked it."

I looked at her and sighed. "I'll have that drink now,

please," I said, figuring the sun had to be over the yard-arm *some*where in the world.

"Of course. What?"

"Vodka and tonic will do me fine."

She used the cordless phone to call her kitchen and order up my drink.

"Lady Cynthia," I said, "why didn't you lock your wall safe?"

"I couldn't be bothered," she said. "That stupid combination—I kept forgetting it and had to rummage through my desk to find it. Besides, I trusted people."

I didn't make the obvious reply to that. We waited in silence until the housekeeper, Mrs. Marsden, a motherly type, brought my drink. It had a thick slice of fresh lime—just the way I like it.

After the housekeeper departed, I said, "I don't mean to get picky about this, but if you couldn't remember the combination to your safe, isn't it possible you forgot where you put the stamps?"

She shook her head. "They weren't just in an envelope or anything like that. They were between clear plastic pages in a little book about the size of a diary. A thin book bound in red leather specially made to hold the Inverted Jennies. It's not something you'd easily misplace. Also, I've torn the house apart looking for it. It's just gone."

"Would you object if I asked how you came into possession of those stamps in the first place?"

"No," she said, "I wouldn't object. Go ahead and ask."

I laughed. "Lady Cynthia, you're pulling my leg."

"I'd love to, lad," she said, leering like Groucho Marx,

"but people might talk. I received those silly upside-down stamps as part of my divorce settlement from my first husband, Max Kirschner. Dear old Max. He loved to wear my lingerie, but he really knew how to manage a bank. He bought the stamps in Trieste. I think he paid ten thousand American for the block of four. But of course that was years and years ago."

"Was he a stamp collector?"

"No, he just liked to own rare things. Like me."

I wasn't making great progress—perhaps because she seemed to be treating her loss so lightly. But that was her way—the dictum of haut monde: Never complain and never explain.

"All right," I said, "if the stamps weren't misplaced, let's assume they were nicked. Anyone in particular you suspect might have sticky fingers?"

The question troubled her. "I'd hate to think it was one of my staff. They've all been with me for years."

"But you said the butler and one of the maids quit. Was this before the stamps disappeared or after you became aware they were missing?"

She thought about that a moment. "No, the stamps were still here after the butler and maid left. I remember now: They quit, and the next day Alan DuPey showed up with his bride. Felice had never seen the stamps, so that night at dinner I brought them down to show her. Then, after dinner, I took them back upstairs and put them in the wall safe. That was the last time I saw them."

"Any signs around the house of a break-in? Jimmied doors or broken windows—anything like that?"

"No. And after the gate is locked at night, Mrs. Marsden always turns on the electronic alarm system."

"Are you certain she turns it on every night?"

"Absolutely. If it's not turned on by midnight, I get a phone call from the security agency to remind me."

"What do you do when you have a party that lasts until the wee small hours?"

"I always hire one or two guards for the occasion. Then, after everyone has gone home, the guards leave, the gate is locked, and the alarm activated."

"Very efficient," I observed, and looked into my half-empty glass. No clues there. "Okay, let's put aside the idea of a break-in or someone on your staff pinching the stamps. Now what about your houseguests?"

"Don't be silly," she snapped at me. "My God, lad, they're *family*. Except for Angus Wolfson, and I've known him for ages."

"Uh-huh," I said. "And are they all well-off?"

"Not one of them is hurting." She paused to finish her drink, then crunched the ice between her teeth. "But of course when it comes to money, enough is never enough—if you know what I mean."

I nodded. "Lady Cynthia, if you expect McNally and Son to make a complete investigation of this matter, you'll have to tell your staff and houseguests about the theft."

She stared at me, outraged. Then: "Shit! If I do that, it'll be all over Palm Beach within two hours."

"True," I agreed, "but that can't be helped."

"But that's why I didn't go to the police. I wanted to keep the whole thing private."

"Can't be done," I said, shaking my head. "How on earth can I make discreet inquiries if people don't know what I'm talking about?"

She considered that. "I guess you're right," she said finally, sighing. "But it means cops, reporters, and maybe the TV people. What am I going to tell them?"

"Lie," I said cheerfully. "Tell them the stamps weren't stolen at all but have been sent to a New York auction house for appraisal."

She laughed. "You're a devious lad, you know that? All right, I'll tell the staff and guests."

"Good. Then I can get the show on the road." I put my empty glass on the umbrella table and stood up. "One more request: I'd like to take a look at the so-called scene of the crime, if I may. Do you mind if I go poking about in your bedroom for a few minutes?"

"Go ahead and poke," she said. "You know your way around the place, don't you?"

"Only the ground floor."

"My bedroom is on the second. South wing. It stretches the width of the house. The east windows overlook the ocean and the west windows look down on the pool and patio. There . . ."

She gestured, and I looked to the second floor where opened windows, screened, were framed by French blue shutters.

"You can pry into anything you like," she said. "Nothing's locked."

"It won't take long," I promised. "Thank you for the drink."

I started away but she called, "Archy," and I turned

36

back, surprised that she had used my name. Usually I was "lad" or, when speaking of me to others, "Prescott's son."

She stared at me a moment, and I waited. "Last night you dined at L'Europe," she said, almost accusingly. "With Jennifer Towley."

"Oh-ho," I said, "the grapevine has been working overtime."

"Are you seeing her?" she demanded.

"Not yet."

"Watch your back, lad," she said. "There's more to her than meets the eye. If I were you, I'd bring that association to a screeching halt. The lady could turn out to be a problem."

I grinned at her. "One never knows, do one?" I said.

I continued on to the house, wondering just what the hell she was implying—and deciding it was merely Palm Beach gossip.

The interior of the Horowitz home was gorgeous, right out of *Southern Accents,* and all the more impressive because I knew the mistress had done the decorating herself. It was an eclectic mix of Victorian, Louis Quinze, Early American, and even a few Bauhaus touches. I know that sounds like a mishmash, but everything fit, nothing clashed, and the predominant colors were rich wine shades, a welcome relief from the sorbet pastels of most South Florida mansions, many of which resemble the lobby of a Miami Beach hotel.

Lady Cynthia's bedroom was large enough to accommodate an enormous four-poster bed lacquered in claret red, a tall wardrobe of carved pine, an escritoire painted with gamboling putti, and much, much more.

There were three huge crystal vases of fresh flowers, one in her dressing room. The walk-in closet contained enough costumes to outfit the female cast of *My Fair Lady,* and the racks of shoes would have made Imelda Marcos gnash her teeth. The bathroom was golden yellow: tile, tub, sink, john, bidet—everything. The faucets were tarnished gold: a nice touch, I thought. One strives for careless elegance, doesn't one?

I didn't search through the desk or turn over chair cushions—nothing like that. I was interested only in the wall safe, and that was easy to spot since it was not concealed behind a painting or camouflaged in any way. It projected slightly from the wall just to the left of the canopied bed. It was nothing special: single dial, single handle. The door opened easily and noiselessly. Inside were several manila envelopes tied with what appeared to be old shoelaces. I didn't inspect the contents, but closed the safe door again, latching it with a twist of the stainless steel handle.

What I was interested in was the distance from the bedroom door to the wall safe. I paced it off. Fourteen long steps. I estimated an intruder could slip into the bedroom, open the safe door, extract the small red leather book containing the Inverted Jennies, close the safe door, and whisk from the bedroom within a minute. Two at the most. It was a cakewalk. But who took the walk?

Then I found another problem. On a bedside table, almost directly below the wall safe, was a large suede jewel case. I lifted the lid: It was like looking into a Tiffany display case. Question: What self-respecting crook would swipe the stamps and then not pause a sec to grab up a handful of those glittering gems? A puzzlement.

Hands in my pocket, I strolled about the bedroom, thinking it was spacious enough to swallow my entire suite at the McNally manse. I believe I was whistling "I've Never Been in Love Before" when I wandered to the west windows and looked down.

Lady Cynthia was paddling around in the swimming pool, obviously naked but still wearing her panama hat and sunglasses. Mrs. Marsden stood waiting on the tiled border of the pool, holding a big bath towel. As I watched, Lady C. came slowly wading out, white body gleaming wetly, and I saw how extraordinary she was.

Usually in the presence of great beauty, one has the urge to leap into the air accompanied by the clicking of heels. But now, seeing that incredible nude emerging from the pool—Venus rising from the chlorine—I felt only an ineffable sadness, realizing I had been born forty years too late.

3

Of all the counties in Florida, Palm Beach is the Ace of Clubs. There is a superabundance: golf clubs, tennis clubs, yacht clubs, polo clubs. Probably the most elegant and exclusive social clubs on Palm Beach Island are the Bath & Tennis and the Everglades. But about five years previously, I got together with a bunch of my wassailing pals, and we agreed what the town needed was another club, so we decided to start one. We called it the Pelican Club in honor of Florida's quintessential bird. Also, most of the roistering charter members resembled the pelican: graceful and charming in flight, lumpish and dour in repose.

We found an old two-story clapboard house out near the airport that we could afford. It was definitely not an Addison Mizner but it had the advantage of being somewhat isolated: no close neighbors to complain about the sounds of revelry. We all chipped in, bought the house, fixed it up (sort of), and the Pelican Club opened for business.

And almost closed six months later. We were lawyers, bankers, stockbrokers, Realtors, doctors, etc., but we knew nothing about running a club bar and restaurant. We were facing Chapter 7 when we had the great good fortune to hire the Pettibones, an African-American family who had been living in one of the gamier neighborhoods of West Palm Beach and wanted out. All of them had worked in restaurants and bars, and they knew how an eating-drinking establishment should be run.

They moved into our second floor, and the father, Simon Pettibone, became club manager and bartender. Son Leroy was our chef, daughter Priscilla our waitress, and wife Jas (for Jasmine) was appointed our housekeeper and den mother. Within a month the Pettibones had the club operating admirably, and so many would-be Pelicans applied for membership that eventually we had to close the roster and start a waiting list.

The Pelican Club was not solely dedicated to merrymaking, of course. We were also involved in Good Works. Once a year we held a costume ball at The Breakers: our Annual Mammoth Extravaganza. All the proceeds from this lavish blowout were contributed to a local home for unwed mothers, since so many of our members felt a personal responsibility. In addition we formed a six-piece jazz combo (I played tenor kazoo), and we were delighted to perform, without fee, at public functions and nursing homes. A Palm Beach music critic wrote of one of our recitals, "Words fail me." You couldn't ask for a better review than that.

It was to the Pelican Club that I tooled the Miata after my stimulating morning with Lady Horowitz. It was then almost eleven-thirty, but traffic crossing Lake Worth on the Royal Park Bridge was heavy, and it was a bit after noon when I arrived at the club.

No members were present when I entered the Pelican, but Simon Pettibone was behind the bar, polishing glasses and watching the screen of a television set displaying current stock quotations.

I swung onto a barstool. "Are you winning or losing, Mr. Pettibone?" I inquired.

"Losing, Mr. McNally," he replied. "But I prefer to think of it as a learning experience."

"Very wise," I said. "A vodka-tonic for me, please, with a hunk of lime."

He began preparing the drink, and I headed for the phone booth in the rear of the barroom. Did you guess I intended to call Jennifer Towley? You will learn that when duty beckons, there is stern stuff in the McNally male offspring; I phoned the Palm Beach Police Department. I asked to speak to Sergeant Al Rogoff.

"Rogoff," he answered in his phlegmy rasp.

"Archy McNally here," I said.

"Yes, sir, how may I be of service?"

When Al talks like that, I know someone is standing at his elbow—probably his lieutenant or captain.

"Feel like a nosh?" I asked. "I'll stand you a world-class hamburger and a bucket of suds."

"Your Alfa-Romeo is missing, sir?" he said. "I'm sorry to hear that. It will be necessary for you to file a missing vehicle report. Where are you located, sir?"

"I'm in the barroom at the Pelican."

"Yes, sir," he said, "I am familiar with that office building. Suppose I meet you there in a half-hour, and you can give me the details of the alleged theft."

"Hurry up," I said. "I'm hungry."

I returned to the bar where my drink was waiting on a clean little mat. I took a sip. Just right.

"Mr. Pettibone," I said, "life is strange."

"Bizarre is the word, Mr. McNally," he said. "*Bee-*zar."

"Exactly," I said.

Sgt. Al Rogoff owned that adjective. I had worked a few cases with him in the past—to our mutual benefit—and had come to know him better than most of his professional associates. He deliberately projected the persona of a good ol' boy: a crude, profane "man's man" who called women "broads" and claimed he would like nothing better than a weekend on an airboat in the Everglades, popping cans of Bud and lassoing alligators. He even drove a pickup truck.

I think he adopted this Joe Six-pack disguise because he thought it would further his career as an officer of the law in South Florida. Actually, he knew who Heidegger was; could quote the lines following "Shall I part my hair behind? Do I dare to eat a peach?"; and much preferred an '82 Médoc to sour mash and branch water. He looked and acted like a redneck sheriff, but enjoyed Vivaldi more than he did Willie Nelson.

He hadn't revealed the face behind the mask voluntarily. I had slowly, patiently, discovered who he really was. He knew it, and rather than be offended, I think he was secretly relieved. It must be a tremendous strain to play a role continually, always fearful of making a gaffe that will betray your impersonation. Al didn't have to act with me, and I believe that was why he was willing to provide official assistance when my discreet inquiries required it.

By the time he came marching through the front door, uniform smartly pressed, the Pelican barroom was thronged with the lunchtime crowd and people had started to drift to the back area where a posted warning said nothing about jackets and ties but proclaimed: "Members and their guests are required to wear shoes in the dining room."

I noticed a few patrons glancing warily at the uniformed cop who had invaded the premises. Did they fear a bust—or were they just startled by this armed intruder who was built like a dumpster? Al Rogoff's physical appearance was perhaps the principal reason for the success of his masquerade. The man was all meat, a walking butcher shop: rare-beef face, pork chop jowls, slabs of veal for ears. And unplucked chicken wing sideburns.

I conducted him to the dining room where Priscilla was holding a corner table for me. We both ordered medium-rare hamburgers, which came with country fries and homemade coleslaw. We also ordered steins of draft Heineken. While waiting for lunch to be served, we nibbled on spears of kosher dill pickles placed on every table in mason jars. The Pelican Club did not offer haute cuisine, but Leroy Pettibone's food adhered to the ribs.

"How much time do you have?" I asked Rogoff.

"An hour tops," he said. "What's up?"

"I want to report a crime."

"Oh?" he said. "Have you sexually abused a manatee?"

"Not recently," I said. "But this may not be a crime at all. It is an *alleged* crime. And the alleged victim will not report it to the police. And if you hear or read about it and question the alleged victim, she will claim no crime has been committed."

"Love it," the sergeant said. "Just love it. Alleged crime. Alleged victim. And I've got to listen to this bullshit for a free hamburger? Okay, I'm not proud. Who's the alleged victim?"

"Lady Cynthia Horowitz."

He pursed his lips in a soundless whistle. "Mrs. Gotrocks herself? That makes the cheese more binding. She's got clout. And what's the alleged crime?"

"Possible theft of a valuable possession."

"The Koh-i-noor diamond?"

"No," I said. "Four postage stamps."

He looked at me sorrowfully. "You never come up with something simple," he said. "Like a multiple homicide or a supermarket bombing. With you, everything's got to be cute. All right, buster, tell me about the four postage stamps."

But then our food was served, and we were silent until Priscilla left. Between bites and swallows, I told him the whole story of the Inverted Jenny and how a block of four of the misprinted stamps was missing from the wall safe in Lady Horowitz's bedroom. The sergeant listened without interrupting. Then, when I finished, he spoke.

"You know," he said, "this hamburger is really super. What does Leroy put in the meat?"

"Probably minced Vidalia onion this time of year. Sometimes he uses chopped red and yellow peppers. The man is the Thomas Alva Edison of hamburgers. What about the Inverted Jennies?"

"What about them? What do you want us to do?"

"Nothing," I said. "If you go to Lady Cynthia, she'll tell you the stamps weren't stolen but have been sent to a New York auction house for appraisal."

"Uh-huh," Rogoff said. "And who gave her that idea—as if I didn't know."

"I did," I admitted. "But she doesn't want any publicity."

The sergeant pushed back his empty plate and stared at me. "You're a devious lad, you know that?"

"You're the second person who's told me that today."

"Who was the first—Lady Horowitz?"

I nodded. "But it's not true," I protested. "I'm not devious. I just want to maintain civility in the world."

"Of course," Rogoff said. "And I'm the Tooth Fairy. So if you're not demanding the PBPD get involved, what *do* you want?"

"A little information."

"It figures," he said mournfully. "There's no free lunch."

"Have another beer," I urged.

"Nope. Coffee and a wedge of Leroy's key lime pie will be fine. I deserve it for listening to your blather."

Priscilla cleared our table, and I gave her Al's order. I settled for just coffee. Black.

"Getting a little tubby?" she teased.

"Nonsense," I said. "I'm still the slender, lithe, bronzed Apollo you've always known."

"Oh sure," she said. "And I'm the Tooth Fairy."

"Two 'devious lads' in one day," I complained to Rogoff, "and now two Tooth Fairies in one day. Does everything come in twos?"

"Everything comes in threes," he said. "You should know that. Now cut the drivel. What kind of information do you want?"

"Those Inverted Jenny stamps," I said. "They're extremely rare. Only a hundred of them were originally sold. I imagine all stamp dealers and most collectors know about them. A block of four recently went at auction for a million bucks. I mean they're valuable and they're famous. So, assuming Lady Cynthia's stamps were pinched, what's the thief going to do with them? It's been bothering me since I was handed the job. He can't sell them to a legitimate dealer; he'd want to know where they came from—the provenance. Ditto for auction houses. So how does the criminal profit from his crime?"

Silence while Priscilla served our coffee and Rogoff's dessert. Then:

"Lots of possibilities," Al said, digging into his pie. "One is ransom. The perp contacts Lady Horowitz and offers to sell her stamps back to her for X number of dollars. Were they insured?"

"Half a million."

"All right, if Horowitz won't play ball, the crook calls the insurance company and tries to make a deal. The insurance people would rather pay out a hundred grand than a half-mil.

"Another possibility is that it was a contract heist. Some collector just *had* to have those cockamamie stamps. He

48

can't afford a million at auction, but he can afford, say, fifty thousand to hire some experienced burglar to lift them. Believe me, there are collectors like that. They'd never put the Jennies on public display; it would be enough to drool over them in private.

"A third possibility is that the thief will use the stamps as collateral for a bank loan. Take my word for it, there are banks here and abroad that accept collateral like stolen bearer bonds without inquiring too closely how the loan applicant got possession. So the crook gets his loan, defaults, and the bank is stuck with hot merchandise while the bad guy is tanning his hide on the French Riviera."

"Fascinating," I said. "I didn't realize it would be so easy to convert the stamps into cash."

"Not easy," Rogoff said, "but it can be done. The simplest way, of course, would be to sell the stamps to a crooked dealer."

"Talking about dealers," I said, "do you know of any local experts who could provide more information about the Inverted Jennies?"

He thought a moment. "There's a guy on the island named Bela Rubik. As in Cube. He's got a stamp and coin shop off Worth Avenue. He knows his stuff. I've used him to help identify stolen property."

"Is he straight?" I asked.

"As far as I know."

"Thanks, Al. You've been a big help. I'll take it from here."

He stared at me. "Why do I have this antsy feeling that I haven't heard the last of the Inverted Jennies?"

"Beats me," I said, shrugging. "I can't see why the Department should get involved."

"The last time you told me that, I ended up in a shoot-out with two crackheads. Remember that?"

"I remember," I said. "You performed admirably."

"Oh sure. And almost got blown away. Thanks for the banquet. Don't call us; we'll call you."

We shook hands and he tramped away. I signed tabs for the lunch and my drinks at the bar, then headed back to Palm Beach. I was satisfied with what I had learned from Rogoff. I don't claim to be yours truly, S. Holmes. I mean I can't glance at a man and immediately know he is left-handed, constipated, has a red-haired wife, and slices lox for a living. I do investigations a fact at a time. Eventually they add up—I hope. I'm very big on hope.

I found Rubik's Stamp & Coin Shop without too much trouble. It was a hole-in-the-wall but appeared clean and prosperous. There was an attractive display of Morgan silver dollars in the front window.

But the door was locked, and I rattled the knob a few times before the man inside came forward and inspected me carefully through the glass. Then he unlocked, let me enter, locked the door behind me. He went back behind the showcase and shoved his glasses, a curious pair of linked jeweler's loupes, atop his bald head.

"Mr. Rubik?" I asked.

He nodded. I fished out a business card and handed it over. He read it slowly, then handed it back.

"I don't need a lawyer," he said. "I already got a will."

I smiled as pleasantly as I could. "I'm not drumming up business, Mr. Rubik. I just need a little information."

He stared at me, silent and expressionless. I figured he was on the downside of sixty, and if his grayish pallor was any indication, he'd never hit seventy. He had a puffy face and his gaze was unfocused and nearsighted. He reminded me of someone I had seen before. Suddenly it came to me: He was Mr. Magoo.

"Information?" he said finally, in a creaky voice. "You lawyers bill by the hour, don't you?"

"That's correct."

"For information," he said, "I do the same. My fee is fifty dollars an hour. Payable in advance for the first consultation."

I took out my wallet, picked out a fifty, and handed it over. "I'll need a receipt for that," I said, trying not to show how miffed I was.

"Of course," he said. "What information do you want?"

"I want to learn something about the Inverted Jenny airmail stamps."

His stare was making me nervous. "Why do you want to know about that issue?" he asked.

I could have demanded, "What the hell do you care? You got paid, didn't you?" Instead I said, "My firm is handling the will of a Boca Raton real estate developer who passed away recently. His estate includes a block of four Inverted Jennies. We'd like to establish an approximate evaluation."

"You want me to make an appraisal without seeing the stamps? Impossible. What condition are they in? Are they glued in an album or what? Are they faded, torn, folded? All these things affect the value."

I sighed. "I don't want you to appraise this particular

51

block of stamps, Mr. Rubik. I just want some general information about Inverted Jennies."

"Nine sheets of the twenty-four-cent airmail stamps were issued in 1918. The printing plate of the blue biplane in the center had been put on the press backwards. Eight sheets were destroyed after the error was discovered. The ninth was sold over the counter in a Washington, D.C., post office to a broker's clerk for twenty-four dollars. A week later he sold the sheet of a hundred stamps to a dealer for fifteen thousand. The sheet was then broken up into blocks and singles. Over the years the value has greatly increased. The block of four that was recently auctioned in New York for a million showed the plate number. A block of four with a printing-plate guideline through the middle went for less than half of that."

"Are there any Inverted Jennies for sale now?"

Rubik shrugged. "Everything is for sale—if the price is right. But many of the Jennies have deteriorated. Like I told you, the value depends on the condition of the stamps."

I tried again. "Are there any on the market now?"

"That I can't say."

"Could you find out? You have contacts with other dealers, I presume. Do you have an association?"

"Yes."

"Will you inquire and see if any Inverted Jennies are being offered for sale?"

"That's a big job," he said. "It'll take time."

"Fifty dollars an hour," I reminded him.

"All right," he said grudgingly, "I'll ask around."

I waited patiently while he pulled down his crazy glasses and wrote out a receipt for fifty dollars in a spidery scrawl. Actually, prorated, he had given me about twenty dollars' worth of time. But I said nothing. If he wanted to believe he had diddled me, so much the better. I have profited mightily by letting people think I am a tap-dancer when, in reality, I am capable of *Swan Lake.*

I took the bill and handed back my business card. "If you hear of any Jennies for sale," I said, "give me a call. If I don't hear from you, I'll stop by again in a week or so."

"I'll have my bill ready," he said without smiling.

He may have been straight, as Sgt. Rogoff had said, but I thought Bela Rubik was a surly character with a galloping case of cupidity. I vowed he would never get my vote for Mr. Congeniality.

My next step was at a nearby sporting goods emporium. In the tennis section I picked out a Spalding graphite racquet I thought would please Jennifer Towley. The clerk promised she could exchange it if the weight and balance didn't suit her. I had it gift-wrapped with a wide ribbon and bow, tossed it into the Miata, and headed for home.

I arrived in time to change and go down to the ocean for my daily plunge. When the surf wasn't too high, I tried to swim a mile up the shore and a mile back. I am not a graceful swimmer, I admit, but I plow along and I get there. Swimming two miles in the late afternoon is an extremely healthful exercise and makes one eager for the cocktail hour.

The gentry must have their ceremonies, of course, and

the cocktail hour was one of ours. Actually, it rarely lasted more than thirty minutes, but it wouldn't be posh to call it the cocktail half-hour, would it?

My mother, father, and I met in the second-floor sitting room, and there the senior McNally would go through the ritual of mixing a pitcher (not too large) of gin martinis. I know it is fashionable to demand *dry* martinis; the drier the better. Some insist on a mixture of eight or ten parts gin to one of vermouth. In fact, I know fanatics who believe having an unopened bottle of vermouth somewhere in the neighborhood is sufficient.

But my father is an ardent traditionalist, and his martinis were mixed in the classic formula: three parts gin, one part vermouth. The result was so odd and unusual that I found it enjoyable. The sire did relax his stern standards to the extent of using olives stuffed with a bit of jalapeño pepper.

On that particular day he had come home early to enjoy the family cocktail hour and then change into black tie since he was scheduled to be the main speaker that evening at a testimonial dinner of our local bar association.

After the martini rite was completed, my father departed, and mother and I dined alone downstairs. That night, as I recall, we had lamb chops with fresh mint sauce. Different from Leroy Pettibone's hamburgers, but not necessarily better. Just different.

Now I must tell you something about my mother since she was fated to play an important role in what I later came to call "The Direful Case of the Inverted Jenny."

Her name was Madelaine, and she was the dearest,

sweetest woman who ever lived but, like all mothers, slightly dotty. She was a native Floridian, which is very rare; most Floridians were born in Ohio. She met my father-to-be when she worked as a secretary in the Miami law firm he joined after becoming a full-fledged attorney. It turned out to be a splendid match.

Not that there weren't disagreements, but they were mostly of a minor nature. My parents could never, ever, agree on the proper temperature setting for their bedroom air conditioner. And my father decried mother's insistence on drinking sauterne with meat and fish courses, while she could never understand why on earth he demanded starch in the collars and cuffs of his dress shirts.

A more serious personal problem was Madelaine McNally's health. My mother was overweight, not obese but definitely much, much too plump. In addition, she suffered from high blood pressure, which probably accounted for her somewhat florid complexion and occasional shortness of breath. Our family physician had put her on a strict diet, and we were bewildered that it resulted in no weight loss. Then we discovered she had been sneaking chocolate truffles while working amidst her begonias in the greenhouse.

But she really was a wonderful woman, and I loved her. I shall always treasure the profound advice she gave me in the first letter I received at New Haven. "Archy," she wrote, "live as if every day may be your last, and always have on clean underwear."

That night, during the minty lamb chops, mother and I chatted of this and that, laughed, and then clapped our hands when Ursi Olson brought us fresh, chilled raspberries topped with a sinful dollop of whipped cream.

"No-cal," Ursi assured my mother.

"I don't care," she said. "I just don't *care*. Life is too short."

Over coffee, I remarked that I had seen Lady Cynthia Horowitz that morning.

"Oh? I hope you gave her our best wishes."

"Of course I did," I said, though I hadn't.

"What an unhappy woman," my mother said, suddenly saddened. "I feel sorry for her."

"Mother! That woman's got everything!"

"No," she said, "she doesn't. She wants it all, and no one can have it all."

I thought she was talking goofy nonsense and made no response. We left the table, and mother returned to the sitting room for an evening of television. I went upstairs to my suite to enter the day's events in my journal.

But first I phoned Jennifer Towley on my private line. I got her answering machine, and after the *beep,* I said, "Jennifer, this is Archibald McNally. It is vitally, urgently, desperately important that I speak to you. Please call me at any hour of the day or night." Then I recited my unlisted number, said, "Thank you," and hung up.

I lighted my *first* English Oval of the day (I was so proud) and wondered again what Lady Horowitz had been hinting about Jennifer. I could not believe that cool, complete woman could be guilty of anything more serious than an ingrown toenail, but it was mildly unsettling to discover she was the subject of Palm Beach gossip.

I had worked on my journal for more than an hour,

jotting down what I had learned that day, when my
phone rang about nine-thirty, and I grabbed it up and
said, "H'lo?"

"Jennifer Towley," she said crisply. "What on earth is
so vitally, urgently, desperately important?"

"Have you decided to see me again?" I asked eagerly.

"I'm still considering it."

"Well, you *must,*" I said. "The Board of Directors of
McNally and Son, in solemn conclave assembled, voted to
reward you with a gift for your splendid cooperation in
the affair of the Frobisher letters. I have made the gift
selection and now must make delivery. And that is why
it's necessary to see you as soon as possible."

She laughed. "What a devious lad you are," she said.

"Three," I said. "Rogoff was right. Now don't tell me
you're the Tooth Fairy."

There was a brief silence. Then: "What *are* you gibber-
ing about?"

"Nothing," I said. "Just idle chatter. Well, when is it to
be?"

"I don't know," she said doubtfully. "I'm going to be
awfully busy. I've landed a new client who wants her
bedroom done over in Art Nouveau. It'll take me forever
to find the right pieces."

"Then you'll need a few hours of relaxation," I said.
"Dinner tomorrow night would be nice. Ever been to the
Pelican Club?"

"No, but I've heard a lot of weird things about it."

"They're all true," I assured her. "Dress informally. I'll
stop by for you around seven. Okay?"

"All right," she said faintly.

57

"And I'll bring your gift," I said. "If I can get three men to help me load it onto the truck."

She was giggling when I hung up. That was a delight, to hear that restrained woman giggle. I went back to my journal with a song in my heart.

I finished making notes and drew up a tentative plan of how I intended to proceed in the Inverted Jenny investigation. Then I poured myself a very small marc from a private stock of spirits and liqueurs I kept in an old sea chest in my sitting room. Pony in hand, I settled down to watch a rerun of *Columbo* on my portable TV set. I had seen that particular segment twice before, but it was still fun.

One more marc and one more English Oval, and I was ready to kiss the day goodbye. I undressed, brushed my teeth, and showered. If I thought of Jennifer Towley— and I did, continually—they were innocent thoughts. Mostly.

I pulled on my pajama shorts, set the air conditioner at 75°, turned out the lights, and went to bed. I slept the untroubled sleep of the pure at heart.

4

I phoned Lady Horowitz after breakfast and asked if she had told her employees and houseguests that the Inverted Jenny stamps had disappeared. She said she had.

"And now *everyone* knows," she said bitterly. "I've already had a dozen phony sympathy calls—including one from a cousin in Sarasota. Bad news certainly travels fast."

"Always has," I said cheerfully. "There's nothing more enjoyable than other people's troubles."

Then I asked if it would be all right if I spent most of the day at her place, making discreet inquiries. She said to come ahead, she would tell everyone I'd be nosing around. But she would not be present.

"I'll be gone all day, lad," she said. "I have scads of things to do."

I asked if that meant Kenneth, the chauffeur, would also be absent.

"No," she said, "I'll take the Jag."

I love it. That casual "I'll take the Jag" meant she would not be chauffeured in her antique Rolls-Royce (a rare 1933 Tourer) but would pilot her spanking-new bronzy Jaguar XJ-S convertible.

I was musing on the unique traits of the affluent when I pulled into the white graveled driveway of the Horowitz mansion. I drove to the left, past the guesthouse, to the broad turnaround in front of the five-car garage. Now *there* was a prime example of conspicuous consumption.

When the long, low building had been erected in the early 1920s, it had been designed as a stable, to house the original owner's riding and carriage horses. Would you believe that this habitat for nags was floored with gorgeous tiles from the palazzo of a bankrupt Venetian nobleman and walled with oak panels from an abandoned Spanish monastery? Money, I decided, has no conscience and no memory.

I climbed out of the Miata and strolled into the shadowy garage where a large, muscular young man (about my age) was sponging down the Rolls. He was wearing the trousers of a chauffeur's uniform but had taken off the jacket. His upper torso was tightly sheathed in one of those tailored T-shirts body-builders affect: nipped-in at the waist and with abbreviated cap sleeves, to display their biceps, triceps and, for all I know, forceps.

"Kenneth Bodin?" I asked.

He looked at me, and for a moment I wasn't sure if he would answer or snap my spine just for the fun of it.

"That's right," he said finally in a high-pitched voice that was shocking to hear issuing from the mastodon.

"I'm Archibald McNally," I said. "Did Lady Horowitz tell you I'd be around asking questions about her missing stamps?"

"She said," he acknowledged and tried a smile. I wished he hadn't; his teeth weren't all that great. "I hope she don't think I swiped them."

"Of course not," I assured him. "She doesn't believe anyone in the house had a thing to do with it. Probably someone from outside."

"Sure," he said. "A cat burglar." When I nodded, he went back to washing the Rolls.

"Just a few questions, Mr. Bodin," I said. "When was the last time you saw the stamps?"

He stopped his work and appeared to think a moment. If he was capable of it. Which I doubted.

"Oh lordy," he said, "I haven't seen those things in years. Maybe two or three."

"You live on the premises?"

"Nope." He gestured toward the end of the garage where a lavender '69 Volkswagen Beetle was slumbering peacefully on the Venetian tiles. "That's mine."

"Beautiful car," I said politely.

"I keep it up," he said proudly. "Anyway, I drive in every day. I live in Delray."

"Long way to commute," I observed.

"Not really," he said. "I start out early. Not much traffic, so I can make time. That's a Miata you got—right?"

"Uh-huh."

"Nice," he said. "I wish I could afford one."

"Mr. Bodin," I said, "you suggested the stamps might

have been lifted by a cat burglar. Have you seen anyone casing the place recently? You know—lurking about or driving past frequently?"

He shook his head. "No one like that. You could ask the Beach Patrol."

"Good idea," I said. "Can you think of anyone—staff or houseguests—who might have been tempted?"

He stopped wiping off the Rolls with a shammy and turned to face me. God, he was a bruiser! Even his muscles had muscles. If the gossip was true—that he had once been Lady C.'s lover—I could understand her brief fling. The guy was a hulk.

But my admiration for his physique stopped at his thick neck. I thought he had the face of a dyspeptic terrier, and his blond hair was too metallic to be credited to the Florida sun. It was carefully coiffed and artfully streaked. Clairol, I was certain, had provided assistance.

"Why no," he said. "To my way of thinking there's no one around here who'd rob the Lady. She's a good boss, and the guests are all family."

"What about the friend, Angus Wolfson?"

"Shit!" he said with unnecessary vehemence. "That old guy's a butterfly. But he seems to be loaded. So why should he cop the stamps?"

"Why indeed?" I said, and couldn't think of any more questions to ask that he might be willing to answer. "Thank you for talking with me, Mr. Bodin. I appreciate it."

"Sure," he said. "Why not? I got nothing to hide."

He turned away, and I saw he had an unlighted cigarette tucked behind his ear. Why he wasn't sucking on a toothpick I'll never know.

I wandered out into the sunlight, heard soft laughter coming from the pool area, and ambled over there. A man and a woman were seated at an umbrella table, working on what appeared to be iced black coffees and a plate of mini-croissants. They looked up as I approached, and the ancient male rose slowly to his feet.

"Good morning," I said, taking off my white linen cap and giving them a 75-watt smile (my max is 150). "I hate to disturb you, but I wonder if I might join you for a few moments. My name is Archibald McNally. I hope Lady Horowitz warned you I might come puttering around asking questions about the missing Inverted Jennies."

"Of course, my dear chap," the man said, offering a halibut handshake. "I am Angus Wolfson, an old friend of Cynthia's. And I do mean *old*—but please don't ask me to be more precise about my age. Growing old is a dreadful thing—until you consider the alternative!" He paused and waited for my laugh.

I gave him a 25-watter. "Maurice Chevalier," I said.

Something changed in his face. "Oh-ho," he said, "an erudite detective."

"Not very," I said, and then tried to make amends for squelching his big boffola. "That's a marvelous jacket you're wearing, Mr. Wolfson."

It was, too: burgundy velvet in the belted Norfolk style. He wore it over creamy flannel trousers. There was a flowered ascot looped casually around his chicken neck. Quite the aged peacock.

63

"Thank you," he said, regaining his good humor. "And this lovely lady is Gina Stanescu, daughter of Cynthia and her—which was it, darling? Third or fourth husband?"

"Third," Ms. Stanescu said with a faint smile and offered me a cool hand to shake. "So nice to meet you, Mr. McNally. Do join us."

I pulled up a webbed patio chair and placed it so I was facing both of them.

"We're having iced coffee," Wolfson said. "Would you care for a glass?"

"Thank you, no," I said. "I never drink on duty." I meant it as a joke, of course—a feeble joke, I admit—but it didn't earn so much as a snigger.

"Shocking thing about those stamps," Wolfson said. "Absolutely shocking."

"It is so unpleasant," Stanescu said in a small voice. "It makes one look at other people with new eyes—wondering."

"Could you tell me the last time you saw the stamps."

They looked at each other. Then Wolfson replied:

"Let me see . . . It was at dinner the night Alan DuPey and his bride arrived. Felice had never seen the Inverted Jennies, so Cynthia brought them downstairs to show. Is that correct, Gina?"

She nodded.

"Did everyone see the stamps at dinner?"

"I believe so," Wolfson said. "The book was passed around the table."

"Yes," Stanescu said. "I looked at them and passed the book along."

"And then? After everyone had seen the stamps?"

"I couldn't swear to it," Wolfson said, "but I believe that after we all left the table, Cynthia took them back upstairs to her bedroom."

"She did," the Lady's daughter said definitely. "I walked up the stairs with her. I was going to my room to get a light sweater because we had all decided to sit outside awhile and have a brandy. I saw mother take the little red book into her bedroom."

"And neither of you saw the stamps after that?"

"No," they said in unison.

"Have either of you noticed any strangers prowling about? Anyone who apparently doesn't belong on the estate?"

Wolfson laughed. "You mean some chappie dressed in black and wearing a mask? No, I've seen no one who even remotely resembles a villain. Gina?"

"No," she said, "no one. Everything has been quite normal."

"Do either of you have any doubts about any member of the staff? I assure you, any accusation you may make will be held in strictest confidence."

"I accuse the chef of putting too much saffron in the rice last night," Wolfson said, "but that's hardly criminal. No, to the best of my knowledge everyone on the staff is honest—and remarkably efficient, I might add."

"I agree with Angus," Stanescu said. "All of mother's people seem to be trustworthy and very loyal to her."

Wolfson gave me a derisive smile. "We're not much help, are we?" he said.

"No," I agreed, "not much."

He took a sip of his iced coffee, started on another

croissant, and I had a moment to eyeball him directly. He must have been a dandy fifty years ago, but now the Barrymore profile had softened. His entire face, in fact, had melted downward, pulling at a broad, high brow that was now pale and shiny with stretched skin.

"Mr. Wolfson," I said, "this has nothing to do with the stamps, and if you feel I am prying unnecessarily, please tell me, but are you retired?"

"Semi," he said. "I was somewhat of a bookman. Had a sweet little shop on the Square. I am also somewhat of a bibliophile, and somewhat of an antiquarian. I have been a somewhat all my life, Mr. McNally, and have done very well at it, I might add. These days my professional activities are limited. Occasionally I am called upon to serve as a consultant to librarians, private and public, and to make appraisals of rare books prior to sale or auction."

"Interesting," I said. "I have a first edition of Mad Comics. Should I sell it, sir?"

"No," he said. "Hold."

We all laughed.

"What about me," Gina Stanescu said. "I feel left out. Don't you want to know about me?"

"I do indeed," I said.

"I am forty-one and unmarried," she stated flatly, "and well on my way to becoming what in your country is called an old maid. A strange fate for the daughter of a mother who has been married six times—is it not? I live in France, in Rouen, where I am the director of an orphanage. And that is the whole story of my life, total and complete."

"An orphanage?" I said. "That must be very rewarding work."

"Rewarding and frustrating. There is never enough money."

"You shouldn't have said that, Gina," Wolfson chided. "Now Mr. McNally will suspect you pinched your mother's stamps to support your home for bastards."

I was offended but she wasn't. She reached out to place a soft hand on one of his veined claws. "Dear Angus," she said fondly. "You talk like a devil, but I know you have a heart of gold."

He snorted. "Of tarnished brass you mean," he said, and lifted her hand to kiss her knuckles.

This Gina Stanescu seemed to me a curious woman. She was swathed in a summery gown of miles and miles of white chiffon and wore a woven straw hat with a wide, floppy brim that sometimes obscured her dark eyes. The floating dress and garden hat gave her a wispy look as if she might go galloping through the heather bellowing, "Heathcliff! Heathcliff!"

But despite that vaporish appearance, her features were as sharp as her mother's. She had a no-nonsense manner, and I suspected those orphans in Rouen did their lessons and cleaned their plates. I wondered, idly, what the body of Lady Cynthia's daughter might be like, hidden beneath those yards of billowing silk. The image that sprang to mind was that of a very elegant Japanese sword.

Wolfson suddenly turned to me. "You are the son of Cynthia's attorney, Prescott McNally, are you not?"

"Yes, sir."

"I have met your father," he said. "A gentleman of the old school." His smile held more than irony but less than scorn.

"He is that," I agreed and rose to make my farewells. I thanked them for their cooperation and warned I might return with more questions. They couldn't have been more gracious, but when I returned to the Miata, I heard their muted laughter drifting across the manicured lawn.

Since no one had invited me to stick around for a spot of lunch, I raced home with a terrible craving for a cold ale and a corned beef sandwich on the sour rye Ursi Olson baked once a week. There was no corned beef in the fridge, but Ursi provided smoked salmon topped with slices of onion, which added up to a very satisfactory substitute.

Sandwich in hand, I sauntered around to the garage where Jamie was planting a few dwarf palms to make the place look less like a barrack.

"What's new?" I asked him.

"Nuthin," he said, so I gave him a nudge.

"I talked to Kenneth Bodin this morning," I said. "You were right; he's a big one."

"Uh-huh."

"And not too much between his ears," I added.

"Air," Jamie said.

I waited patiently.

"Girlfriend's name is Sylvia," he said finally. "Sylvia Montcliff or Montgrift or Montgrief. Something like that. Lives in Delray Beach."

"Sure she does," I said. "So does he. Thanks, Jamie."

I took what remained of my sandwich up to my lair and

scribbled in my journal awhile. I figured I might not have the energy after what I hoped would be an enjoyable engagement with Jennifer Towley that evening.

By two-thirty I was back at the Horowitz estate, and this time I entered the main house by the back door and went directly to the kitchen. Jean Cuvier, the chef, was seated at a stainless steel table, the usual Gitane dangling from his lower lip. He was poring over a handicap sheet for the races at Calder. Instead of the white toque of his calling, he wore a New York Yankee baseball cap, the beak turned to the rear.

If girth was any indication of culinary talent he should have been a Cordon Pourpre instead of a Cordon Bleu. I mean he was a *humongous* man with three chins, two bellies and, I presumed, jowls on his kneecaps. He was also living refutation of the popular belief that all fat men are jolly, being peevish and cranky. But his genius with a saucepan excused all.

"Bonjour, maître," I said.

He squinted up at me through a swirl of blue smoke. "Bonjour, Ar-chay," he said.

The following conversation was entirely in French. My years at Yale weren't a total loss.

I asked him when was the last time he had seen the Inverted Jenny stamps. He shrugged and said years and years ago. I asked if he had seen a small red book being passed around the dinner table on the night Alan DuPey and his wife arrived. He shrugged and said no.

I asked if he thought anyone on the staff might have taken the stamps. He shrugged. I asked if he had seen any nogoodnik-types skulking about. He shrugged and said no. Then I asked if he thought any of the houseguests might be capable of such a nefarious deed. This time he didn't shrug, but slowly stubbed out the minuscule butt of the Gitane in a white china saucer.

"Perhaps," he said.

"Who?"

"The English son," he said. "Harry Smythe and his wife."

"Why them?"

Then he shrugged. "They are very cold people. And the last time they were here, they left me no tip. A month of meals, and no tip. I thought they were tight people. Cold and tight. But perhaps they are in need of money. They see the stamps and think the madam is rich and will not miss them. So they collar the stamps. Simple, no?"

I was about to shrug when a young woman in a maid's uniform entered the kitchen. I recognized her from those dinners my family had enjoyed at the Chez Horowitz. I knew she was addressed as Clara but didn't know her last name. I introduced myself and learned she was Clara Bodkin—and you didn't have to be a Shakespearean scholar for the phrase "bare bodkin" to leap to mind, for she was a toothsome creature, a bit plumpish but excellently proportioned. Her flawless, sun-blushed complexion was especially attractive.

I ran through my list of questions, in English, with meager results. Yes, she had seen the stamps being passed around the table at the DuPey dinner. That was the last time she had seen them. No, she did not believe anyone on the staff or any of the houseguests was capable of the theft. And while she had seen no strangers hanging about,

70

it was her theory that some fiend had sneaked into the house while everyone slept, and took the Inverted Jennies from madam's wall safe. It gave her, Clara, chills to think about it.

I listened to all this somewhat absently. My attention was elsewhere. For as Clara spoke so volubly, she stood alongside Jean Cuvier's chair, and he was steadily stroking her rump in a thoughtful fashion. She did not move away.

He must have seen astonishment in my face, for after Clara finished talking, he lighted another Gitane and said to me, in French, "It is all right, Ar-chay. Clara and I are to be married."

"Congratulations," I said heartily.

"For one night," he added, and gave a great shout of laughter.

"What did he say?" Clara demanded of me. "Is the blimp talking dirty again?"

"Not at all," I said hastily. "He told me that I can accept every word you say as gospel since you know everything that's going on in this house."

"That I do," she said, nodding. "But I see no evil, hear no evil, speak no evil."

"Very wise," I assured her.

When I left, she was tickling the back of his fat neck. I do believe she might have seated herself on his lap—if he had one.

I decided I had earned my salary for the day, and besides, asking the same questions continually had the same effect as the Chinese water torture. I drove home, changed, and went down to the beach for a swim. I resolutely did my two miles and returned home in time to dress for the family cocktail hour and my date with Jennifer Towley.

Mother remarked how handsome I looked, father stared disgustedly at my acid green polo shirt, and I ingested my share of the martini pitcher's contents. Then I bid them good night and departed for what I hoped would be an evening of a thousand delights. I didn't forget Jennifer's tennis racquet. Talk about Greeks bearing gifts!

She lived across Lake Worth, south of the Royal Park Bridge. It was an old neighborhood of short streets west of Flagler Drive. The homes were small but pleasant, the grounds limited but neatly groomed. Jennifer rented the ground floor of a two-story stucco building painted a sky blue. Her apartment was her antique shop; everything in the place was for sale—except the lady herself, of course.

She greeted me at the door, and I entered into a foyer (Edwardian) and then was ushered into the living room (Victorian). I had suggested she dress informally, but she was impeccably upholstered in a black dress so simple and *nothing* that it must have cost a fortune. The only jewelry she wore was a pale amethyst choker. Elegant? On a scale of 1 to 10, I'd rate her a 12.

The tennis racquet was an instant success; after hefting it and trying a few swings, she declared the weight and balance were perfect. I received a kiss in gratitude. It was a very small kiss but much appreciated.

I held the Miata door for her, and she slid in with a flash of bare tanned legs that made me want to turn cartwheels on her lawn. But I controlled my rapture and we sped off to the Pelican Club. I called her attention to the full moon I had ordered for the occasion.

"I may turn into a werewolf," I cautioned.

"I'll get some garlic at the restaurant," she said.

"Garlic is for vampires," I told her. "And frogs' legs. There is no known defense against a werewolf."

"I have a black belt in karate," she claimed.

"I have a white belt in Indian wrestling," I said. "Perhaps later this evening you will permit me to demonstrate."

She laughed. "What am I going to do with you?" she asked.

"Love me," I replied, but I did not say it aloud.

We were early enough to beat the usual dinner crowd, and Priscilla showed us to my favorite corner table. Jennifer looked about with interest.

"It resembles a fraternity house," she said.

"It was intended to," I said. "Strictly stag. But shortly after the club was organized, the ladyfriends and wives of several founding members threatened a lawsuit if they were not allowed to join. They said they would claim sex discrimination because we were carrying on business networking at the club. Actually, the only networking going on was an active exchange of hangover remedies, but we surrendered graciously to their demands. Now the Pelican Club is a coed establishment. The roster is full, but I chair the Membership Committee and might be able to finagle a quid pro quo and get you a card if you're interested in joining."

"Thank you," she said, giving me the cool, level gaze, "but I think not. If I want to visit I'll ask you to invite me."

73

"Splendid idea," I said, and looked around for Priscilla. She was standing at the kitchen door, and when she caught my eye she pointed at Jennifer and made a loop with thumb and forefinger in the A-OK sign. It was gratifying to have her approval.

She came over to the table and posed, hip-sprung. "Something to wet the whistle, folks?" she said.

"Let's have a champagne cocktail," I suggested to Jennifer.

"Oh my," she said, "you'll spoil me."

"That's my intent," I said. "We'll have champagne cocktails, Priscilla. And what is Leroy pushing tonight?"

"Roast pork or broiled yellowtail."

"How's the yellowtail?"

"I wouldn't know," she said. "I eat at McDonald's."

Jennifer smiled.

"Priscilla," I said, "behave yourself."

She grinned and sashayed away to fetch our cocktails.

It turned out to be a very pleasant dinner indeed. We both had the yellowtail, shared a big Caesar salad, and had lemon ice for dessert.

Jennifer ate like a trencherwoman—which always pleases the guy who's picking up the tab. She spoke very little but that was okay; I like to talk, as you may have guessed, and I kept her laughing throughout the meal.

I do not consider myself a womanizer. Most of my relationships with women have been lasting, some as long as three or four months, and one for an entire year, almost. I have always favored jolly ladies who are not too intent on trotting up the aisle while an adenoidal soprano belts out "Oh Promise Me."

We moved out to the bar where we had a brandy stinger because it seemed the glam thing to do. I had a vague romantic notion of suggesting a long drive down the coast during which the full moon shining off a calm sea would work its libidinous magic. But Jennifer, now suddenly serious, if not solemn, said she'd like to return home since she had an important appointment early the next morning. The moon promptly went behind a cloud.

So I drove her back to her pad, disappointed but not devastated. In addition to playing the clown, one must have an endless reserve of patience. We pulled in front of her trig little house, and I killed the engine, hoping against odds that she might invite me in for a nightcap.

She turned on the seat to face me and took up my hand. Good start.

"Archy," she said, "there is something I must tell you."

"Oh?"

"I'm divorced."

It was my turn to laugh. "Jennifer, you say that as if it was an awful perversion, like collecting thimbles. A lot of people are divorced. Some of my best friends are divorced. It's really not a mortal sin."

"I just wanted you to know."

"Thank you. Now I know."

She hesitated, and I thought she was about to reveal more. But apparently she changed her mind. Instead, she said, "Then it won't change things between us?"

I stared at her, and my mouth might have fallen open just a wee bit. "Of course not," I said, thinking that this *couldn't* be what Lady Horowitz warned me about. Divorce is as widespread in Palm Beach as jock itch in the

75

Major Leagues. "I don't see why it should change anything."

"Would you like to come in for a nightcap?" she asked.

Strange, enigmatic woman!

5

On the following morning I went to the office with my father. He drove his Lexus the way he did everything else: slowly, carefully, and with a deep respect for thou-shalt-nots. I mean we'd come to a red light, no traffic to be seen in either direction, and he'd stop and wait for the green. What an upright man he was! But never a prig; he was simply worshipful of the law. His tombstone might justifiably bear the inscription: "Prescott McNally: He never stole a hotel towel."

"About Lady Horowitz's missing stamps," he said, eyes determinedly on the road. "Are you making any progress?"

"Not really, sir," I said. "So far I've spoken to three of the staff and two houseguests and learned very little."

He was silent a moment, and I knew the gears were turning. Not meshing yet, but turning.

"What is your feeling about this, Archy? Have the stamps merely been misplaced or were they stolen?"

"All I can do right now is guess," I told him. "I'd guess they were pinched."

Then the gears meshed, and he nodded. "I think it would be prudent to act on that assumption. I'll call Lady Cynthia and suggest she report the disappearance of the Inverted Jennies to the police immediately. Or, if she prefers, I'll do it for her."

"Father!" I said, offended. "I've just started my investigation."

He gave me a brief glance, then hastily turned his attention back to the road. "Archy, I don't mean to bruise your ego, but if the stamps are not recovered—a possibility, you'll admit—and Lady Horowitz puts in a claim for the insurance, it is vitally important that there is a police record attesting to the fact that she reported the theft. You can understand that, can't you?"

"Yes, sir," I said resignedly. "Does this mean I'm off the case?"

"Not at all. I want you to continue your discreet inquiries."

"That means the cops and I will be walking up each other's heels," I said. "Interviewing the same people twice."

"You've worked with the police before," he pointed out. "And very successfully, I might add. Besides, as you well know, it is frequently wise to ask a witness to repeat his or her story twice or more. It's an effective method of uncovering discrepancies."

"All right then," I said, "I'll keep at it. You might suggest to Lady Cynthia that she report the theft to Sergeant Al Rogoff. If he catches the squeal, he may be assigned the investigation. Al and I get along well together."

I didn't think it necessary to tell him that Rogoff already knew of the theft. We drove along in silence a few minutes while I debated whether the injection of officialdom into what I considered *my* case would prove a help or a hindrance.

"Pleasant evening last night?" my father asked idly.

"What?" I said, startled. "Oh yes, sir, very pleasant."

"Anyone your mother and I know?"

"I don't think so. Jennifer Towley, the lady who returned the Frobisher letters. I gave her the tennis racquet."

"And was she appreciative?"

"Extremely."

"You are attracted to her?"

"Exceedingly."

He sighed. "It seems to me I have heard that several times in the past."

I laughed. "Father, I know very well that you and mother would like to see me happily married, settled down, and producing grandchildren at regular intervals. That time may come—but not yet."

"We'll try to be patient," he said dryly.

McNally & Son was not a rinky-dink operation. We occupied (and owned) a five-story edifice of glass and stainless steel on Royal Palm Way. The architecture was not to my father's taste, but he admitted the gleaming modernism seemed to impress clients, potential clients, and IRS auditors.

Most of the firm's work was in estate planning, taxes, revocable and charitable trusts, and dull stuff like that. But we also had associates skilled in litigation; real estate; copyrights, trademarks and patents; divorce; malpractice; personal and product liability; and even one old codger who knew more maritime law than anyone south of Chesapeake Bay. McNally & Son was, in fact, a legal supermarket.

My office was possibly the smallest in the building, and I often thought I was condemned to that cell so that Prescott McNally could easily refute any charges of nepotism. But I really didn't mind since I rarely occupied the office. Naturally I wasn't assigned a secretary, but on those rare occasions (about once a year) when I had to compose a letter, my father's personal secretary, Mrs. Trelawney, helped me out and corrected my spelling. I never could remember if there were one or two *c*'s and *m*'s in "accomodate."

The reason I visited headquarters that morning was to prepare my monthly expense account, which might be a contender for the Pulitzer Prize for Fiction. I dug out all my bar and restaurant tabs, the bill for Jennifer's tennis racquet, the signed receipt from Bela Rubik (the stamp and coin man), bills for dues paid to various clubs, and bits of this and that. I added them all up, and the total seemed to me woefully inadequate.

So I tacked on a few imaginary cash expenditures: cab rides I had never taken, bribes to informants I had never made, gas purchases for the Miata. I did not go hog-wild, of course; I am not a swindler. But as I added more fanciful items, my swindle sheet grew satisfyingly.

I was still hard at it when my phone rang. I was shocked. I mean, my phone almost *never* rings. And then it's usually a wrong number.

"Archibald McNally," I answered.

"The Machiavelli of Palm Beach?" Sgt. Al Rogoff said. "I just wanted to check that you're in. What a pleasant surprise! I'll be right over."

"What for?" I asked.

"Hah!" was all he said before hanging up.

A half-hour later he was squirming uncomfortably on the one folding steel chair allotted to me for visitors, regarding me more in anger than in sorrow.

"Rat fink," he said accusingly. "Oh, excuse me. I should have addressed someone who's a pal of Lady Horowitz as *Mister* Rat Fink."

I held up my palms in surrender. "Al, I swear I didn't know until this morning that she was going to file a complaint. I really thought it was going to be my headache. I had no idea it would end up on your plate."

"Yeah?" he said, staring at me. "Maybe. And maybe not. You been looking into it?"

"Only for two days."

"What have you got?" he demanded, taking out his notebook.

I gave him the names of the staff and guests residing at the Horowitz home. I recited the gist of the conversations I had with Kenneth Bodin, Angus Wolfson, Gina Stanescu, Jean Cuvier, and Clara Bodkin. I described Lady Cynthia's bedroom, and told him about the unrifled jewelry box close to the wall safe.

He scribbled rapid notes in his little book, and when I finished, he looked up at me suspiciously. "And that's all you've got?"

"That's all."

"Come on, Archy, don't try to kid a kidder. You're holding out on me."

I had already polished the bone I intended to toss him.

"Well, there *is* something," I said hesitantly, "but I don't think it's important."

"Let me play the judge. What is it?"

I told him that a few weeks before the stamps disappeared, a butler and a maid had left Lady Horowitz's employ, claiming they couldn't stand the heat of a Florida summer.

"But the Inverted Jennies were seen after they left," I pointed out, "so they couldn't be involved in the snatch. Unless they sneaked back in."

"Uh-huh," Al said. "Or told some light-fingered buddy about the stamps. Okay, I'll look into it." He closed his fat notebook and put a rubber band around it. "You figure to keep sherlocking on this thing?"

I nodded. "I planned to go out there this afternoon and check out some of the people I haven't talked to yet."

He considered that awhile, and I awaited his decision. If he ordered me off the case, I'd have to take a walk. He had the badge, not me.

"All right," he said finally, "you keep nosing around and

we'll compare notes. Nothing held back. Is that under-
stood?"

"Of course," I said. "I wouldn't have it any other way."

He sighed and hauled himself to his feet. "I hate Beach
cases," he said. "Those richniks treat me like the hired
help."

"Don't give it a second thought," I advised him.
"They're just as innocent and just as guilty as anyone else.
And don't forget the gifts at Christmastime."

"Yeah," he said sourly. "A box of stale Girl Scout cookies." He started for the door, then paused and looked
about my infinitesimal office. "You really rate," he said.

"The boss's son," I reminded him.

He was laughing when he left.

What I hadn't told him, of course—and didn't intend
to—was the rumor that a few years ago Lady Horowitz
had been enjoying fun and games with her chauffeur. It
seemed to me the doyenne was the type of woman who'd
terminate that relationship; it wouldn't be Kenneth
Bodin who split; he'd never want the gravy train to stop.

And, assuming he was unceremoniously dumped, it was
possible he had entertained dim-witted thoughts of revenge against the wealthy woman who had suddenly
taken him up and then just as suddenly dropped him,
either from boredom or because she found another lover
with Bodin's physical excitement plus the brains he
lacked. So the muscleman, enraged by this slight to his
machismo, decided to swipe the Inverted Jennies to teach
the rich bitch a lesson.

Thin stuff, you say? Of course it was. I knew it was. But

it was all I had so far, and I wanted to check it out before handing over the results to Sgt. Al Rogoff.

I finished composing my expense account, dropped it off at our treasurer's office, and then stopped by the employees' cafeteria. The luncheon specialty of the day was something called a "mushburger," apparently made of minced mushrooms, carrots, black olives, and rhubarb. What, no turnips? Anyway I passed. But I did drink a glass of unsalted tomato juice and ate two rice cakes. Feeling healthy as all get-out, I leaped into the Miata and headed for the Horowitz domain.

I rang the front-door chimes and, as I had hoped, the oak portal was opened by the housekeeper, Mrs. Marsden. We exchanged pleasantries, and I asked if we could talk privately for a moment.

"I was wondering when you'd get around to me," she said—a steely smile there—and led the way into the first-floor sitting room, which could have held the Boston Pops. We sat in chintz-covered armchairs in a secluded corner and leaned toward each other, speaking in hushed voices as if we were trading state secrets.

She was a majestic woman with the posture and manner of a sergeant major. She was a widow, and I happened to know she had put two kids through college by enduring all the craziness of the Horowitz ménage. She had been with Lady C. a long time, and I doubted if any outrage her mistress might commit would surprise her. She knew she was working for a loony and accepted it.

I took her through the usual questions, and she gave a firm negative to all. Then I sat back and regarded her gravely.

"Mrs. Marsden, you know I'm not a lawyer, but I do represent my father, Lady Cynthia's attorney. So in a sense I am bound by the same rules of lawyer-client confidentiality. What I'm trying to say is that it's the job of McNally and Son to protect the interests of Lady Horowitz. With that in mind, is there anything at all you can tell me about the disappearance of the stamps? I assure you it'll be held in strictest confidence."

She was silent for a long while, which was a tipoff in itself. If there was nothing, she would have said so immediately.

Finally she stirred restlessly. "It's nothing I can spell out," she said. "Nothing definite—you understand?"

I nodded.

"A feeling," she said. "That's all it is, a feeling. I see people talking, and they shut up when I come close. And people meeting people they shouldn't be meeting."

"Which people?" I asked.

But she ignored my question. "Just the mood," she said, almost ruminating. "Like something's happening, something's going down, but I don't know what it is. That's not much help, is it?"

"More than you think," I told her. "I trust your instincts. If things become a little clearer, will you contact me?"

"Yes, I could do that."

"I know you have our phone numbers, at home and the office. I'd really appreciate it if you'd give me a call. This business is nasty."

"That it is," she said, nodding vigorously. "I-do-not-like-it-one-bit."

"I won't take up any more of your time, Mrs. Marsden. Anyone else around I can talk to?"

"Harry Smythe and his wife are out on the north terrace. Playing chess."

"Nice people?" I asked her.

"I wouldn't know, sir," she said, the perfect servant.

I found my way to the north terrace—the one in the shade—and walked into a family squabble. Nothing vulgar, but as I arrived he swept the chessboard clear with a sweep of his arm and she gave him a high-intensity glare. If looks could kill, he would have been dead on the scene. And these were the people chef Jean Cuvier had described as "cold"?

I stooped to pick up a rook and a pawn, and set them upright on the board. "Checkmate," I said with what I hoped was a soothing smile. It wasn't.

"And just who the hell are you?" he demanded in a BBC accent.

I was tempted to give him a brash response like "Mickey Mouse" or "King Tut" but obviously neither of them was in the mood for levity.

"Archibald McNally," I said. "And you must be Doris and Harry Smythe. Surely Lady Horowitz told you I'd be around asking questions about her missing stamps."

"It's got nothing to do with us," the woman said in the surliest way imaginable. "So bug off."

Unbidden, I pulled up a chair, sat down, crossed my legs, and gave them a taste of the McNally insolence. "Of course it concerns you," I said stonily. "You were on the premises when the Inverted Jennies disappeared. So naturally you are suspect. The theft has now been reported to the local authorities. If you refuse to answer my questions, I shall be forced to report your uncooperative attitude to Sergeant Al Rogoff, who is heading the official investigation. He has been known to make recalcitrant witnesses talk by beating them about the kidneys with a rubber truncheon."

I really thought I had gone too far, and they'd immediately dismiss me as a demented freak. But perhaps it was the influence of American movies and TV shows that caused them to stare at me in horrified astonishment, wondering if I might be telling the truth about the interrogative techniques of Florida cops.

"We know absolutely nothing about it," Harry Smythe said, tugging at his ridiculously wispy Vandyke.

"Not a thing," his wife chimed in.

I looked at them. What a pair they were! Both long and stretched, all pale skin and tendons. Both wore their hair parted in the middle, but his was sparse and straw yellow while hers was thick chestnut and quite long. And both had the dazed eyes and clenched jaws of the luckless. I hoped Mrs. Marsden would count the silver before they left.

I spent an unpleasant twenty minutes putting the Smythes through my inquisition. But as I seemingly accepted all their answers without objection, their aplomb returned, and Harry took to staring at my pastel silk sports jacket with chilly disdain. He was wearing a Harris tweed with suede patches on the elbows—in South Florida yet!

I didn't find it bothersome if he thought me foppish. That was his opinion—and my father's. *His* idea of sartorial splendor is wearing a Countess Mara tie.

"There is nothing you can add to what you've already told me?" I asked finally.

"I think someone on the staff took the stamps," he offered.

"Thank you both very much," I said, rising. "I'll probably be back with more questions, and I imagine Sergeant Rogoff will want to hear your story as well. Now go back to your chess game. It's such a lovely day for it."

I marched back into the house and met Lady Cynthia Horowitz entering from the front door. She looked like a million dollars. But I speak metaphorically. Actually she looked like a hundred million dollars which, according to Palm Beach gossip, was her approximate net worth. Anyway, she was smashing in a Donna Karan sheath of beige linen. She also had a tennis bracelet of diamonds around one bare ankle.

"Hi, lad," she said breezily. "How's the snooping coming along?"

"Slowly," I said. "I've just been talking to Doris and Harry Smythe."

"Monsters, aren't they?" she said. "I just can't believe that stiff is my son. And that shrew he married! The two of them are so dull."

"You invited them," I pointed out.

"Come with me," she ordered, crooking a forefinger.

I followed her down the long hallway to a shadowed game room complete with billiard table, card tables, and a small roulette wheel. There was also a zinc wet bar built into one wall, and that's where Lady Cynthia headed.

"What'll you have?" she asked.

"Nothing, thank you," I said. "But you go ahead."

"I intend to," she said, and I watched with fascination as she swiftly and expertly constructed a gin-and-bitters.

"Let me tell you about my son Harry," she said, "and my sweet daughter-in-law. They're professional guests. That's how they live: London to Paris to Antibes to Monte Carlo to Palm Beach to Newport—wherever they have acquaintances, friends, or relatives who'll put up with them for a weekend, a week, a month—whatever. Neither Harry nor Doris has ever worked and probably never will. The only capital they have can be packed in four suitcases. I give Harry a yearly allowance, just enough so they can fly tourist-class to their next invitation. Sponges, both of them."

"A sad way to live," I observed. "What kind of a future can they have?"

She gave me a crooked grin. "They're waiting for me to die," she said, then hoisted her glass. "Cheers!" she said.

I wished then I had asked for a drink because what she said touched me. Sad bravery always does.

"Ma'am," I said, "I'd like to ask you something I hope won't offend you. If the Smythes are constantly on their uppers, as you say, do you think it possible they might have stolen the Inverted Jennies?"

She considered that a moment, head cocked to one side.

"Nope," she said at last. "Out of character. Petty stuff maybe, but not a *big* crime. They just don't have the balls for it. They're really small people, lad. Which is why I have Mrs. Marsden count the silver before they leave."

I laughed. "The idea had occurred to me. You and I think the same way."

She looked at me strangely. I could not interpret that look.

"Do we?" she said.

I departed soon afterward, having had my fill of the Inverted Jenny Case for one day. I drove home, took my swim, attended the family cocktail hour, and dined with my parents.

I announced my intention of spending the evening in my den getting caught up on personal correspondence. My father suggested I might like to take a break later and come downstairs for a nightcap in his study. Prescott McNally never commanded, he suggested.

I brought my journal up to date, paid a bill for a tapestry waistcoat (couldn't put *that* on my expense account), and dashed off a few short notes.

I also phoned Jennifer Towley and got her answering machine. While waiting for the *beep* I wondered idly if it was a Victorian or Edwardian model. I left a message thanking her for an invigorating evening and asking that she call so that we might arrange an encore. I hung up, curious about where she might be at that hour. I am not afraid of competition, you understand, but I would much prefer the cool Towley gaze be leveled only at me. And my ego is such that I refused to believe she could have found a more ardent swain. Grumbling with frustration,

I clumped downstairs to my father's study for that night-cap.

He was still fighting his way through *Little Dorrit,* but put the volume aside when I entered and invited me to help myself from his port decanter. He waited until I was fueled and seated before he spoke:

"I suppose you know that the police have been notified about the disappearance of Lady Horowitz's stamps."

I nodded.

"As you had hoped, Sergeant Rogoff has been assigned to the investigation."

"Yes, sir," I said. "I had a talk with him this morning and gave him what I have, which isn't much."

He looked at me narrowly. "You gave him *everything*?"

"Not *quite* everything," I said, and told my father the wild theory I had that Kenneth Bodin, the chauffeur, might have pinched the stamps to get back at the rich lady who had an affair with him and then gave him the boot.

My father rose from his club chair and strode over to the pipe rack on his marble-topped sideboard. He selected a handsome silver-banded Comoy and began to pack it from a walnut humidor. His back was turned to me.

"You really believe that, Archy?" he asked. "About the chauffeur?"

"I'll have to check it out," I said, "but at the moment it's all I have."

He lighted his pipe with a wooden kitchen match and returned, puffing, to his chair.

91

"Sounds farfetched to me," he said.

"Yes, sir, it does," I agreed. "And if I had anything better I'd zero in on that. But I still have three more people to talk to, and something might turn up. By the way, I spoke to Lady Horowitz this afternoon. She seemed remarkably chipper."

"She doesn't appear devastated by her loss," he admitted. "But as I'm sure you're aware, it represents a small fraction of her net worth. Couldn't that rumor about Lady Cynthia and her chauffeur be merely idle gossip, with no truth to it?"

"It could be," I acknowledged. "But I'm always amazed at how often local gossip turns out to have at least a kernel of truth. And she does have the reputation of being rather free with her favors, in addition to her six husbands."

"Yes," he said, "I suppose so."

And then he said nothing more about the Inverted Jenny Case. I made some idle conversation about the dwarf palms Jamie had planted about the garage, and he responded mechanically. I finished my port, thanked him, and rose to leave. He didn't urge me to stay.

He said merely, "Keep at it, Archy."

I went back upstairs and prepared for bed. My father is a deep, deep man, and I couldn't help wondering why he had quizzed me in such detail about the missing stamps. Usually he hands me an assignment and never asks questions until I bring him the results. I could only assume he wanted McNally & Son to provide exemplary service to a valued client. There are a lot of hungry attorneys in South Florida, where many wealthy people switch lawyers as often as they do proctologists.

6

The following morning I overslept (a not infrequent occurrence) and dashed down to the kitchen where I found Ursi Olson doing something violent to a pot of yams. Our cook-housekeeper is a stalwart woman who looks as if she could plow a field, pause to drop a foal, and then continue plowing.

"Breakfast?" she asked.

"Sure," I said. "But I'm on a diet."

"No eggs Benedict?"

"I lied to you," I said. "I'm not on a diet. Eggs Benedict, by all means."

"You got a phone call from your father's office," she said. "Mrs. Trelawney. She wants you to call her."

While Ursi rustled up my eggs, I used the kitchen phone to call my father's secretary.

"I have your expense account check," she told me.

"Bless you!" I said fervently.

"Can you pick it up?"

"You betcha," I said. "Later today. Okay?"

"Whenever," she said.

Sounds like a silly, innocuous phone call, doesn't it? But later I was to reflect on how important it turned out to be. Because if Mrs. Trelawney hadn't called me, and I hadn't agreed to stop by the office and pick up my check, then I—but I'm getting ahead of myself. At the time it happened I felt nothing but joy at the news that funds awaited me. My checking account had become a bit emaciated. I don't mean that poverty loomed, but one sleeps better with a few shekels under the mattress, doesn't one?

After breakfast I hustled to the Horowitz mansion. I wanted to talk to the remaining residents before they were braced by Sgt. Rogoff and his henchmen. Al is a very capable investigator, but subtlety is not his long suit. First of all, he *looks* menacing, which makes a lot of people lockjawed—especially the guilty. I look like a twit, which fools many into telling me more than they intended.

I headed directly for the ground-floor office of Consuela Garcia, Lady Cynthia's social secretary and my lost love. She was on the phone when I entered and motioned me to a chair.

"But I mailed the invitation myself, Mrs. Blair," she was lying smoothly. "I really can't understand why you didn't receive it. Our dreadful postal service! Well, Lady Horowitz is planning a big Fourth of July bash, and I'll make every effort to make certain you receive your invitation. And again, I'm so sorry you were disappointed last time."

She hung up and grinned at me.

94

I rubbed one stiff forefinger against the other in the "shame on you" gesture. "Liar, liar, pants on fire," I said.

"Listen, you," she said, "I hear you were at the Pelican with a looker. Who is she?"

"My sister," I said.

"Since when does a guy buy his sister champagne cocktails?"

"Oh-ho," I said. "Priscilla's been talking."

Connie, who's a member of the Pelican Club, said, "Priscilla never blabs and you know it. But my spies are everywhere. How are you, Archy?"

"If I felt any better I'd be unconscious. And you?"

"Surviving, barely. Half the calls I get are from yentas who want to know who snatched the madam's stamps. I suppose that's why you're here."

"You suppose correctly. Have the cops been around?"

"Not yet."

"They will be."

"That's all I need," she said mournfully. "The reporters are bad enough. Okay, let's get it over with."

I ran her through my shortened version of Twenty Questions and learned nothing important. Consuela had last seen the Inverted Jennies about six months ago when Lady Cynthia passed them around at a charity benefit. Everyone knew they were kept in an unlocked wall safe, and anyone could have snaffled them: staff, houseguests, or even brief visitors.

I stared at her as she spoke and saw what had attracted me originally: She was a shortish, perky young lady with cascading black hair. Once, in our brief escapade, I had the joy of seeing her in a string bikini. The memory lingered. But there was more to her than just a bod; she had a brain as well. She ditched me, didn't she?

"Connie," I said, "give me something, no matter how wild. Who do *you* think could have stolen those stupid stamps?"

She pondered a long while. "Not an outsider," she said finally. "Not an over-the-wall crook. I don't buy that. It was an inside job."

I groaned. "Thanks a lot," I said. "Five people on the staff, six houseguests. That's eleven suspects."

"Including me," she said, grinning again.

"That's right," I agreed. "And the cops know it."

"Oh, that's beautiful."

"What about Harry Smythe and his wife?"

"What about them?"

"I don't like them," I said.

"Who does?" she asked, reasonably enough. "But if I had to make guesses, they wouldn't head the list. They're too mean."

"Who would head the list?"

She hesitated just a moment. Then: "Alan DuPey and his wife."

"Why them?"

"They're too nice."

I came close to slapping my thigh in merriment. "The FBI could use you, Connie. What a sleuth you are!"

"Well, you asked me for wild ideas."

"So I did," I said. "I haven't talked to the DuPeys yet. Are they around?"

"No one's around. The madam is at the hairdresser's

and the rest of the crowd has gone out for the day on Phil
Meecham's yacht."

"That old roué?" I said. "He'll make a play for all the
women and most of the men. All right, I'll catch the
DuPeys another time. Thanks for your help, Connie."

I was starting out when she called, "Archy," and I
turned back.

"Who is she?" she asked again.

"You never give up, do you?" I said. "Well, it's no secret; her name is Jennifer Towley."

Connie's smile faded. "Oh-oh," she said. "You've got
trouble, son."

I stared at her. "What *is* this?" I demanded. "You're the
second person who's warned me. Why have I got trouble?
What's wrong with my dating Jennifer?"

"Nothing," she said, busying herself with papers on her
desk. "Now get the hell out of here. I have work to do."

I knew there was no use pushing it so I got the hell out
of there as ordered. I drove to headquarters debating
which mystery was more maddening: the missing stamps
or Jennifer Towley. About equal, I reckoned.

In the cool lobby of the McNally & Son Building, the
receptionist, a white male heterosexual (we were an equal
opportunity employer), handed me a pink message note.
It stated that Bela Rubik had phoned me about an hour
previously and wanted me to call him as soon as possible.

But first things first: I went upstairs and collected my
check from Mrs. Trelawney. She was a delightful old bird
who obviously wore a wig and looked like everyone's
maiden aunt. But she loved raunchy jokes, so I spent ten
minutes with her, relating the most recent I had heard.

She had a couple of good ones herself. Then I went to my office and phoned Rubik.

"Archibald McNally," I said, "returning your call. Do you have anything for me, Mr. Rubik?"

"Yes," he said. "Something important."

"What is it?"

"Not on the phone," he said. "Come over as soon as you can."

"All right," I said. "I'll be there shortly."

I stopped at my bank, a block away, and deposited the expense account check. I could have ambled down to Rubik's shop—it was a nice stroll—but the day was becoming brutally hot, and I decided to drive. I found a place to park near Worth Avenue and walked over to the stamp and coin store, wishing I had worn my panama.

There was a cardboard sign taped to the glass door: BACK IN AN HOUR. I am not ordinarily a profane man, but I admit I may have uttered a mild oath, pianissimo, when I read that. Not only had I told the idiot I was on my way, but the sign gave no indication of when Rubik had left. Back in an hour could mean I'd have to wait three minutes or fifty.

Not at all gruntled, I started to walk away, then stopped. Suddenly I realized that stupid sign had been taped to the *outside* of the glass door. How often have you seen a merchant do that? Never. They fasten their signs on the *inside* of the glass so they can be removed and used again. Tape it outside and some nut will come along, rip it off, and toss it in the gutter just for the fun of it.

I retraced my steps and inspected the sign more

closely. It seemed to have been hastily scrawled and was attached to the glass with a ragged piece of masking tape. I shielded my eyes and tried to peer within. I saw no movement, but on the tile floor alongside the showcase I spotted the stamp dealer's crazy spectacles with the twin loupes. They were twisted and one of the lenses had popped out.

"Oh Jesus," I said aloud.

I tried the doorknob. It turned easily. I opened the door a few inches. "Mr. Rubik," I called, "are you here?"

No answer.

I entered cautiously, moving very, very slowly. He was lying on the floor behind the showcase. His bald skull had been dented so many times it looked like a crushed paper bag. It was clear that his spirit had flown. And next to his smashed skull lay what seemed to be the weapon: a crystal paperweight. There was very little blood coming from the shattered skull.

I am not a stranger to violent death, but I don't think I'll ever get used to it. I hope not. I looked around, then stepped carefully over the corpse to a back office that was large enough to hold a big double-doored safe. No one was in sight and no one was crouched behind the desk ready to leap out and shout, "Boo!" The tiny lavatory was also empty.

I used the phone on Rubik's desk, handling it lightly with my silk foulard pocket square. I called the PBPD, praying Al would be in. He was.

"Sergeant Rogoff," he said.

"Archy McNally," I said. "I'm in Rubik's Stamp and

Coin Shop. He's on the floor waiting for the meat wagon. Someone smashed in his skull."

Al didn't miss a beat. "All right," he said. "I'm on my way."

"Make it fast, Al," I urged. "I'm lonely."

"Don't touch a thing," he ordered. "Go outside and wait for me on the sidewalk."

"I know the drill," I said crossly, but he had already hung up.

I went back outside and stood guard at the door. I stuck my hands in my pockets to hide the tremble. There were pedestrians moving lazily along, and some of them gave me a friendly nod the way people do in Florida. One old codger said, with a perfectly straight face, "I don't think it's too cold, do you, partner?" I wanted to top him by casually mentioning, "Hey, partner, there's a murdered man in this store." But I didn't.

It seemed like an eternity but it probably wasn't much more than ten minutes before I heard the sound of an approaching siren. What a sweet song that was! Then the police car pulled up with a squeal of brakes. Al and another uniformed officer climbed out, taking their time. The other cop was a stranger to me, but he seemed awfully young, which means I'm getting awfully old—right? Anyway, he was trying to look stern and purposeful, and he kept his hand resting on his gun butt.

We all moved inside and looked down at the crumpled remains of Bela Rubik.

"Thanks a lot, Archy," Al said to me. "And it's not even my birthday."

The young officer squatted by the corpse and fumbled at the neck. I don't know what he thought he was doing— probably feeling for the carotid. He looked up at Rogoff. "He's stiff, sarge."

"No kidding?" Al said. "Are you sure he's not faking it?" He turned to me. "Go back to your office, Archy," he ordered, "and don't leave it even to take a pee. After I get the wheels turning here, I'll give you a call and you come over to the palace and dictate your statement."

I nodded. "That paperweight—" I offered. "It's called a millefiori. It's made by cutting cross sections of glass rods of different colors and shapes."

"Thank you, professor," the sergeant said. "That certainly is a valuable clue. Now beat it."

I didn't go directly back to my office. I stopped at the nearest bar and had a double Pinch. My shaking finally stopped. When I arrived at headquarters, I went to my father's office, but Mrs. Trelawney said he had left for lunch with a client. So I retired to my cubbyhole and lighted my first English Oval of the day. I thought I deserved it.

I sat there for more than an hour, counting the walls and trying not to think about *anything*. But it didn't work. I couldn't stop reflecting on chance. If Mrs. Trelawney hadn't phoned me about that expense account check, I wouldn't have come into the office that morning. And if I hadn't come into the office, I wouldn't have received the message that Rubik had called. And if I hadn't wasted time trading jokes with Mrs. Trelawney, I'd have left sooner. And if I hadn't paused to deposit the check but hustled over to Rubik's shop immediately, I might have walked in on a horrendous murder. But what was the use of imagining. Life is all ifs, is it not?

Then Sgt. Rogoff called. "All right," he said, "come over now. We're ready for you."

I drove over to the building on County Road Al liked to call the "palace." His office was larger than mine (whose wasn't?), and the decor was Police Station Moderne. I sat in an uncomfortable wooden armchair and dictated my statement into a tape recorder, with Al and two witnesses in attendance.

This time I omitted absolutely nothing. I told of my first meeting with Bela Rubik and how he had agreed to ask other dealers if a block of four Inverted Jenny stamps had suddenly come on the market. Then I stated how he phoned me that morning, saying he had something of importance to tell me that he didn't want to discuss on the phone.

I described how the sign attached to the outside of the glass had aroused my curiosity. I said I had entered after seeing Rubik's broken glasses on the floor. I noted that when I first visited the shop, the door had been locked and apparently the proprietor would not admit anyone he didn't know who appeared threatening.

I said I had touched nothing but the doorknob and the phone on Rubik's desk. I had seen no one leaving the shop as I approached. I had smelled no perfume, cologne, or any other scent inside the store. The stamp dealer had mentioned nothing to me of prior robberies or assaults. And that was all I knew.

The tape was taken away to be transcribed, and Sgt. Rogoff and I were left alone. He pulled out a cigar, sliced off the tip with a penknife, and began to juice it up.

"You come up with some doozies, you do," he said. "You figure it had something to do with the Inverted Jennies?"

"I think that's a reasonable assumption," I said. "Unless it was plain and simple robbery. Was anything missing?"

"Didn't look like it. The showcase was locked and intact. So was the safe in the back office. Rubik still had his wallet, untouched."

"Al, was he married?"

"Yeah," the sergeant said softly. "His wife's in a nursing home. Alzheimer's. He's got one daughter with the Peace Corps in Africa. We're trying to notify her. He had two sons but both were killed in a light-plane crash last year. 'When troubles come, they come not singly but in battalions.'"

"Why, Sergeant Rogoff," I said, "that's beautiful. But you've got it wrong. It's 'When sorrows come, they come not single spies, but in battalions.'"

"Troubles or sorrows," he said, "what's the diff? So you figure it was someone he knew?"

"Someone he recognized," I said. "Someone he had dealt with before."

"What do you think was important that he wanted to talk to you about?"

I shrugged. "I asked him to find out if any Inverted Jennies were being offered for sale. Maybe he found out."

"And was killed for it?"

"It's possible."

Al grinned at me. "Anything is possible," he said. "It's even possible that you're holding out on me."

"I wouldn't do that," I protested. "Not about murder."

Rogoff thought a moment. "How are you coming along with the Horowitz clan?" he asked suddenly.

"Still at it. Nothing to report."

"Stick with it," he said. "You handle the stamp theft—those people will tell you more than they'll tell us—and I'll concentrate on the Rubik homicide. How does that sound?"

"Makes sense," I said. "And I think eventually we'll discover we're working the same case."

"You think someone in the Horowitz group offed Rubik?"

"Yes," I said. "Don't you?"

But "Could be" was all he'd say. The stenographer came in with my typed statement: original and four photocopies. I signed them all, and Rogoff gave me one of the copies for my file.

"If you think of anything else," he said, "let me know."

"I just did," I said. "That sign on the door—did the killer bring it with him? I mean, was the whole thing planned?"

The sergeant shook his head. "I doubt it. There was a stack of cardboard like that in the bottom drawer of Rubik's desk. He probably used it to stiffen envelopes when he mailed stamps. He also had a roll of masking tape."

"So it was a spur-of-the-moment thing?"

"I'd say so. He and the perp got in an argument about

something, and it ended up with him getting his skull cracked."

"And the killer hung out the sign to give himself more time to get far away?"

"That's the way I see it."

"Did they dust the sign? The tape? The paperweight?"

"They're still at it," Al said. "Don't hold your breath."

"May I go now?" I asked.

"Sure," he said. "You better go home, have a belt, and lie down. You don't look so great."

"I don't feel so great," I said. "Thanks for your prompt assistance, sergeant. Sorry I had to dump this on you."

"If not this," he said, sighing, "it would be something else. It never ends." He paused a moment. Then: "I didn't much like Rubik, did you?"

"No," I said. "Still . . ."

I drove slowly and carefully back to the McNally spread. I wondered why I was driving in that Medicare fashion and realized it was a whiff of mortality that had inspired my caution. One never knows, do one?

I garaged the Miata and entered the house through the side door. My mother was standing at the sink in the kitchen, arranging cut flowers from our garden in a crystal vase. She looked up as I came in.

"Hello, Archy," she said brightly. "Isn't it a splendiferous day!" She paused a beat, doubting. "Did I use the right word?"

"Exactly the right word," I assured her.

"Good! And what have you been doing today?"

"Oh," I said, "this and that. Right now I'm going to change and take my swim."

"Do be careful," she said. "It's rough out there. Now these are the last of the roses, Archy. The heat just eats them up."

I watched a moment as she worked, bending over the sink and smiling as she clipped stems and placed the blooms in the vase just so.

"Mother," I said, "how have you been feeling lately?"

"Tiptop," she said. "Couldn't be better."

"Are you taking your medication?"

"Of course. Every day."

I swooped suddenly to kiss her velvety cheek, and she looked at me with pleased surprise.

"Oh my!" she said. "What was that for?"

"I got carried away," I said, and left her laughing with her flowers. She had a little girl's laugh.

I changed, took up my beach bag and towel, and trotted across A1A to the ocean. I saw at once that mother had been right; it was rough out there, with a pounding surf and big patches of seaweed lifting and falling on the waves farther out. I decided not to dare it.

So I smeared on sunblock and sat on the sand in the latticed shade of a palm tree. I stared out at that turbulent sea and tried to review the events of the day. I did all right with my mental rerun until I got to the strip of film where I stood staring down at the crushed skull of Bela Rubik. And that became a freeze-frame; I couldn't get past it.

I never thought I could shiver on a blazing late-May afternoon in South Florida, but I did. It required almost a physical wrench to dissolve that morbid scene from my memory. I did it by resolutely focusing my mind's camera on more positive images. Jennifer Towley's classic elegance. Consuela Garcia in a string bikini. And similar recollections of love, joy, and calm seas. All to keep the specter of sudden death at bay.

Listen, I'm no hero.

7

My parents had a local couple in for a rubber of bridge that evening, and I didn't have a chance to speak to my father. But after breakfast the next morning I asked if we could talk for a few minutes before he left for the office. He led the way into his study.

"What is it, Archy?" he asked rather testily. The governor hates to have his routine disturbed.

I told him about the murder of Bela Rubik. His face grew bleak. He pondered a long time.

"Distressing," he finally pronounced. "Do you think the homicide is connected with the theft of Lady Horowitz's stamps?"

"Yes, sir," I said. "I'd bet on it."

"Sergeant Rogoff also thinks so?"

I nodded.

He moved slowly about his den, picking things up and

putting them down. "I hope he won't reveal the possible connection to the media."

"I doubt if he will, sir. Al is an intelligent man, and prudent when it comes to dealing with Beach millionaires. He'll tell the reporters Rubik's death was probably due to an attempted robbery. The stamp dealer put up a fight and was killed. That will protect Lady Horowitz and also give the perpetrator a false sense of security. Rogoff likes to come on as a heavy, but he can be foxy when it's called for."

"I'm glad to hear that. In view of the murder, do you wish to continue your discreet inquiries?"

I was offended. "Of course," I said heatedly.

My father turned to face me. "I am not questioning your courage, Archy," he said quietly. "I am merely suggesting that this case has taken on a gravity we didn't anticipate. Our firm will do its best to protect our clients' interests, but I am not certain that includes a homicide investigation."

"Sergeant Rogoff will handle that," I told him, "and I will try to solve the Inverted Jenny theft. Al and I agreed on that."

Another long pause for heavy ratiocination.

"Very well," the lord of the manor said at last. "Let's do it that way. Please keep me informed."

I nodded, and he started out, then paused to look back at me.

"Be careful," was all he said, but I appreciated even that small expression of his concern.

I waited a few moments, watching out the window. When I saw the Lexus pull away, I dug out his telephone directories again. This time I consulted the Yellow Pages for North Broward County. There were a half-dozen stamp dealers listed. I tore the whole page out of the directory and stuffed it in my pocket.

This was my reasoning:

If Rubik had discovered that a block of Inverted Jennies was suddenly being offered for sale, there seemed to be no reason why another stamp dealer couldn't do the same thing. But I didn't want to endanger the skull of another local philatelist. I figured employing a dealer miles away from the scene of the crime would offer sufficient protection—unless I was followed, and I intended to make certain I wasn't.

Usually the trip from Palm Beach to Fort Lauderdale along A1A is one of the most scenic drives in the Sunshine State. As you proceed south, the Atlantic Ocean is on your left, and on your right are the lavish dormitories of the *rich* rich. On one side: nature, on the other: civilization. But the depredation of the beachfront didn't bother me. I figured that sooner or later nature would even the score with a juicy hurricane.

But that morning I had little time for environmental musings. As I drove along at a lively clip, I revised the agenda I had drawn up for my investigation. The brutal killing of Bela Rubik had shuffled my priorities and, despite my agreement with Sgt. Rogoff, I decided the homicide took precedence over the theft.

Incidentally, during my trip southward I passed through Delray Beach and made a mental note to get cracking on Kenneth Bodin, to prove or disprove that Mr. Deltoids was involved in this meshugass. I also remembered to check my rearview mirror frequently to see if I could spot a tracker. Nothing.

I had selected the Lantern Stamp & Coin Shop in Fort Lauderdale only because I found the name attractive. And when I found the place on East Commercial Boulevard, I was pleased to see an antique lantern hanging over the entrance. I approved of that since I am a great fan of Diogenes. But lettered on the plate-glass window in gilt script was the legend PROP.: H. LANTERN. So apparently the store had been named for the owner, not the lamp.

The door was locked, and when I rattled the knob a formidable fiftyish lady came forward and peered at me through the glass. I held up my business card so she could read it. She unlocked the door and allowed me to enter.

"Yes?" she said.

"May I speak to the owner, please?"

She stiffened. "*I* am the owner," she said haughtily.

"I beg your pardon," I said. "I assumed that—"

"I know what you assumed," she interrupted. "That it's impossible for a woman to own and run an independent business, and therefore I must be a salesclerk or the wife or daughter of the owner."

"Nothing of the sort," I said. "It's just that—"

"Let me tell you something," she carried on. "There are no secrets of business management known only to the male gender. There are many women who own and manage successful enterprises."

"Very admirable, I'm sure," I said, "but you are inferring a prejudice that simply doesn't exist. I have known several stamp dealers in my lifetime, and without exception they have all been old, crotchety gentlemen. So naturally I was surprised to find a young, attractive female in the trade."

And I gave her a 100-watt smile that had no effect whatsoever. She stared at me with narrowed eyes, obviously debating whether or not I was conning her, which, of course, I was. Finally she relented.

"All right," she said, "I'll accept your apology."

I wasn't aware that I had offered one, but didn't dare tempt this gorgon's wrath by mentioning it.

"Now then," she continued, all business, "what can I do for you?"

I gave her the same song and dance I had given Bela Rubik: My law firm was handling the estate of a recently deceased Boca Raton real estate developer. Included in the inventory of his personal effects was a block of four Inverted Jenny postage stamps. For tax purposes we would like to establish the value of the stamps by determining the market price of a similar block currently being offered for sale.

H. Lantern shook her head. "Can't be done," she said decisively. "All stamps have different values, even those of the same issue. The value depends on the condition of the stamps."

"You know that," I said, "and I know that, but the IRS doesn't know that. Quite frankly, we fear they are aware that a block of four Inverted Jennies was recently auctioned for a million dollars, and they are liable to insist that value be placed on the stamps included in the estate of our deceased client."

"I could do an appraisal for you," she offered.

I uttered a short, bitter laugh. "You think the IRS would

accept that? Never! Right now their estimate of market value is the million-dollar sale in New York that received so much publicity. The only way we can counter that is by quoting the price of Inverted Jennies currently being offered for sale. We will pay fifty dollars per hour for your time if you would be willing to take on the job of discovering if any blocks of Inverted Jennies have recently come on the market and, if so, what the asking price is. I'm sure it's less than a million dollars."

I could see she wasn't totally convinced by my scam, but the fifty dollars an hour was alluring, and I'm certain she asked herself what possible harm could she suffer by agreeing to my proposal. I could have enlightened her, but didn't.

"A down payment?" she asked, and I knew I had her.

I gave her fifty in cash, took a signed receipt, and left her my business card. She promised to call as soon as she had made inquiries, talked to other dealers, and consulted philatelic periodicals. We shook hands, and she smiled before I departed. What a pleasant surprise!

Because I was so close, I cut over to Oakland Park Blvd. and took it eastward to the ocean. I decided to have a small lunch at Ireland's Inn, a place I recalled from previous excursions to Lauderdale.

The day had started out clear and bright, but Florida's weather is mercurial, and now the air was clotting up, a dark cloud bank was moving in from the south. So instead of lunching outside, practically on the beach, I opted to sit indoors at a window facing the sea. I ordered a turkey club sandwich, which I dearly love, and a bottle of non-

alcoholic beer, for which I was developing a taste, and I
hope you will not think the less of me for it.

There is no delicate method of eating a thick club sandwich; one must gobble. So while I gobbled and swigged
my Buckler, I reviewed the interview with H. Lantern,
whose given name turned out to be Hilda. She was a
prickly woman (she would be incensed by that adjective),
but I thought her competent enough and was convinced
she'd do a conscientious job.

The rainsquall came over as I lunched. It really poured,
then suddenly stopped, the sky blued, the sun shone. I
paid my bill, went outside, and found to my delight that
the parking valet had had the great good sense to move
my open Miata under the portico before the deluge. I
gave him a heavy tip and assured him that one day he
would be president.

I was back in Palm Beach by three o'clock, drove past
my home, admiring that dignified, stately edifice, and
turned into the driveway of the Horowitz fiefdom. I asked
Mrs. Marsden if the DuPeys were present, and she di-
rected me to a Georgian-styled gazebo framed in a small
grove of bottle palms beyond the pool area.

There I found the newlyweds lounging at a set of cast-
iron garden furniture. On the table was a pitcher of what
appeared to be iced sangria, along with a stack of plastic
tumblers. I introduced myself, they introduced them-
selves and invited me to help myself to a drink. I did and
sipped cautiously. It was intended to be sangria, all right,
but made with some awful plonk. Dreadful stuff.

I congratulated the DuPeys on their recent nuptials,

and they laughed heartily as if the marriage had been a lark and no one appreciated the joke more than they. They were holding hands when I arrived, and they continued to clasp paws during the entire interview. It was easy to see they were both sappy with love.

I started to address them in French, but Felice asked me prettily to speak English as she wasn't certain of the syntax and also wanted to learn as many American idioms as possible. I obliged. I would have granted her every wish, for she was charming, a kitten with a mischievous grin and a full inventory of pouts and moues.

Alan, the benedict, was onion soup personified. I mean, give him a beret and a pencil-thin mustache and you'd have Lucky Pierre in the flesh. But he was bubbling with gaiety that not infrequently slopped over into hilarity. Did I hear the pitch of desperation there, as if he thought it better never to stop laughing or he might start screaming?

They were perfectly willing to answer questions about their personal lives. He wrote book reviews for a monthly Parisian literary journal, and she was an apprentice at Chanel, and wasn't life grand? I began to understand what Consuela Garcia meant when she had condemned them for being "too nice." The DuPeys' happiness seemed excessive, almost cloying. You wouldn't make an entire meal of caviar, would you? You would?

I resolutely turned to business, asked the usual questions, and heard nothing new. Chuckling Alan had seen his mother's misprinted stamps several times in the past. Giggling Felice had seen them for the first time at dinner the evening they arrived. Neither had the slightest notion

116

of who, staff or guests, might have nobbled the Inverted Jennies. And it was obvious from their manner that the theft ranked far down on their anxiety list.

It seemed nothing was to be learned from these love-birds, and I was about to withdraw when I casually asked if they had enjoyed the cruise on Phil Meecham's yacht the previous day. My innocent query elicited another eruption of uncontrolled glee.

"We never went," Alan explained after his spasm of mirth had subsided. "The captain of the yacht—a splen-did vessel!—said the sea was much too rough and we would all suffer mal de mer. So Monsieur Meecham pro-posed we remain tied to the dock and have a party right there."

"Ooo, la!" his wife cried.

"And what a party," Alan went on, rolling his eyes. "Four cases of a very good champagne—Moët Brut Impé-rial, you know—and the food! A *orgie!*"

"Four cases for the six of you?" I said. "I'd say that was ample."

"More than six," Felice said. "There were also fourteen other guests."

"Ten," her husband corrected her gently. "Because the Smythes, Gina, and Angus left after the cruise was can-celed. But I can tell you that those of us who remained put a big dent in Monsieur Meecham's wine supply."

"He was so fonny," his wife added. "He wanted to make love to *all* of us!"

"I can imagine," I said, bid them farewell, and departed while they were still convulsed with laughter and still holding hands.

117

I tried to tumble-dry my thoughts and realized that last bit of information was a lone sock. Here's the scenario:

The time of the murder was reasonably well established. The clobbering of Bela Rubik's occiput had occurred between the moment I spoke to him on the phone from my office and the moment I found the corpus delicti.

I had previously learned that all the six Horowitz houseguests were afloat on a cruise aboard Phil Meecham's yacht the previous day.

That meant that if anyone in the Horowitz household was the killer, it had to be one of the staff.

But now I had learned that Doris and Harry Smythe, Gina Stanescu, and Angus Wolfson had left the moored yacht when the cruise was canceled. That meant I had to restore them to the list of suspects.

I consoled myself by reflecting that the original roster of eleven possibles had now dwindled to nine.

It's called progress.

I drove away in a melancholy mood, wondering if I might achieve a more fulfilling life by becoming a real estate agent like everyone else in South Florida. Then I had another mournful thought: If Lady Cynthia's butler hadn't quit two weeks before the crimes were committed, he would have been the prime suspect. All the tomes I had read on criminal behavior were quite firm on that point: The butler *always* did it.

But my spirits rose when I arrived home, for Mrs. Olson informed me that Jennifer Towley had phoned while she was cleaning my suite.

"She sounds nice," she said.

"She *is* nice," I shouted back as I dashed upstairs to phone.

I lay back on my bed as I spoke to Jennifer and kicked my heels in the air, thinking the DuPeys' happiness might be contagious. We talked of weighty things like the weather, the cost of fresh snapper, and the outrageous attempts by the State of Florida to ban thong bikinis on public beaches.

"Enough of this idle chitchat, Jennifer," I said finally. "When may I see you again?"

"That's why I called," she said. "I'm having dinner with a client tonight, but I should be home by ten o'clock at the latest. Could you come over for a drink? There is something very important I want to say to you."

"You're going to propose?" I asked.

"No," she said, not laughing. "This is very serious, Archy. I should have told you sooner, but I didn't have the courage. Now I've decided to tell you before you hear it from someone else."

"All right," I said, my joy balloon deflating, "I'll be there at ten."

"I won't keep you long," she promised.

"Keep me as long as you like," I told her.

Then she did laugh, but it was a feeble one.

I hung up somewhat disquieted. It was her statement "This is serious, Archy" that put the quietus to my brief felicity. I've already told you what a carefree cove I am, or strive to be. I blame most of society's ills on seriousness. Believe me, if everyone would sit on a whoopee cushion at least once a day, it would be a better world.

I know I was uncharacteristically withdrawn and silent that evening because my mother remarked on it. She asked if I was coming down with something. I was tempted to reply, "Love," but instead I assured her I was in perfect health but merely distracted by the press of business. I don't believe mother knew exactly what it was I did, but she accepted my explanation, although advising that a nice glass of warm milk before bedtime would enable me to sleep better.

I was at Jennifer Towley's home a few minutes after ten o'clock, and she had something better to offer than warm milk: a liter of Absolut plunged into a crystal bucket of ice cubes. She had set out two tall shot glasses that looked like bud vases.

She was wearing one of her elegant Little Black Dresses. This one appeared to be conservatively cut, with a high neck and long sleeves. But when she turned around, I saw that it had no back whatsoever. As Felice DuPey might say, "Ooo, la!"

"I shall pour your first drink, Archy," she said, "and then you must help yourself to more. I think you may need it."

"Oh-oh," I said, "that sounds ominous."

"Not ominous," she said. "Perhaps upsetting."

She seated herself in a low armchair and tugged her skirt down to cover her bare knees. Now *that* was upsetting.

"I told you I was divorced," she stated. "Towley is my maiden name. My married name was Bingham. My husband was Thomas Bingham. Does the name mean anything to you?"

I shook my head.

She sighed. "Several years ago he was arrested and convicted of felony theft. He stole about fifty thousand dollars from his employer, a wholesaler of plumbing supplies."

I took a heavy gulp of my vodka. "Where did this happen?"

"Boca Raton. He did three years and four months at Raiford."

It was my turn to sigh. "Jennifer, were you divorced before or after he was convicted?"

"About a year before," she said. "Thank God. If I hadn't, I wouldn't have divorced him after he went to prison, would I?"

"I suppose not," I said, thinking there were many women who would have, and admiring her.

"He was a gambler," she said. "Absolutely addicted. He was handsome, well-educated, well-spoken. And a dynamite salesman. At a party one night the president of the company told me that Tom had a bright future: sales manager and then into the executive suite. He might even become CEO. He could have had all that, but he couldn't stop gambling."

"On what?"

"On everything! Horse races; dog races; baseball, football, and basketball games; lotteries; elections; the weather—you name it. And on his selling trips he always managed to get to Las Vegas or Atlantic City."

"You were aware of his addiction?"

"Of course I was aware," she said angrily. "How could I *not* be aware? I saw what was happening to our bank accounts, a second mortgage on our home, the dunning letters from creditors. And the interest on his credit card charges! It was a horrendous situation. I pleaded with him to get professional help: a psychologist, Gamblers Anonymous, talk to our minister—anything. But he refused to admit that he had a problem, that he was hopelessly addicted. You don't have any addictions, do you, Archy?"

"One," I said. "You."

I do believe she blushed, but it may have been the rosy glow coming from the Tiffany lamp on the table. I helped myself to more Absolut. I couldn't serve Jennifer; her full glass was untouched.

"I did everything I could," she continued. "I loved Tom, I really did. He could be a splendid husband: kind, gentle, understanding. Except he had this terrible sickness."

"I had a friend who was like that," I said, lying but trying to be sympathetic. "And it *is* a sickness."

"Things began to disappear from our home," she went on. "Crystal, silverware, a few of my antiques. He was selling them. He was involved with loan sharks, and rough men began coming to our house or parking outside all night. I really couldn't take any more of it so I filed for divorce. He wept and begged and swore he would stop betting. But he had done that a dozen times before, and I knew it was no good. I think the final straw was when I realized he was stealing money from my purse. So I divorced him. And a year later he went to prison."

"A sad story," I said.

"A soap opera," she said with a strained smile. "It happens all the time, all over the country. I talked to a counselor who specialized in treating addictions, and he said no improvement could be expected until the addict acknowledged he was out of control and sought help voluntarily. Tom wouldn't do that."

There was silence awhile. She sat with her head lowered, and I hoped she wasn't going to cry. I'm an absolute klutz when it comes to dealing with weeping women.

"Something I haven't asked you," I said. "Any children?"

"No," she said, lifting her chin to look at me, and I saw she was clear-eyed; her calm, direct gaze had returned. "Do you think it would have changed Tom if we had?"

"I don't know," I said. "Who can predict human behavior? Did you say he's out of prison?"

"Yes. He was released about a month ago."

"Did you visit him while he was inside?"

"No."

"Write to him?"

"Not really," she said. "Just birthday and Christmas cards. But he wrote me frequently. He said being behind bars had made him realize how he had screwed up his life, and mine. He swore he was a changed man, and when he was released he'd never gamble again as long as he lived."

"Do you believe him, Jennifer?"

"No."

"Has he called you since he's been out?"

"Four times."

"And he wants you to take him back?"

Her eyes grew round. "How did you know?" she asked.

"Because that's exactly what I'd do if I were in his place. Will you take him back?"

123

"Never!" she cried. "Archy, have you ever had night-mares?"

"Not often. Perhaps a half-dozen in my lifetime."

"Well, I had a nightmare that lasted almost four years. I don't want to go through that again."

I asked, almost idly, "Where did he call you from—Boca?"

"No," she said, "he's living in Delray Beach."

I think I stared at her with a look akin to the wild surmise of the men of stout Cortez, silent upon a peak in Darien. Although how they managed to spot the Pacific Ocean from Connecticut I've never been able to understand.

"Delray Beach?" I repeated, and my voice sounded like a croak. "What's he doing there?"

"He says he has a good job selling hurricane shutters, mostly to people who live in high-rise condos. He claims his boss knows about his prison record but is willing to give him a chance. Tom says he makes a small salary but does well on commissions. I believe that. I told you he's a super salesman."

I nodded, thinking that Jennifer was probably his toughest prospect. She leaned forward and took my hands in hers.

"Archy," she said, "I'm sorry to dump this on you. I realize it's depressing. But I know how people talk, and I wanted to tell you myself rather than have you hear it secondhand."

"I appreciate that," I said.

She sat back and slumped. "I feel wrung-out. Just talking about it brings back so many memories. All of them painful."

"I can understand that," I said. I stood up. "I suppose you want me to go."

Finally, finally, she took a sip of her vodka, then looked up at me with that cool, level gaze. "Whatever gave you that silly idea?" she said.

There was something demonic in her lovemaking that night, as if she sought to exorcise thoughts, feelings, perhaps those painful memories. I profited shamelessly from her anguish.

Popular wisdom has it that the way to a man's heart is through his stomach. Don't you ever believe it.

8

I banished all my problems for the weekend and lived the life of a blade-about-town. On Saturday I played tennis at a friend's private court. After he scuttled me in straight sets, he phoned a couple of jolly ladies. They came over, and we all frolicked in his pool, had a few drinks, and laughed a lot.

On Saturday night after dinner (tournedos with foie gras), I headed for the Pelican Club. I found a few of my cronies already in attendance, and I won five dollars throwing darts. That made me the big winner, and I had to stand a round of drinks that cost me twenty.

On Sunday I took my ocean swim early, then drove out to Wellington where I watched a polo match from my father's box. I had brought my Tasco zoom binocs along, but I saw no one in the stands who excited my interest. Jennifer Towley, I decided, had elevated my taste. How ya gonna keep 'em down on the farm after they've seen Paree?

On Sunday night my parents and I made a short trip down A1A to a Palladian-style mansion owned by a wealthy client of McNally & Son. Along with thirty other guests we enjoyed a boisterous cocktail party and cookout that featured Maine lobsters and Louisiana prawns. The grill was presided over by a uniformed butler wearing white gloves and a topper.

But Monday rolled around all too quickly, and then it was back to the Sturm und Drang.

You may think a detective's best friend is his revolver, magnifying glass, or bloodhound. Wrong. It is a telephone directory—the handiest aid to any inquiry, discreet or otherwise. I looked up the home address and phone number of Kenneth Bodin in Delray Beach, and scrawled them on the inside of a book of matches. Then, just for the fun of it, I tore out the Yellow Pages listing places that sold hurricane shutters. There were a lot of them, but most seemed to be located north of Boynton Beach. I found only a few in the Delray–Boca Raton area.

By ten o'clock I was on the road again, and it was not a day that would bring a prideful smile to the mug of Florida boosters. The sky had the color and weight of a wet army blanket, not a wisp of air was moving, and even the palm fronds looked dejected. It was an oppressive atmosphere, as if a storm was lurking nearby and might pounce at any moment.

I stopped for gas in Delray Beach and made my phone call to Kenneth Bodin's residence from the station. As I had hoped, a woman answered.

"Hello?" she said in a squeaky little voice.

"Sylvia?" I asked.

"Yes. Who's this?"

"My name is Dooley, and I'm in South Florida for a convention. I threw my back out, and I need a massage. A friend suggested you might be able to help."

"Yeah?" she said suspiciously. "What friend?"

I named the most active roué I knew. "Phil Meecham," I said. It worked.

She squealed with delight. "What a crazy guy!" she said. "How is Phil?"

"Sitting up and taking nourishment," I said. "How about that massage?"

"Aw, I'm sorry, Dooley, but I'm not in that line of work anymore. My boyfriend won't let me."

"Well, I can understand that," I said. "But is he home right now?"

"No. He works up at Palm Beach."

"Well, then . . .?" I suggested.

"No can do," she said firmly. "I gave him my sacred promise. And besides, he might come home unexpectedly."

"That's too bad," I said, sounding disappointed. "Then I guess I made the trip for nothing."

"Listen, Dooley," she said. "I'm working as a cocktail waitress at a lovely place on the beach. The joint opens at noon. Why don't you stop by, have a few drinks, and maybe we can work something out."

"Sounds good to me," I said, and she gave me the name of the lovely place on the beach and told me how to find it.

I killed an hour by driving around to stores that sold and installed hurricane shutters. I hit pay dirt on the fourth. Yes, Thomas Bingham worked there, but at the moment he was out estimating a job. I was relieved to hear it, having absolutely no idea of what I would have said to him if he had been present. I think I just wanted to size him up, see what a man looked like who would sacrifice Jennifer Towley for the sake of a dog race.

I left no message for Bingham but said I'd stop by again. Then I headed for Sylvia's place of employ, wishing I knew what the hell I was doing. But sometimes chance and accident prove more valuable than the most detailed plan. That's what I told myself.

At least I had sense enough to park my car a few blocks away and walk back. I had no desire for Sylvia to remark casually to Bodin, "A young buck stopped by today, driving a flag-red Miata." His porcine ears would have perked up immediately.

When I entered Hammerhead's Bar & Grill, I was tempted to do a Bette Davis impersonation: flap my elbows, suck an imaginary cigarette, and utter those immortal words: "What-a-*dump*!" I suppose I was being elitist, but it was a bit of a culture shock, after that deluxe weekend at Palm Beach, to be faced by so much Formica with naked fluorescent tubes flickering overhead.

The bar was crowded with what appeared to be a fraternity of construction workers and commercial fishermen. I took a bandanna-sized table in the corner, and in a moment a zoftig blond lady came jiggling over to me. She was wearing a hot-pink miniskirt and a hot-green

tank top that may have been sprayed on with an atom-
izer.

"Hiya," she said.

"Sylvia?" I said. "I'm Dooley."

"Well!" she said, giving me a really nice smile. "Pleased
to make your acquaintance, I'm sure. In town for long?"

"Oh, maybe a week or so," I said. "I'm staying in Boca
with a friend."

"Man or woman?" she asked, leering at me.

"Man," I said. "Unfortunately."

"Maybe we can do something about that," and she actually winked at me. "What can I bring you?"

I know that in a place like that, the only safe choice
would be something with a cap on the bottle. But I feared
if I asked for nonalcoholic beer, the proprietor and patrons might toss me to the sharks skulking offshore.

"A bottle of beer, please," I said. "Do you have Heineken?"

"Of course," she said. "This is a high-class joint."

She brought my beer and a bowl of salted peanuts.
Then, unbidden, she took the chair opposite me, and I
was aware that a few customers at the bar glanced at me
enviously.

"You're awfully young to be a pal of Phil Meecham,"
she said.

"You know Phil," I said. "He never discriminates because of age, sex, color, creed, or country of national origin."

"You can say that again," she said, laughing. "Once I
saw him try to make a chimpanzee. Can you believe it?"

"Easily," I said. "May I buy you a drink?"

"Maybe a diet Coke," she said. "Okay? I'm trying to lose weight."

"Don't you dare," I said.

"Oh *you!*" she said.

She came back with her drink and then dug into my bowl of peanuts.

"What time do you get off work, Sylvia?" I asked.

"Well, that's the problem," she said. "I leave around eight when the night girl comes on. Then I have to go right home or my boyfriend will have the pip. Or sometimes he comes in here when he gets off work, and then we go home together. He keeps me on a short leash."

"What's doing there?" I asked her. "Wedding bells?"

"Maybe," she said, scoffing more peanuts. "It depends on my mood."

"So really the only time you have free is in the mornings?"

"That's about it," she agreed. "Ken leaves for work early to beat the traffic. And I have to get up early to make him breakfast."

"I'll be around awhile," I said. "May I call you some morning?"

"Of course you can, Dooley," she said. "We could take a ride down to your friend's place in Boca."

"Good idea," I said, and finished my beer. "I'll give you a ring." I stood up. "How much do I owe you, Sylvia?"

"It's on the house," she said. "Maybe you'll come back. You've got class; I can tell."

"Thank you," I said, and slipped her a ten for her keen discernment. I waved and started away. Then I had one of my wild ideas that always shock me because I can't understand where they come from.

"By the way," I said, turning back, "my friend in Boca lives in a high-rise condo, and he's thinking of installing hurricane shutters. You know anyone around here who sells them?"

"Sure," she said. "Tom Bingham. He drops by almost every evening when he gets off work."

"Fine," I said. "The next time you see him, will you get me a business card?"

"A pleasure," she said. "Tom's a good guy. Him and Ken and me spend a lot of time together."

See what I mean about chance and accident? But sometimes you have to nudge them a bit.

I drove home through a darkling day. It hadn't yet started to rain, but the sky pressed lower, and gulls were straining to beat their way against a freshening wind. Where *do* gulls go during a storm?

But I had more on my mind than the homing habits of sea gulls. I was computing that if Kenneth Bodin, girlfriend Sylvia, and Thomas Bingham were buddies, maybe all three—or at least the two men—had planned and carried out the theft of the Inverted Jennies. My main reason for considering this a distinct possibility was that Bingham had served time for stealing fifty thousand dollars.

That may sound prejudicial to you, but law enforcement officers the world over know that if a former felon is anywhere near the scene of a crime, the odds are good that he or she was actively involved. It's not bigotry; it's a knowledge of recidivist rates. Leopards don't change their spots, and ex-cons rarely change their stripes.

You may smugly believe that I had a more personal reason for suspecting Bingham, that I hoped to end what I thought was a determined effort on his part to win back the affection of his ex-wife. And if you ask if that was indeed my motive, or an important part of my motive, I plead the Fifth Amendment—the one dealing with self-incrimination.

I was a short distance from home when I felt the first spatters of rain. I gave the Miata the automotive equivalent of giddyap and made it into our garage just before the deluge. Sgt. Al Rogoff's pickup truck was parked outside on the gravel, and he lowered the window of the cab long enough to beckon me over.

I dashed through the rain and climbed in. It was air conditioned but rank with old cigar smoke.

"You don't have to light up a fresh stogie," I told him. "You can just drive around inhaling yesterday's smoke."

"Talking about cigars," he said, "I spent all day at the Horowitz place, and that crazy dame wouldn't let me flame a cigar anywhere. Not just in the house, she said, but nowhere on the grounds. She's only got a hundred acres—right?"

"Maybe a little less."

"Well, I couldn't even go out in the woods and grab a puff. She's a bird, that one."

"A rich bird," I said. "Is that why you're wearing civvies and driving your own heap?"

"Yeah. She didn't want any uniforms or police cars hanging around. I guess she thought it would lower the tone of the neighborhood. Where have you been?"

"Down in Delray Beach checking out Kenneth Bodin, the chauffeur."

"Learn anything?" Al asked.

"Less than a soupçon," I said. "He's living with a cup-cake, but if that's a crime, half the guys in South Florida would be behind bars. No signs or talk of sudden wealth."

"Heavy debts?"

"I can check that out through bank and credit agencies up here. How did you make out on the homicide?"

"Not too bad," the sergeant said. "We're lucky because the time of death can definitely be established within an hour or so. At that time the five members of the staff were all on the estate. I admit they alibi each other, which could be a conspiracy, but I doubt it. Lady Horowitz says she was at the hairdresser's. I'll have to check that out. As for the houseguests, the DuPeys claim they were partying on a docked yacht and were seen by dozens of people. Something else to check out. That leaves Mr. and Mrs. Smythe, Gina Stanescu, and Angus Wolfson. All four claim they left the yacht after the cruise was canceled and were wandering around the shops on Worth Avenue at the time Bela Rubik got pasted in the Great Stamp Album in the Sky. The actual whereabouts of those four at the time of death will be a migraine to pin down, but I guess it can be done with a lot of legwork."

"You're convinced that the homicide and the theft of the Inverted Jennies are connected?"

"The only reason I'm convinced," Al said, "is that I've got nothing else. There's no evidence at all pointing to an attempted robbery. Maybe it was a weirdo, a serial killer on the loose, but I don't buy that. Those missing stamps and what Rubik said to you on the phone are the only leads I've got. Archy, what's your guess—was it a man or a woman?"

I considered a moment. "I'd guess it was a man. Look, the human skull isn't an eggshell, you know. You can give it a pretty sharp bop without breaking it. So there was physical power behind that paperweight."

"It could have been a strong woman."

"Could have been," I agreed, "but bashing in a skull just doesn't seem to me something a woman would do, even if she was insane with rage."

"Yeah," Rogoff said, "it doesn't seem likely, does it? By the way, he didn't die of a bashed skull."

I stared at him. "Would you run that by me again."

"Bela Rubik didn't die from repeated blows to the cranium. According to the ME, they would have knocked him out for sure, and they damaged the brain, but he actually died of cardiac arrest, a massive heart failure brought on by the assault. That still makes it a homicide, of course."

"Of course," I said, "but it opens up a whole new can of worms. Maybe the attacker didn't intend to kill him. Just knock him out or hurt him."

"I'm not interested in the killer's intent," Al said. "That's for the courts to decide. I just want to nab the perp and then let the lawyers argue about intent."

"I'm not sure that's the way to go," I said slowly. "Perhaps knowing the intent is the only way to find the killer."

The sergeant groaned. "You know, you have a taste for complexity. I'll bet you like black olives, too."

"Love 'em," I admitted.

"It figures," Al said mournfully. "All right, the rain's letting up, you can run for the house without getting soaked. I have to get back to work. Keep in touch."

"For sure," I said. "I expect to be in all night. Give me a call if anything breaks."

That evening my parents left to attend a dinner being given for a septuagenarian couple celebrating their 50th wedding anniversary. I was invited but begged off. Long hours of fruit punch and charades are not my idea of a hot time in the old town tonight.

So I had dinner in the kitchen with the Olsons. Ursi dished up a concoction she called McNally Stew: a spicy mix of chunks of beef, chicken, hot Italian sausage, and shrimp, all in a red wine sauce and served over a bed of wide noodles. Kiss your diet farewell.

After that gluttonous debauch I went upstairs, thankful I was wearing an expandable belt, and set to work on my journal, with the original cast album of *Guys and Dolls* playing on my stereo. I may even have sung along with "Sue Me." This was after I phoned Jennifer Towley, got her answering machine, and hung up without leaving a message.

I was still scribbling when *my* phone rang. It was Sgt. Rogoff.

"Wake you up?" he asked.

"Come on, Al," I said, "it's not even ten o'clock. What's up?"

"After I left you I hit the streets. First I went to the hairdresser where Lady Horowitz claims she had an appointment at the time Rubik was aced."

"And?"

"She had an appointment all right, but she never showed up."

I was silent.

"Hello?" Rogoff said. "You there?"

"I'm here," I said. "Just trying to catch that curve ball."

"Yeah," he said. "It's screwy, isn't it? Listen, Archy, do me a favor, will you? I don't want to brace that old dame with what I know and demand she spill the truth. She scares me; I admit it. She's got a lot of clout in this town and could make things sticky for me if she wanted to. You follow?"

"I follow," I said. "All right, Al, I'll try to find out where she was at the time Rubik was killed. Did you tell her that the theft of her stamps was connected to a homicide?"

"Hell, no! I didn't tell her or any of the others there was probably a link. I just said we had a good lead on the identity of the stamp thief, and I had to check out their whereabouts at a specific time to eliminate the innocent."

"You think they bought that?"

"Everyone but the killer," Al said. "Talk to the old biddy for me, will you, Archy? She likes you."

"She does?" I said, somewhat surprised.

"Sure. She told me so herself. Something else you can do for me . . ."

I sighed. "And I get a piece of your salary—right?"

"Wrong. Your father drew up Lady Horowitz's will, didn't he?"

"That's correct," I said, knowing what was coming.

"Can you find out who inherits if she croaks?"

"Probably," I said, "but I'm not going to tell you. That's privileged information."

"What do I have to do to get it?"

"Get her permission first. I'll ask my father."

"Do that, will you?"

"Sure. But why do you want to know who inherits?"

"Because maybe someone, family or friends, perhaps one of the houseguests, *doesn't* inherit, knows it, and decided to pinch the stamps to get what they could. And that led to the homicide."

"Sergeant Rogoff," I said, "you're brilliant."

"It's taken you this long to find out? What a lousy detective. Let me know what your father says."

It was about ten-thirty when I heard the crunch of gravel, went to the window, and saw the Lexus pulling into the garage. I waited another half-hour, smoked my first cigarette of the day, and brooded about what Rogoff had told me. I wasn't looking forward to telling Lady Cynthia she had been caught in a lie. She was quite capable of canning McNally & Son instanter.

The door of my father's study was closed, but when I knocked I heard his murmured, "Come in." He was plumped down in his club chair, still wearing his dinner jacket, but he had loosened tie and collar. I thought he looked old and tired.

"Good party?" I asked.

"Wearing," he said with a wan smile. "You were wise not to attend. Not your cup of vodka at all."

"Speaking of that, sir," I said, "may I bring you a glass of port? You look a mite bushed."

He stared a brief moment. "I think a tot of brandy would do more good. Thank you, Archy, and help yourself."

I poured us small snifters of cognac from his crystal decanter and seated myself in an armchair facing him. We raised glasses to each other, took small sips.

"Sorry to bother you at this hour, father," I said, "but Sergeant Rogoff just called and asked me to speak to you."

I explained what Rogoff wanted and why he wanted it. The guv listened closely.

"I couldn't possibly release that information," he said, "without Lady Horowitz's permission."

"I told Al that. He wants you to try to get it."

Long pause for heavy thought. Then: "I can understand Rogoff's reasoning. It's a nice point: A disinherited relative or friend might wish to profit immediately. You were right, Archy; the sergeant is a foxy man."

"Yes, sir. Will you ask Lady Horowitz if details of her will may be given to the police? On a confidential basis, of course."

He sighed wearily. "All right, I'll ask."

"Do you think she'll agree?"

He looked at me with rueful amusement. "Who can possibly predict what that extraordinary woman might or might not do? I'll ask her; that's all I can tell you."

"Good enough," I said, finished my brandy, and rose. "Sorry to have disturbed you, sir."

"Not at all," he said.

I tramped upstairs, thinking he was not so much wearied as troubled. And seeing my father troubled was like viewing a statue of a worried Buddha.

9

I had a lot of important things to do the next morning—such as dumping the contents of my wicker laundry hamper into a big canvas bag, adding four pairs of slacks to be dry cleaned, and lugging everything downstairs to be picked up by our laundry service. I also balanced my checkbook, which came out three dollars more than my bank statement. Close enough. And I called a florist to deliver an arrangement of whatever was fresh to Jennifer Towley.

So it was a bit past ten-thirty before I headed for the Horowitz empire. I knew quite well that all those putzy things I had busied myself with that morning were sheer cravenness on my part: an attempt to postpone the moment when I'd have to face Lady C. and ask, "Why did you lie to Sergeant Rogoff?" When Al told me she scared him, I could empathize; she scared me, too. She was a woman of strong opinions and fierce determination. And her millions gave muscle to her whims.

I found Lady Horowitz lying on a chaise at poolside. In the shade, of course. She was wearing a mint-green silk burnoose, the hood pulled up, and I soon learned she was in a scratchy mood.

"That policeman," she said wrathfully, "that insufferable *cop,* positively *reeks* of cigar smoke."

"I know," I said, "but he—"

"And his idiotic questions!" she ranted on. "Why, he treated me like a common criminal."

"He's just trying to do his job," I said as soothingly as I could. "He's really on your side, you know. He'd like to recover the stamps as much as you would."

"Cowpats!" she said. "He's just trying to make my life miserable because I gave him work to do when he'd rather be somewhere else swilling beer and belching."

"He's really a very efficient police officer."

She stared at me. "He's a friend of yours, lad?" she demanded.

"We've worked together several times," I acknowledged. "And successfully, I might add."

But she'd have none of it. "That's all I need," she fumed, "two amateur sherlocks stumbling around on their flat feet. I suppose that's why you're here—to ask more questions."

She hadn't invited me to sit down, so I didn't. But I moved into the shade of a beach umbrella and leaned on the back of a chair, looking down at her.

"Well, yes," I admitted. "I'd just like to get a clarification of something you told Sergeant Rogoff."

"A clarification?" she said suspiciously. "Of what?"

"The sergeant has a good lead on the identity of the thief, but needs to pin down the whereabouts of everyone involved at the time the crime was apparently committed. You told him you were at your hairdresser's. But when Rogoff checked, he discovered you had an appointment but didn't show up. Would you care to comment?"

"My first comment is that I'm going to get a new hairdresser," she said. "The stupid snitch!"

"Please, Lady Horowitz," I said, "where were you?"

"I've had a touch of arthritis in my knees, and didn't want anyone to know I was going to an acupuncturist. That's where I was." She looked at me. "You're not buying that, are you?"

"No," I said.

"All right," she said almost cheerfully, "let's try this one: I was sitting in a dyke bar slugging Black Russians. No? How about this: It was such a lovely day I decided to drive the Jag up the coast to the country club. How does that grab you?"

I sighed. "I gather you're not going to tell me where you were."

"You gather correctly, lad. The whole thing is so moronic it's sickening. Does Rogoff think I swiped my own stamps?"

"Of course not."

"Then why in hell should I tell him where I was at such and such a time? My private life is my private life, and I don't have to account for it to anyone. Period. That includes you, lad."

I nodded. "Thank you for your time."

She tried to smile but couldn't. "You're pissed at me, aren't you?"

"Somewhat," I admitted. "It seems to me you're making Mount Everest out of a very small molehill indeed."

"That's what you think," she said, and I looked at her with perplexity because she appeared to be stiff upperlipping it, and I couldn't understand why. But then she waved me away with a gesture of dismissal, and I went.

Ordinarily I am an even-tempered johnny. I don't curse when a shoelace snaps. Stepping on a discarded wad of chewing gum might elicit a mild "Tsk." And I've been known to laugh merrily after spattering the front of my white shirt with marinara sauce. But that go-around with Lady Cynthia definitely cast a shadow on the McNally sunniness. It was not, I felt, going to be my day. How right I was.

I went into the main house to search for Mrs. Marsden, hoping she might be willing to describe in more detail those forebodings she had mentioned. But as I passed the game room, I heard the unmistakable sounds of a female sobbing, and since the door was ajar I had no scruples about entering and looking about for the sobber.

I found Gina Stanescu leaning against the billiard table and trying to stanch a freshet of tears with a hanky no larger than a cocktail napkin. I've told you that I'm usually a klutz when dealing with lacrimating ladies, but in this case I believe I responded sympathetically if not nobly.

"Hi, Miss Stanescu," I said. "What's up?"

Her answer was more sobs, and I reacted to the crisis in my usual fashion by heading directly for the nearest source of spirits—in this case, the wet bar. The first bottle I put my hand on was ouzo, which I thought would be excellent shock therapy. I poured the tiniest bit into a snifter, brought it to her, and pressed it into her hand.

It worked to the extent that she found she couldn't cough and weep at the same time. The weeping stopped and, eventually, so did the coughing.

"What is wrong?" I asked. "Is there anything I may do to help?"

She shook her head, then took another sip of the ouzo, which emptied the glass.

"More?"

She cleared her throat. "Thank you, no. You have been most kind, Mr. McNally. I should have closed the door. But it came upon me very suddenly. Do you have a handkerchief, please? I'm afraid mine is a mess."

I supplied the linen, happy it was fresh and unwrinkled. She used it to dab her eyes dry, but they remained swollen.

"I received some bad news," she said. "The Rouen authorities wish to close my orphanage. The roof leaks dreadfully, you see, and the plumbing is in very bad repair. Also, the electrical wiring must be replaced. It would all cost a great deal of money."

"That's a shame," I said, suddenly wary, I admit, because I feared this might be a prelude to an attempted financial bite. "Surely your patrons or contributors would be willing to provide the funds."

"I think not," she said, now speaking evenly and decisively. "We have just been scraping by as it is. People give what they can afford. I will not beg."

"Very admirable," I said, "but sometimes it's necessary. What about your mother?"

She looked at me as if questioning my IQ. "Who do you think has been making up the losses all these years? I will not ask her for more. I cannot. She has been so generous. Just incredible."

Why did I feel this was the first false note in what she was telling me? I knew that her mother made small annual contributions to several charities, but she was Lady Horowitz, not Lady Bountiful. Unless, of course, she splurged on her daughter's orphanage. That was possible, but after the morning's snappish interview I found it difficult to credit her mother with any generosity, of spirit or purse.

"I don't know about France," I said, "but in this country there are fund-raising organizations. For a fee, they recommend methods of increasing the income of worthwhile charities. Direct mail campaigns, for instance. Auctions of donated art objects. Even lotteries."

She shook her head again. "We are too small," she said, "and too local. We can only exist with the kindness of our benefactors. But the cost of the repairs far exceeds what we can expect."

"Surely you don't intend to close down?"

"No," she said determinedly, "not yet." And her sharp features hardened. Then she did resemble her mother. "Not until the very last moment. There is still a slim chance we may pull through."

"And what is the slim chance?"

"A miracle," she said solemnly. "Mr. McNally, thank

you for your interest, and the loan of your handkerchief. I shall have it laundered and returned to you."

"No need," I said, but she was already sweeping from the room. She was wearing one of her voluminous white gowns, and it billowed out behind her. But now it made her look less like a romantic heroine than a fleeing ghost.

Nothing was making much sense to me. First, Lady Cynthia refused to reveal her whereabouts at the time Bela Rubik was killed. Now Gina Stanescu refused to ask her mother for funds to repair her orphanage although, according to her, mommy dearest had been a generous contributor in the past. I suspected Ms. Stanescu had been telling me the truth, but not the *whole* truth.

What I needed at the moment, I decided, was one of Leroy Pettibone's creative hamburgers and a pail of suds. A lunch like that would goose the disposition and bring roses back to my cheeks.

But when I arrived at the Pelican Club, I found it mobbed with the midday crowd, all apparently ravenous, because when I glanced into the dining room, I saw no vacant tables. I concluded I would be forced to lunch at the bar, but then a bare feminine arm was raised, waved, and beckoned me. I peered and saw it was Consuela Garcia, sitting alone at a table for two. I dodged over immediately.

"Hiya, babe," I said huskily, twirling an imaginary mustache. "You come here often?"

"Oh, shut up and sit down," she said. "You look hungry."

147

"*And* thirsty," I said, sitting. "How are you, Connie?"

"Miserable," she said.

"Well, you look great," I assured her. "Just great."

That was the truth. She was wearing a white linen sundress that enhanced her deep tan beautifully. Big gold hoop earrings dangled, and her glossy black hair was unbound. I happened to know it was long enough to touch her buns.

Priscilla came over to take our order and glanced at me. "Connie," she said, "you're not allowed to pick up strange men in the club."

"You're going to get it," I said to her threateningly.

"I hope so," she said. "But when?"

Connie and I laughed, ordered hamburgers and beers, and started nibbling on the pickle spears.

"Why are you miserable?" I asked her.

"It's that nuthouse I work in," she said. "I had to get away for an hour or I'd be climbing walls."

"What's the problem? Lady Cynthia?"

"You've got it, Archy. She's been in a snit lately."

"Oh?" I said, suddenly curious. "Since when? Since her stamps were stolen?"

"No," Connie said, "that didn't seem to bother her. It's only been in the last few days that she's become a holy terror. You know what I heard her called the other day?"

"Lady Horrorwitz?"

"That's old stuff. I was at a cocktail party and heard some old bitch refer to her as Lady Whorewitz. People can be awfully cruel."

"Awful *and* cruel," I said. "Ah, here's our lunch."

Connie asked for hot salsa to put on her burger, but I passed. I recalled that during our brief and intimate joust she amazed me by nibbling on chipotles, those peppers that can scorch your tonsils. Connie popped them like macadamia nuts.

"Tell me something," I said casually, working on my food, "when the madam takes off alone in her Jag, does she tell you where she's going?"

"Sometimes," Connie said, "and sometimes not. And she hates it if anyone asks. She's really a very secretive person."

"Maybe too secretive. Sergeant Al Rogoff asked her where she was at a particular time, and she lied to him. Then I asked her, and she as much as told me to stuff it."

"That sounds like her."

"She lied to you, too," I said quietly.

Connie stopped eating long enough to stare at me. "When was this?"

"The day everyone was supposed to go out on Phil Meecham's yacht. You told me Lady C. went to her hairdresser's."

"That's where she said she was going."

"I'm sure she did. But she never showed up at the salon."

"That's odd," Connie said, frowning. "As I told you, she either tells me where she's going or she doesn't. But I can't recall her ever lying to me. How do you figure it?"

"I can't," I said. "Perhaps she enjoys being a mystery woman."

"Archy, that's nonsense. She's about as mysterious as a fried egg. She has only one rule: Just do everything exactly her way, and you'll get along fine with her."

"I don't suppose you'd care to ask her where she went instead of the hairdresser's."

"No, I would not," Consuela said firmly. "In spite of my kvetching I happen to like my job and want to keep it."

We cleaned our plates and sat a moment in silence, finishing our beers.

"You still seeing Jennifer Towley?" Connie asked idly.

I nodded.

"Did she tell you her history?"

"She did."

"That her ex-husband is also an ex-con?"

"She told me," I said patiently.

"You ever see him, Archy?"

"No, I never have."

"I have," Connie said. "He was pointed out to me last Saturday."

"Oh?" I said, interested. "What kind of a dude is he?"

"Well, he certainly doesn't look like he's done time. I mean he's well-dressed, got a nice tan, looks to be in good shape. I'd guess he's an inch or two shorter than you. No flab. Pleasant-looking. Not a matinee idol, but presentable enough. He laughs a lot."

"Where did you see him, Connie?"

"Down at Dania Jai Alai."

"What on earth were you doing there?"

"My Significant Other and I decided to do something different on Saturday, so we drove down to catch the games."

"And that's where you saw Thomas Bingham?"

"Oh-ho," she said, "so you know his name. Yes, he was there. My guy knew who he was."

"Connie," I said, "was he betting?"

"Bingham? Like there was no tomorrow."

I signed the tab, we left the club, and Connie gave me a warm kiss on the cheek and thanked me for lunch. I waved when she drove away in her Subaru. A sterling lady, I reflected, and our abbreviated affair was something I'd remember when I was playing checkers in a nursing home.

I got into the Miata and squirmed a bit on the sun-heated cushions. I lighted an English Oval and pondered my next move. Al Rogoff was wrong; I did not enjoy complexity. I liked things clear and uncomplicated. But now I seemed to be involved in a maze of maybes. The uncertainties were so overwhelming that I was tempted to take off for Hong Kong immediately and not return until all problems had been solved.

But instead of flying to Hong Kong, I drove to a car rental agency in West Palm Beach. I flashed my plastic and hired a black Ford Escort GT for a week. I asked the clerk if I could leave it right there on the lot.

He looked at me as if I were a new variety of nut. "For a week?" he asked incredulously.

I nodded. "I'll pick it up every now and then," I told him. "Whenever I feel the urge." And I gave him a twenty-buck tip.

"Of course, sir!" he cried heartily. "Absolutely no problem."

I didn't wish to explain my motive to him. To wit: The

Miata is a spiffy little car that catches the eye, especially when it's a screaming red. If I was going to do any tailing, I wanted wheels that wouldn't attract a second glance.

I drove back to the McNally & Son Building and parked the Miata in our underground garage. I went upstairs and asked Mrs. Trelawney if my father was available. She said he was in, but conferring with a client; she'd give me a buzz when he was free. So I went to my office which, for some reason, seemed smaller than ever. I thought of it as an Iron Maiden without the spikes.

I sat there for more than a half-hour reviewing the morning's tête-à-têtes with Lady Cynthia, Gina Stanescu, and Consuela Garcia. Very frustrating. Instead of clarifying matters, all three women had succeeded in adding to my professional and personal woes. They had tossed me more oddly shaped pieces on the table, the jigsaw puzzle kept getting larger, and I hadn't yet found two parts that fit.

Mrs. Trelawney phoned and said the boss could give me fifteen minutes before his next appointment, so make it snappy. Before I left for my audience, I tugged out my breast pocket handkerchief a bit to display it more conspicuously. It happened to be a square of brightly colored Pucci silk in a wildly abstract pattern, and I knew it would make my father's teeth ache. I really don't know why it pleased me to rile the old man occasionally. Perhaps it was just a sophomoric way of asserting my independence.

He was standing alongside his big rolltop desk when I entered his office, and I saw his gaze go immediately to the Pucci square. He made no comment, but one hairy eyebrow rose a good half-inch.

"Sorry to bother you, sir," I said, "but I wondered if you've had a chance to speak to Lady Horowitz about her will."

"I have," he said, "and she absolutely refuses to reveal any of its contents to the police."

"I expected that," I said, "but as you observed, she's unpredictable, and there was always a chance she might agree. Sergeant Rogoff will be disappointed."

There was silence, and I could tell by his thousand-yard stare that he was conducting one of those long inner debates that always preceded his dicta.

"I trust your discretion, Archy," he said finally. "If I didn't, you would not occupy the position you do in this organization. For your information—and I emphasize, *only* for *your* information—approximately half of Lady Horowitz's estate will go to several charities. Then there is a long list of specific bequests to individuals, including servants, friends, and even, I might add, all her ex-husbands who are still alive. The remainder of the estate is to be divided equally amongst her five children, three of whom are presently her houseguests."

I nodded. "I appreciate your confidence in my discretion, father. Without revealing any of the details to Sergeant Rogoff, may I tell him that you informed me there is nothing in Lady Cynthia's will that would aid his investigation?"

Again that long pause while he considered all the possible consequences of granting my request. Prescott McNally was one great muller.

"Yes," he said at last, "you may tell him that, but no more. How is the investigation proceeding?"

153

" 'A riddle wrapped in a mystery inside an enigma,' "
I quoted. "Winston Churchill."

"*Sir* Winston Churchill," he corrected me gravely, always the stickler for titles. "No suspects at all?"

"Too many suspects," I said. "Including Lady Horowitz
herself."

He stiffened and almost glared at me. "Surely you are
not suggesting our client stole her own stamps and murdered the dealer."

"Oh no, sir," I said hastily, "nothing like that. But she
refuses to reveal her whereabouts at the time Rubik was
killed." Then I told him of the inability of Al Rogoff to
determine where she was, capped by my own failure that
morning. "Not necessarily guilty conduct," I admitted,
"but worth a little more digging, wouldn't you say, father?"

"I suppose so," he said slowly, and I sensed the return
of that troubled state of mind I had noted the previous
evening.

"One final question, sir," I said. "You told me that approximately half of Lady Horowitz's estate will go to several charities. Do you happen to recall if one of them is
an orphanage in Rouen operated by her daughter Gina
Stanescu?"

He thought about that, but only for a moment this time.
"No," he said definitely, "it is not."

"Thank you, father," I said.

I drove home in a pensive mood; "pensive" meaning
that I devoted no thought at all to the Inverted Jenny
Case, but spun my mental wheels trying to decide
whether or not to tell Jennifer Towley that her ex was

gambling again. If I did tell, was it to save her from potential heartbreak or further my own romantic prospects? There was a nice moral choice involved there, and I solved the problem in my usual fashion: I postponed my decision.

I found my mother standing at the wooden workbench in the potting shed. She was sorrowfully regarding what was possibly the most decrepit plant I had ever seen: stalk drooping, leaves withered, the soil in the white pot dried and cracked.

"Mother," I said, "what on earth *is* that thing?"

"Isn't it sad, Archy?" she said, and I feared she might weep. "It's a 'Dancing Girl' begonia. Sarah Bogart brought it over to see if I could save it."

"What did she *do* to it—feed it Drāno?"

"Neglect," mother said angrily. "Just sheer, brutal neglect. The sick little thing is on its last legs."

"Can you save it?"

"I'm certainly going to try," she said determinedly. "I shall repot it in proper soil, water and fertilize, coddle it—and talk to it, of course."

She set to work with a marvelous set of stainless steel gardening tools my father had sent her during a business trip to Edinburgh. Her ministrations were slow, gentle, and purposeful. I had no doubt at all that the "Dancing Girl" would be kicking up its heels within a fortnight.

"Mother," I said, "have you noticed that father seems unusually troubled lately?"

"The poor thing," she said, and it took me a beat to realize she was referring to the bedraggled begonia.

"I realize he works very hard," I went on, "and is probably under a great deal of stress. But that's nothing new, and I've always felt he was coping."

"Tender, loving care is what's needed," mother said.

"But recently," I continued, "he seems almost distraught. Do you know of anything in particular that might be disturbing him?"

"You're going to be well again real soon," my mother promised the plant. "You'll have gorgeous, healthy leaves and all the scarlet flowers you could want."

I gave up and started away, but she called me back. "You must think positively, Archy," she said, "and always look on the bright side of things."

"Yes, mother," I said.

10

I really hated to scam Consuela Garcia. I thought her a lovely woman, perhaps not as sophisticated as she believed, but there was no malice in her. And I knew that despite her complaints, she was intensely loyal to her employer. So I had a swindle devised and rehearsed before I tooled up to the State of Horowitz on Wednesday morning.

I found Connie in her office, talking on the phone as usual. She waved me to a chair and continued her conversation. Apparently it involved a reception Lady Cynthia planned for a famous tenor who was about to visit Palm Beach.

Connie hung up and rolled her eyes heavenward. "The first crisis of the morning," she said, "and now you. What's on your mind, Archy?"

"A request," I said. "But please hear me out before you decide. Yesterday at lunch you told me that sometimes when Lady Horowitz takes off alone in her Jag, she doesn't tell you where she's going. Right?"

Connie nodded.

"What I'd like you to do," I said, "is the next time that happens, give me a quick telephone call."

"So you can follow her?" she said, outraged.

"Please listen a moment. You know I've been working closely with the police on the theft of the Inverted Jennies. We have good reasons to believe Lady Horowitz is being blackmailed, and she turned over the stamps as part payment."

"Blackmail!" Connie gasped, but she sounded more dismayed than disbelieving. She had been around long enough to know that Palm Beach is to a blackmailer as a chicken coop to a fox.

"All the evidence points to it," I lied on. "Regular cash withdrawals from her bank account, for instance. Now you know that if the cops or I ask her the direct question, 'Are you being blackmailed?' she'll tell us to get lost. Our best bet to stop this nastiness is to follow her to the blackmailers, identify them, and either put them behind bars or kick them out of the county. With no publicity; I can promise you that."

She looked at me, then took a deep breath. "I don't know," she said slowly. "I suppose she's done some things in her life she could be blackmailed for."

"Haven't we all?" I said. "Will you do it, Connie? Will you call me the moment you learn she's taking off in the Jag?"

"I'll think about it."

"Please do that," I said, rising. "I know you want to end this dirty business as much as I do."

I left her shaken and fumbling for a cigarette with trembling hands. Did I feel guilty about giving her that song and dance? No. The end doesn't *always* justify the means, but sometimes it does.

I exited the main house and heard sounds of laughter and splashings coming from the pool area. I strolled over there and found Felice and Alan DuPey frolicking in the water like baby dolphins. The newlyweds were wearing matching mauve swimsuits and aqua bathing caps.

I waved to them, and they waved to me. Their terry robes were piled on an umbrella table, and I pulled up a chair there and sat in the shade. I watched them cavort, yelping and dunking each other. Why did I feel so old? And why did I feel faint stirrings of envy? Tinged with a smidgen of regret, of course.

They came scrambling out of the pool laughing and peeling off their caps. They pulled on their robes, joined me, and we all exchanged greetings.

"Having a good time?" I asked. A silly question; they both looked like they had found Eden in South Florida.

"Oh, it is *so* lovely here," Felice said, looking about with shining eyes. "I never want to leave."

"But we must," her husband said, clasping her hand. He turned to me. "We depart Saturday morning."

"Sorry to hear it," I said. "Can't you stay a bit longer?"

He shook his head. "Sadly, no. We must return to our jobs. Back to the salt mines."

"You go, Alan," his wife said saucily, "and I shall stay. Mr. McNally will take care of me."

"I'd be delighted," I said, and we all laughed.

But it disturbed me. The DuPeys ranked close to the bottom of my list of suspects, but I didn't want to see them gone from the scene. If they were somehow involved in the theft and subsequent homicide, it would be extremely difficult if not impossible to prove their guilt if they were half a globe away.

Even more important, if they were totally innocent, as I believed, they still might have information they hadn't yet divulged, information they thought insignificant but which could be useful. Alan gave me the opening I needed.

"Tell me, Mr. McNally," he said, "have you discovered who stole mother's stamps?"

"Not yet," I said. "The investigation goes on. Perhaps you and Felice can help. When you all went aboard Phil Meecham's yacht, you were told the cruise was canceled because of high seas. Is that correct?"

"Yes," he said, "but we stayed to party."

"You and Felice did," I said. "But the Smythes, Gina Stanescu, and Angus Wolfson took off. I believe that's what you said. Have I got it right?"

They both nodded.

"Did they tell you where they were going?"

"Shopping," Felice said promptly, paused, then jabbered at her husband in such rapid French I couldn't follow it.

"Window-shopping," Alan explained. "I don't think

they were planning to buy anything, but they said they wanted to see the shops on Worth Avenue."

"Such expensive shops!" his wife said. "Ooo, la!"

"Aren't they," I agreed. "So as far as you know, they were just going to wander about and do the tourist bit?"

The two looked at each other, then nodded again, vigorously this time.

"They all left the yacht in a group—the four of them?"

He frowned, trying to recall, but his wife supplied the answer.

"No," she said, "not all together. Gina and Angus departed first and then, perhaps a half-hour later, the Smythes. I remember because . . ."

Suddenly both burst out laughing, sharing a mutual joke.

"What's so amusing?" I asked.

Alan calmed down long enough to reply. "I shouldn't peach on them," he said, "but when Harry and Doris left, they took a bottle of Monsieur Meecham's champagne with them."

"We saw it," Felice said. "It was so funny. Harry tried to hide it under his jacket."

"In case they got thirsty while window-shopping," I suggested. "Well, I'm sure Phil Meecham never missed it. But Gina and Angus went off together?"

"Oh yes," Alan said. "They are very close, those two."

"Do you suppose—" his wife started, then stopped and bit her knuckle.

"Suppose what?" I urged her.

"It's nonsense," Alan said, looking at his new wife

161

fondly. "Felice believes there may be more than friendship there."

"Oh?" I said. "A romance?"

"It is not nonsense," Felice said, pouting prettily. "A woman knows these things, and I say there is definitely a feeling, an emotion between them."

"Impossible," the husband said firmly. "First of all, he is at least twenty years older than she, and also he is gay."

"Those things are of no importance," the wife said just as firmly. "Perhaps they are both lonely."

"That's possible," I admitted. "I hoped to have a talk with Mr. Wolfson this morning. Do you know if he's around?"

"No, he is not," Alan said. "He went down to the beach about an hour ago."

"I hope he's not going to swim," I said. "It's choppy out there today, and the radio warned of an undertow."

"Oh no," Felice said. "He can't swim; he told us so. He said he's just going to take a walk and perhaps pick up a few shells."

I nodded and stood up. "I'll see if I can find him. Thank you for the talk. I'm sure I'll see you again before you leave."

"You are not married, Mr. McNally?" she asked suddenly.

"No," I said, "I am not."

Felice looked at me speculatively. "I have a beautiful cousin," she said. "About your age I would say. Also unmarried."

"Felice!" her husband cried, and clapped a palm lightly

over her mouth. "Please to excuse," he said to me. "She is *such* a matchmaker."

His wife took his hand away. "I just want everyone to be as happy as we are," she said.

I left them holding hands and gazing at each other with bedroom eyes. Enough already!

The Horowitz estate fronted on Ocean Boulevard. Across the road was a paling of sea grape and then a waist-high concrete wall. Beyond that was the beach, the Atlantic Ocean and, eventually, Morocco.

But I wasn't going that far. I walked northward to a break in the wall where a weather-worn wooden staircase led down to the sand. During the season you might see dozens of bathers in both directions. In late May I saw a family group of four swimmers to the north and two supine sun-worshipers to the south. Palm Beach Island is definitely not Coney.

I also saw, to the north, the distant, approaching figure of a solitary stroller I decided could very well be Angus Wolfson. I kicked off my loafers (no socks) and plodded through the sand. As we came closer it indeed proved to be the Boston bibliophile, carrying his sandals and sloshing through the shallows like a kid kicking his way through puddles of rain.

He was wearing white flannel bags and a silk shirt with flamboyant collar and billowing sleeves that Lord Byron might envy. Atop his head was a yellowed boater with a tatty band that he wore with an insouciance I admired, and he stabbed at the sand with the tip of a Malacca cane.

As I came up, he recognized me and swept off his ridiculous hat with a gesture of mock politesse and bowed slightly. "Mr. McNally," he said, "what a delightful surprise."

"Planned," I told him. "I heard you were walking the beach and hoped to have a talk. May I accompany you, sir?"

"Only if you cease calling me 'sir.' It's one notch from 'pop.'"

"Old habits die hard," I said. "I was taught to address male elders as 'sir' as a mark of respect."

"Sometimes we don't deserve it," he said lightly. "By all means, walk along. An absolutely *brilliant* day."

It was. An ocean breeze took the edge off the sun's heat, and the blue sky was mottled with popcorn clouds. But the sea was undeniably choppy with a steady surf that came pounding in to swirl milky foam about our bare ankles.

We meandered slowly southward, Wolfson occasionally leaning heavily on his cane. I didn't think he looked at all well. The sagging flesh of his face had a grayish tinge, and once or twice he pressed his free hand to his abdomen as if to restrain a persistent pain.

"Are you feeling all right?" I asked.

"A temporary malady," he said blithely. "It will soon pass."

"What is it, Mr. Wolfson?"

"Living," he said and looked to me for an appreciative chuckle. I obliged as best I could. He asked: "And are you still snooping about after those silly stamps?"

I was offended by that derisive description of my discreet inquiries, but let it pass. "I'm still investigating, yes."

He stopped a moment to lean on his cane and stare out at the dim horizon. "I really don't understand why you're making such a fuss about the disappearance of those misprinted bits of paper. I assure you that Lady Cynthia is not losing any sleep over their loss."

"If the stamps are not recovered, an insurance claim will be filed. My father wants to make certain that both his office and the police have made a good-faith effort to find the stamps or the thief or both."

He made no reply but resumed his slow walk. His head was lowered, the wide brim of his hat hid his eyes.

"And why did you wish to talk to me?" he inquired. "I've already told you what little I know of the matter."

"Just a few more questions," I said. "You left Phil Meecham's yacht with Gina Stanescu after the cruise was canceled. Do you mind telling me where you went?"

"Yes, I do mind," he said. "I resent this interrogation since it seems to imply there may have been something suspicious in my activities that day. However, I have nothing to hide so I shall answer. Gina and I found our way to Worth Avenue and visited several shops. We separated in a department store because I was weary of walking about. We made plans to meet in an hour. I stopped briefly in a bookstore but found nothing that interested me. I then went to the Cafe L'Europe, sat at the bar and had an excellent vodka gimlet, ice cold and razor-sharp. Gina eventually joined me and had a glass of white wine. We finished our drinks—I had a second—and phoned Kenneth. He came for us in that marvelous Rolls, and we rode home in style. Satisfied?"

"I am," I said, "but you know what the police are like; they'll want to check your story with Gina, the clerk at the bookstore, the bartender at L'Europe, and Kenneth."

"Let them do all the bloody checking they want," he cried with unexpected fury. "I don't give a good god-damn!"

I looked at him with astonishment. The sudden spasm of anger seemed to have weakened him. He swayed, I feared he might fall, and put a hand on his elbow to steady him.

"Are you all right?" I asked anxiously.

"I'm beginning to feel the heat," he said with what I can only describe as a vulpine grin. "I think we better go back."

"Of course," I said. "Would you care to lean on my arm?"

He glared at me. "I am stronger than you may think," he said coldly. "I am not yet decrepit, I do assure you."

But we retraced our steps slowly, Wolfson with his head bowed and using his cane. He stopped abruptly, lowered his head a little more to peer at the sand.

"Look at that!" he said. "A lovely shell! Will you retrieve it for me, please."

I bent to pick it up, shake out the sand and hand it to him. It was a common whelk, chipped and encrusted, but he turned it tenderly in his fingers as if he had found a treasure.

"Is it rare?" he asked.

I could not lie but I could dissemble. "All shells are rare

along this stretch of coast," I told him. "We've had very slim pickings for the past few years."

"I shall give it to Gina," he said. "She'll love it."

We finally got back to the Horowitz mansion, and Wolfson left me to go to his room. "A short nap," the antiquarian said, "to recharge my batteries."

I went out to the Miata and saw Kenneth Bodin puttering about in the garage. He was wearing one of his skimpy T-shirts, muscles popping in all directions. I joined him and proffered my box of cigarettes. He selected one and examined it closely.

"English Ovals, huh?" he said. "I never smoked one. Imported?"

"Yes," I said. "From Virginia."

"I'll have it after lunch," he said, and tucked the cigarette behind his ear. "You find those stamps yet?"

"Not yet," I said. "Perhaps you can help. On the day all the houseguests were supposed to go for a yacht cruise, did you get a call around one o'clock to pick up Gina Stanescu and Angus Wolfson?"

"That's right," he said. "The cruise was canceled, so they went shopping. Then they wanted a ride back. They could have called a cab, I guess, but that's what I'm here for—right?"

"Right," I said. "Where did you pick them up?"

"Outside the Cafe L'Europe," he said promptly. "They were waiting for me on the sidewalk."

"And you drove them directly back here?"

"Sure. Hey, has this got something to do with the stamps?"

"One never knows, do one?" I said, and left him flummoxed.

I returned home for lunch. But before digging into the chef's salad Ursi had prepared, I made two phone calls. The first was to Sgt. Al Rogoff.

"Hiya, sherlock," he said. "What's up?"

"You're having lunch," I said. "I can hear you masticating."

"Nah," he said, "I haven't done that since I was in the navy."

"Not a bad pun," I admitted. "What are you eating?"

"Anchovy pizza."

"Rather you than me," I said. "Can you chew pizza and make notes at the same time?"

"Sure."

I repeated what Angus Wolfson had told me of his activities during the time Bela Rubik was getting his skull smashed.

"Okay," Al said. "Thanks. I'll check it out."

"I've already questioned the chauffeur," I told him. "He says yes, he picked up Stanescu and Wolfson about one o'clock. Do you believe him?"

"I don't believe anyone," Rogoff said.

"Does that include me?" I asked.

"Especially you," he said.

My second call was to Jennifer Towley, and I was pleasantly surprised when she replied instead of her answering machine.

"Sorry," I said, "but I can't talk until you *beep*."

"*Beep*," she said.

"How about dinner tonight?"

168

"Love to," she said at once.

"Are you sure you wouldn't like to consider it for—oh, say two seconds?"

"I did," she said, "and I'd love to have dinner with you tonight. What shall I wear?"

"Clothes would be nice—but if you'd rather not . . ."

"I'll wear clothes," she said firmly.

"Listen," I said, "I just had an earthshaking idea. I haven't done the black-tie bit in ages. Why don't we glam it up just for the fun of it?"

"Groovy," she said. Then: "Do people still say groovy?"

"No."

"Well, I think glamming it up for an evening is a marvy idea."

"No one says marvy anymore either."

"Keep it up," she warned, "and you and your black tie will end up alone at the Pelican Club."

"See you around seven," I said.

"That's keen," she said. "Also neat."

I hung up, thinking she was in a delightfully antic mood.

At the family cocktail hour that evening, father eyed my white dinner jacket with his usual distaste for my duds. He once observed that wearing a white dinner jacket made a man look like a trombonist in Guy Lombardo's band.

Mother had news. She had received a handwritten note from Lady Cynthia Horowitz. The three of us were invited to attend an informal dinner for Felice and Alan DuPey on Friday night. It was to be a farewell party prior to their departure for France on Saturday morning.

"Shall we accept, Prescott?" she asked. (She had once addressed him as "father," and he had instructed her in no uncertain terms that since he was not her father, he did not appreciate the designation. All very well and good, and I agreed with him, but I noted that on more than one occasion he had addressed her as "mother." How do you figure that?)

"I think we should," he said, and turned to me. "You've met the DuPeys, Archy?"

"Yes, sir. I spoke to them today."

"A pleasant couple?"

"Newlyweds," I said, "and disgustingly in love. It can't last."

"Don't be so sure of that, Archy," my mother said, sipping her martini.

I know it's fashionable to be late, but early in our relationship I had sensed that Jennifer was a woman who preferred punctuality in her business and personal dealings. So I rang her bell a minute or two after seven o'-clock, duded up in dinner jacket, black tie and cummerbund, as promised.

She came to the door, and I almost shouted with delight. If that wasn't a Hanae Mori she was wearing, it was an awfully good ripoff. The beaded gown fell to her ankles and looked as if it had been painted by van Gogh, perhaps as a study for "Starry Night." It was all swirls of vibrant colors that caught the light and gave it back deepened and intensified.

Jennifer must have seen my admiration, for she struck a model's pose and twirled. "Glamorous enough for you?" she asked.

"Magnificent," I said. "I think I better cancel our reservation at Burger King. We'll go to a fancier place."

"We better," she said. "I shot my bank account on this little number."

Actually, I had made a reservation at The Ocean Grand, a new hotel down the road a piece. It's an elegant resort, and if anything could top the painted silk murals on the walls of the dining room, it could only be that scintillant gown Jennifer was wearing.

I'm not going to describe our dinner in detail because you'd gain weight just reading about it. I'll merely mention our entrees: Jennifer had sautéed breast of pheasant with kumquats, and I had wood-grilled tenderloin flavored with tamarind and guava. Isn't that enough to set your salivary glands atwitter?

After dessert and espresso, we moved to the lounge, where a harpist was strumming something that sounded suspiciously like "The Darktown Strutters' Ball." We sat at the bar and ordered S.O.B.s. You may not be familiar with that drink. The full name is Sex on the Beach, and I believe it's indigenous to South Florida. I don't wish to reveal the ingredients lest it achieve wide popularity and undermine the democratic institutions of this great nation.

"Oh Archy," Jennifer said, sighing, "what a scrumptious dinner! I must have put on five pounds."

"Nonsense," I said. "It was all no-cal—didn't you know?"

"Liar," she said. "But I don't care; I'll go on a diet tomorrow."

"Famous last words. Just play a few sets of tennis in the

171

hot sun; that'll melt the avoirdupois. Jennifer, have you used your new racquet yet?"

"Not yet. I can't tell you how busy I've been. I was hoping to take an hour off yesterday for a lesson with the club pro, but something came up."

I didn't ask.

"As a matter of fact," she said, looking down at her drink, "my ex phoned. He was going to be in West Palm Beach and wanted to have lunch."

"Uh-huh," I said. "And did you?"

She nodded. "I thought about it and decided there was no point in being uncivil. After all, we *were* married. And having a quick lunch with Tom didn't send a signal that I wanted him back, did it?"

I didn't answer that. "It's your decision," I said, but suddenly the evening didn't seem quite as perfect as it had ten minutes ago.

"Well, I saw him," she went on. "I think it was more curiosity than anything else. I wondered if those years in prison had changed him."

"And?"

She gave a short laugh. "I think they helped. Physically, at least. He's thinner and has a good tan. He looks very fit. And he's as optimistic as ever. I suppose salesmen have to be that way."

"What about the gambling?"

"He says that's all finished. He claims he hasn't made a bet since his release, and he swears he'll never gamble again as long as he lives."

"Do you believe him?"

"Oh Archy, how can I? He told me the same thing so many times when we were married, and he always broke his promise. No, I don't believe him."

"I think that's wise."

"I hope he means it this time," she said thoughtfully. "For his sake. But I wouldn't bet on it."

"Good," I said. "Don't you start betting."

She gave me a sad smile.

We finished our drinks and left. I drove slowly on the trip homeward while Jennifer chattered on about her crazy clients and their wild decorating ideas. I had never known her to be so voluble, and it suddenly occurred to me that she—like Gina Stanescu and Angus Wolfson—might be lonely. Lonely in the sense of lacking someone in her life with whom to share intimacies, even if they were only the mundane details of living: What did you have for lunch? Did you get caught in the rain? Is your headache better? Did you remember to pick up the dry cleaning?

In other words, she lacked a partner. And I wasn't yet certain I wanted to apply for the job. The reason is obvious, isn't it? Cowardice.

She invited me in for a nightcap, and I accepted gratefully because I did admire this woman. She really demanded nothing from me, and I knew she wouldn't. She gave generously and in return, I think, she wanted me to respect her independence. And so we circled each other in comfortable orbit, but never collided. That would have meant destruction or merger, and I don't believe either of us had the moxie to chance it.

That evening, in her Victorian four-poster, her horizontal aerobics were as fervid as ever. At least her body responded enthusiastically to stimuli. But I had the feeling that her thoughts were away and drifting.

11

I had Thursday carefully planned: things to do, people to see, questions to ask. And then my carefully crafted schedule just fell apart, and chance and accident took over again, with no help from me this time.

I was heading out to the garage after breakfast when the phone rang. I scampered back into the kitchen with a premonition that the day was not going to proceed as planned.

"The McNally residence," I said.

"May I talk to Mr. Archibald McNally, please."

A woman's voice, deep and throaty. I had heard it before but couldn't place it.

"Speaking," I said. "Who is calling?"

"This is Mrs. Agnes Marsden."

"Mrs. Marsden! How nice to hear from you. Sorry I didn't recognize your voice. How are you?"

"Very well, thank you. Mr. McNally, are you coming over today?"

"I intend to," I said, "but later this afternoon."

"Could you come right away?" she said, almost pleading. "There's something I should tell you, and I want to get it off my chest now. If I wait till this afternoon, I might change my mind again."

"Don't do that," I said. "I'll be there in ten minutes. Thank you, Mrs. Marsden."

She opened the door of the Horowitz mansion while I had my hand raised to use that enormous brass knocker: the head of Bacchus surrounded by vine leaves. The housekeeper led me into the mammoth first-floor sitting room, and we occupied a corner as we had before. She sat stiffly upright, but her fingers were interlaced and gripped tightly.

"Young man," she started, "can I trust you?"

"Of course you can," I said, oozing sincerity. "Whatever you tell me is strictly confidential. It will go no farther, I promise you."

"See that you keep your promise," she said tartly. "I mentioned to you that I have seen strange goings-on that disturb me."

I nodded.

"I have decided to tell you about them. They may mean nothing, and I hope they do. But a crime has been committed in this house, Mr. McNally, and something of great value has been stolen. Being black, I am naturally the one the police will suspect."

"No, no," I protested, infinitely saddened.

"Yes, yes," she said ironically. "Don't attempt to teach

me the ways of the world, young man. So I have a personal reason for helping your investigation any way I can."

"I appreciate that," I said, "and I welcome it. But believe me, Mrs. Marsden, you are not a suspect and never have been."

She ignored that, obviously not believing it. "First of all," she said, "Gina Stanescu and Angus Wolfson have become very close. Closer than you might expect for two people who have known each other such a short time. I see them together frequently: taking walks, sitting on the terrace or in the game room. Once or twice she was crying, and he was comforting her."

I nodded again, not wanting to interrupt her recital.

"That could be completely innocent," she said. "A man and a woman getting close—nothing wrong about that. What is wrong is the way Wolfson has been carrying on with Ken Bodin, the chauffeur."

I was surprised at Wolfson's temerity, but not shocked. "Carrying on?" I said.

Her back became ramrod straight and she looked sternly at me. "People's personal lives are their own. I don't interfere, and I don't expect them to interfere with me. But private things should be kept private. They can do anything they wish, but I don't want to know about it. Do you understand what I'm saying?"

"Yes, Mrs. Marsden, I think I do."

"That Mr. Wolfson just doesn't care who sees what he's doing or who hears what he's saying to Kenneth. I don't like it one bit."

"And how does Kenneth take all this?"

She made a grimace. "That boy is a noodle," she said. "Nothing between his ears. He just eats it up when Mr. Wolfson comes on to him. He grins and laughs and shows off his muscles."

"I get the picture," I said, and thought a moment. Then: "Do you think Wolfson is giving Kenneth money?"

"I wouldn't be a bit surprised," the housekeeper said, stood suddenly, and smoothed the wrinkles from her bombazine dress.

I rose also. "Thank you for the information, Mrs. Marsden. It may be of help. One final question: Do you think Lady Horowitz has been acting oddly lately?"

She stared at me, face expressionless. "Oddly?" she asked. "What do you mean?"

"Oh, driving off in the Jaguar by herself without telling anyone where she's going."

"No," she said firmly, "I've noticed nothing like that."

And she swept swiftly from the room, leaving me standing there with more unlinked pieces to add to my jigsaw puzzle.

I drove the Miata to the McNally Building on Royal Palm Way, foolishly believing I was going to get back to my planned schedule. I parked in the underground garage and strolled over to the glass-enclosed booth inhabited by Herb, our security guard. He's a spindly, hipless bloke whose gunbelt always seems in danger of slipping down around his knees.

"Herb," I said, "may I use your phone?"

"Sure thing, Mr. McNally," he said. "It's a scorcher out there today."

"True," I said. "It gets hot in the summer and cold in the winter. I don't understand it."

I called for a cab to come pick me up. While I waited, I chatted with Herb about tropical fish. According to what I had heard, his mobile home was wall-to-wall aquaria, and he liked nothing better than to debate the virtues of Black Tetras versus Mickey Mouse Platies. I am not an expert on tropicals, but I once owned a Zebra Danio named Irving. It died.

The cab finally showed up, and I asked the driver to take me to that car rental agency in West Palm Beach where I intended to pick up the black Ford Escort GT I had hired for tailing purposes. This was what I was thinking:

If I received a call from Consuela Garcia telling me that Lady Horowitz was going to take off alone in her Jaguar, destination unknown, I wanted my anonymous car closer than West Palm Beach. And I couldn't park it in the McNally driveway or my father would be sure to ask me its purpose. And if I told him I had rented it so that I could follow McNally & Son's wealthiest client without fear of detection, he would have had me committed.

I switched from cab to Escort and drove back to Royal Palm Way. I parked next to the Miata and told Herb I was going upstairs to get a windshield sticker issued to employees. All cars parked in our underground garage must have them or they get towed away. We had a small outside parking area for visitors and clients.

I asked Mrs. Trelawney for a numbered decal, and she wanted to know why I needed it since I already had one for the Miata. I told her it was for my new skateboard. She hooted one laugh and handed it over. I stopped at my office and found two telephone messages on my desk. One was from Sgt. Al Rogoff, the other from Hilda Lantern, the stamp dealer in Fort Lauderdale. Both asked me to call as soon as possible.

I phoned Hilda Lantern first. She sounded excited for such a dour woman and told me she had a report regarding the current market value of a block of four Inverted Jenny stamps, and thought it important that I be informed at once.

"That's fine," I said. "What is it?"

"Not on the phone," she said sharply. "You better come here."

I wasn't about to argue with that dominative lady and assured her I'd be delighted to spend three hours driving to and from Fort Lauderdale to hear what she had to relate. I hung up and may have screamed, "Drat!" Or possibly some other four-letter word.

I stuffed Al Rogoff's message in my jacket pocket, returned to the garage, and slapped the identification sticker onto the corner of the Escort's windshield. Then I headed the rented car southward to Lauderdale, glumly reflecting that when R. Burns penned his aphorism regarding the best laid schemes o' mice and men, he must have been referring to the Thursday schedule of A. McNally.

The drive south didn't lift my mood. It was a hot day all right, but humid and cloudy. So instead of beaching, everyone in South Florida decided to go malling. Traffic was horrendous, and by the time I hit East Commercial

Boulevard I was as cantankerous as Hilda Lantern and figured I could match her peeve for peeve.

But I found the lady in a dulcet mood. Of course that may have been due to the whopping bill she handed me for her labors to date on behalf of McNally & Son. The charges, she claimed, were for time spent and phone calls made to stamp dealers, trying to establish the current market price of a block of four Inverted Jenny stamps.

"None of them ever handled such a rarity," she reported. "I couldn't get any quotes."

That was understandable. Asking the average stamp dealer what he would pay for an Inverted Jenny was akin to asking the average jeweler for a quote on the Star of India.

"But then," she went on, "I got a return call from a dealer out on Powerline Road near Palm Aire. He said that early this morning, right after he opened, a woman showed up with a block of four Jennies and asked if he wanted to buy."

I tried to conceal my rush. "Did she mention how much she wanted?"

"Half a million. He examined the stamps and told her they were too rich for his blood; he just couldn't swing the deal."

"How were the stamps presented? Mounted? In an envelope? Or what?"

"Between plastic sheets in a small red book," Ms. Lantern said. "About the size of a daily diary."

"Uh-huh," I said. "And did the dealer describe the would-be seller?"

Hilda delivered a short, scornful laugh. "Not your run-of-the-mill stamp collector," she said. "A young blond woman wearing short-shorts and a halter top. I suppose she was what you men would call well-endowed."

"I suppose," I agreed. "Did the dealer happen to note the car she was using?"

"He didn't mention it," Lantern said, looking at me curiously. "Why do you ask?"

"Just wondering," I said, naturally hoping it had been a lavender Volkswagen Beetle. "So she left with her stamps, and that was that?"

"Not quite," she said almost triumphantly. "The block of four Inverted Jennies she tried to sell him were counterfeit."

I clenched my teeth to keep the old jaw from drooping. "Counterfeit?"

She nodded.

"A forgery?"

"Absolutely. No doubt about it."

"How could the dealer be so sure after such a brief inspection?"

"You know anything about the history of the Inverted Jennies?" she demanded.

"Some," I said. "The original sheet of a hundred stamps was bought in 1918 at a Washington, D.C., post office by a broker's clerk. He paid twenty-four dollars. About a week later he sold the sheet to a stamp dealer for fifteen thousand."

"That's right," Lantern said. "And a week after that, the dealer sold the stamps to a collector for twenty thousand. But the collector kept only twenty of the stamps and gave the dealer permission to break up the remainder of the sheet into singles and blocks and sell them. When the dealer did that, he made light pencil marks on the back of each stamp, showing the name of the buyer. Practically all the Inverted Jennies in existence have those penciled notations on the back. If they don't, the chances are good that they're counterfeits. In this case, the Palm Aire dealer who called me said there were no marks on the backs of the stamps. And when he examined the face with a magnifying glass, the printing appeared slightly fuzzy and the inverted biplane in the center was slightly off register. Also, the number of perforations along the edges of each stamp was one less than the government printing office uses. Those stamps were definitely fakes."

I drew a deep breath. "Did the dealer tell that to the woman who was trying to sell them?"

"No. He didn't want to get involved. He just told her that he couldn't afford them and got her out of his shop as quickly as possible."

"That was probably the smart thing to do," I said. "Well, I don't think we can use the asked-for price of forged stamps as a benchmark for our deceased client's block of four, but I certainly appreciate the information. Will you continue your inquiries, please."

"If you want me to," she said. "When can I expect payment?"

"You'll have a check within a week," I promised. "Or I can pay now by credit card if you'd prefer."

"I'll wait for the check," she said, and we parted with a firm handshake.

I drove back to Delray Beach as speedily as traffic and the law allowed. Of course you know what I was thinking:

In all of South Florida there couldn't be more than one blond young woman, wearing short-shorts and halter top (and "well-endowed"), trying to peddle a block of four Inverted Jenny stamps. And those placed between plastic sheets in a small red book. Tallyho!

I entered Hammerhead's Bar & Grill and looked about for Sylvia. Not present, which pleased me. I stood at the Formica bar and ordered a beer from a T-shirted bartender who appeared to be in the full flower of middle-aged louthood.

"Sylvia around?" I asked casually.

"Nah," he said. "It's her day off."

"Oh," I said, "I didn't know. Maybe I'll try her at home."

"Won't do you no good," he said with a louche laugh. "It's her boyfriend's day off, too. They was going to drive down to the Keys."

"Thank you very much," I said, and meant it.

I finished my beer, left a tip large enough to shock the publican, and headed for the hurricane-shutter emporium where Thomas Bingham was employed. Now if it was also *his* day off, my happiness would be complete.

My motive was contemptible; I admit it. I wanted desperately to involve Bingham in the snatch of Lady Cynthia's stamps and the subsequent murder of Bela Rubik. My excuse was simply that I was smitten by Jennifer Towley. I had felt similar emotions about other women—similar but far less intense. Then it had been mostly a matter of testosterone. Now it was a matter of heart. I wanted that cool, elegant woman for my very

own, and the ex-husband represented a threat to my felicity.

Not a very noble reason for hounding a man, is it? But
I make no claims to nobility. After all, my grandfather was
an expert at pratfalls.

My luck foundered with Tom Bingham. He was in the
store, and when I asked for him, he came forward smiling.

"Yes, sir," he said, "what can I do for you?"

Vanish, I wanted to say, but didn't.

"Mr. Bingham," I said, "I'm from out of town, but I'm
staying with a friend in Boca. He's got a condo in a high-
rise and wants to get hurricane shutters. He asked me to
find someone who could do the job."

"And how did you get on to me?" he asked, still smiling.

"I was having a drink at Hammerhead's," I said, "and
Sylvia suggested I contact you."

"Good for Sylvia," he said. "She's great people, isn't
she?"

"She certainly is."

"I party with her and her boyfriend," he went on in the
most open and honest way imaginable. "We have a lot of
laughs together. Would you like me to come to your
friend's condo and give you an estimate? No charge."

"The problem is that he works during the day," I explained, "and I'm about ready to head up north. Could
you possibly come out in the evening?"

"Of course," he said promptly. "Anytime. And that includes Saturday or Sunday. Whatever's convenient for
him."

Connie Garcia had been right; he was a pleasant man,

not terribly handsome but with more than his share of easy charm. I could understand why he was a dynamite salesman; he gave the impression that satisfying your every wish was his foremost priority. There was something almost puppyish in his desire to please.

"Suppose I have my friend give you a call," I said. "Then the two of you can set up a time."

"Sounds good to me," he said, and I wondered if he slept with that genial smile.

"Thank you, Mr. Bingham," I said, started to leave, then turned back. "Oh, by the way," I said, "is there any place nearby where I can buy lottery tickets?"

The smile expanded. "You play the lottery, do you?"

I nodded. "Since I've been in Florida I've been hooked."

"Me, too," he said cheerfully. "Totally addicted. I play Lotto, Fantasy Five, the scratch-offs—everything. It keeps me poor. Sure, there's a liquor store on the corner that has a computer. They'll sell you as many tickets as you want. As they say in the commercials, 'You never know.' "

"That's right," I agreed. "Hit once and you're set for life."

"Now you're singing my song," he said, and I left him with his smile intact.

I still wasn't ready to forget his complicity in the Horo-witz heist. If playing the lottery kept him poor, he could be in as deep as Kenneth Bodin and Sylvia, and the two men had elected the woman to try to sell the swag. But one thing I definitely knew to be true: Thomas Bingham

186

hadn't been cured of his compulsion to gamble by those years he had spent in the slammer.

I pondered these things on my homeward drive. I decided the biggest puzzle was this: What on earth did Jennifer Towley, a lady of taste and discernment, *see* in this guy? There was nothing exceptional about him that I could spot. He was a loser, a salesman of plumbing supplies and hurricane shutters, an ex-convict with a monkey on his back. But Jennifer had married him, sent him birthday cards in prison, taken his phone calls after his release, met him for lunch. She was demeaning herself and I couldn't compute it.

Does that make me an elitist snob? I guess so.

I drove directly to the Pelican Club. It was then about three-thirty, and the place was deserted except for Simon Pettibone behind the bar. He was reading *The Wall Street Journal* through his B. Franklin specs. I waved to him, went to the public phone, and called Sgt. Al Rogoff.

"*So* nice to hear from you," he said. "Have you had a pleasant day? A tennis match perhaps? A chukker of polo?"

"Oh, shut up," I said. "I think you and I better get together and have a talk."

"No kidding?" he said. "What a brilliant idea. Where are you now?"

"In the bar of the Pelican Club."

"I should have known. Can you stay sober for a half-hour until I get there?"

"I never drink to excess," I said stiffly.

187

"Now you *are* kidding. If I ever need a liver transplant, with my luck I'll get yours. Wait for me."

I returned to the bar and swung onto a stool. "Mr. Pettibone," I said, "you have a few years on me and infinitely more wisdom. Tell me, what do *you* do when life threatens to overwhelm and problems become too heavy to be borne?"

He thought a moment, peering at me over his square glasses. "I usually kick my cat, Mr. McNally," he said.

"Good suggestion," I said. "I must purchase a cat. Meanwhile I'll have a wee bit of the old nasty in the form of an Absolut on the rocks, splash of water, chunk of lime. And if I attempt to order a refill, I want you to eighty-six me. An officer of the law has just cast aspersions on my liver."

I carried my drink over to a booth and nursed it until Sgt. Rogoff came stalking in. He looked around, saw me, and came lumbering. He slid in opposite me and stared stonily.

"What are you drinking?" I asked.

"Hemlock," he said. "I know you're not totally to blame, but every time you drop something on my plate I start thinking about early retirement. You know how I spent yesterday?"

"Haven't the slightest."

"Checking out the whereabouts of Doris and Harry Smythe at the time Rubik was iced. They claimed they left Meecham's yacht and went to Testa's for what Harry called 'a spot of lunch.' Bushwa! No one at Testa's remembered them. So I went back to the Smythes, and they finally admitted they had lunch at a Pizza Hut. So I checked on that, and the people at the Pizza Hut remembered them all right. You know why?"

"They left a nickel tip?"

"That, too. But mostly they were remembered because they asked for two plastic glasses and uncorked a bottle of champagne they had brought along. Archy, can you believe this insanity?"

"Easily," I said, laughing. "They swiped the bubbly from Meecham's yacht. So you figure they're cleared?"

"Looks like it."

"Al, have you started checking out Gina Stanescu and Angus Wolfson?"

"Not yet. You believe Wolfson's story?"

"Not completely," I said. "He flared up when I started to ask questions. There really was no need for it if he was totally innocent. But maybe he was just being crotchety. I think the man is sick."

"Sick?"

"Ill. He seems to be in pain. Get out your notebook, Al; I have more for you."

While I had waited for him, sipping my vodka daintily, I had decided how much to tell him. Everything about Hilda Lantern, Kenneth Bodin and Sylvia, but nothing about Thomas Bingham. That's all Rogoff would have to hear: an ex-con possibly implicated in crimes under investigation. He'd have zeroed in on Bingham like a gundog on point. And I didn't want Jennifer Towley involved in any manner whatsoever.

When I completed my recital, Al looked at me thoughtfully. "What made you go to the stamp dealer in Lauderdale?"

I pondered my answer carefully. I really needed the sergeant's cooperation and didn't want to stiff him or send him sniffing along false trails. But there were things I didn't wish to reveal at this stage of the investigation. My reasons will, I trust, become apparent later.

"Take your time," Al said, peeling the cellophane from a cigar. "Meditate. Cogitate. Consider all the permutations and combinations. And what about your karma? I can wait."

"Look," I said, hunching forward, "when I hired Rubik I fed him a farrago. I told him my firm was handling an estate that included Inverted Jenny stamps, and we wanted to establish an evaluation. I asked Rubik to make inquiries and see if he could determine the current price. That's what I *told* him. What I hoped was that he'd discover a block of Inverted Jennies had recently come on the market. You follow?"

"Way ahead of you," Rogoff said, lighting his cigar. "You figured the thief would try to unload as soon as possible. Right?"

"Right. And Rubik obviously discovered something of importance but was killed before he could pass it along to me. So I decided that if Rubik could get the information, another stamp dealer might be able to do the same thing. I just happened to pick Hilda Lantern's name out of the Yellow Pages, and she came through. How do you like that bit about the stamps being counterfeit?"

"Love it," Al said. "You think that was the important information Bela Rubik uncovered and wanted to tell you before he was iced?"

"Possibly," I said.

Rogoff thought a moment, then puffed a plume of blue smoke over my head. "That Palm Aire dealer who examined the stamps—do you think he told Bodin's girlfriend they were fakes?"

"Hilda Lantern said he didn't."

"That means the villains still believe they're holding loot worth half-a-million. I think what I better do is contact every stamp dealer from Miami to Fort Pierce and tell them to stall anyone who comes in and tries to sell a block of Inverted Jennies. They can say they need a day or two to raise the cash. Then the dealer can give me a panic call, and I'll have someone in the store and the place staked out when the crook returns. How does that sound?"

"It's got to be done," I agreed. "It's a big job, but it's doable. I think you'll nab Bodin and Sylvia, but that's my opinion—not something you can take to the SA. The only way you're going to make a case is to pinch the thieves in the act of trying to sell. The fact that the stamps are fakes doesn't change things; they're still stolen property."

"Yeah," Al said sighing, "all that work for itty-bitty pieces of worthless paper. Well, I better get back to the palace and start the wheels turning."

"Just two more short items," I said. "I struck out with Lady Horowitz. She just won't tell me where she was when Bela Rubik was killed. And she refuses to let you take a look at her last will and testament. But my father said I could tell you that there's nothing in that document that could have any possible effect on your investigation."

"How does he know?" the sergeant said bitterly. "He's no cop."

"True," I said, "but he's no simp either. And he's also a man of probity with a high regard for the law. Believe me, Al, if there was anything at all in the will that would help solve a theft and a homicide, he'd reveal it even if it meant breaching client-attorney confidentiality. My father's morals are stratospheric. Sometimes I think he's training to take over God's job in case He resigns."

Rogoff laughed, flipped a hand at me, and strutted out, chewing on his cigar. I went back to the bar and slid my empty glass toward Mr. Pettibone.

"Another, please," I said.

"You told me to cut you off," he reminded me.

"I lied," I said.

But the second was a sufficiency. Florida police are rough on even slightly tipsy drivers, and I had no desire to get racked up on a DUI charge. I drove the Escort back to the McNally Building at a sedate pace, switched to the Miata, and continued my homeward journey.

I had time for an abbreviated ocean swim and arrived bright-eyed and bushy-tailed at the family cocktail hour. I dined with my parents that night and made a mindless jape about feeling exactly like our entree—soft-shelled crabs. Mother and father smiled politely.

I retired to my suite and scribbled furiously in my journal until I had recorded everything that had happened, including my last conversation with Rogoff. Then I phoned Jennifer Towley and was happy to find her at home.

"I miss you," I told her.

"And I miss you, too," she replied. Divine female!

"Good," I said. "Then how about lunch tomorrow?"

"Oh Archy, I'd love to," she said, "but I just can't. I've *got* to get caught up on my bookkeeping: billing, clients' accounts, my own checkbook, and nonsense like that. I simply *must* spend the day at it."

Suspicion flared, and I wondered if she was actually meeting her ex-husband for lunch.

"You've got to take a break in your accounting chores," I said. "Why don't I pick up some edible takeout food and show up at your place around noon. We can have a nosh together, and then I'll take off and leave you to your ledgers."

"Marvelous idea," she said at once. "Absolute genius."

"I thought so," I said with a considerably leavened heart. "See you at noon tomorrow. Sleep well, dear."

"You, too," she said, then added faintly, "darling."

I hung up delighted with her response and mortified at my initial jealous reaction. I must, I thought, learn to trust this woman who had invaded my right and left ventricles. It was not yet a Grand Passion but, like my mother's begonias, my love needed only TLC to flower.

I idly flipped the pages of my journal, resolutely turning my thoughts back to the theft of the Inverted Jennies. I set to work brooding, an activity aided by a very small tot of marc and the haunting wails of a Billie Holiday tape.

Maybe, I acknowledged, Sgt. Al was right after all, and I did have a taste for complexity. Because I found I could not really believe that this whole foofaraw was simply a case of a lame-brained and resentful chauffeur stealing from his employer. I didn't *want* to believe that, perhaps because it reduced the entire investigation to banality and my own role to that of an office manager catching a junior clerk swiping paper clips.

But it wasn't complexity I favored so much, I finally decided, as intrigue and the convolutions of human hungers. I wished the Case of the Inverted Jennies to hold hidden surprises, unexpected revelations, and a startling denouement.

I should have remembered what Aesop once told me: "We would often be sorry if our wishes were gratified."

12

I breakfasted with my parents on Friday. Then my father departed for the office in his Lexus, mother scampered into the greenhouse to bid a bright "Good morning!" to her begonias, and I moved to the kitchen to have a heart-to-heart with our cook-housekeeper.

"Ursi, luv," I said, "I've contracted for a picnic today—a very special picnic for two. What would you suggest?"

She accepted my question as a serious challenge, as I knew she would, and inspected her refrigerator and the shelves of her cupboards.

"Lemon chicken," she decided. "Baked, then chilled. German potato salad. The greens should be arugula and radicchio. For dessert, maybe a handful of those chocolate macaroons your mother bought."

"Sounds super to me," I said. "I'm hungry already. Where's our picnic hamper?"

"In the utility room," she said. "And don't forget a bottle of wine."

"Fat chance," I said.

I brought her the wicker picnic hamper that had been in our family since Year One and contained enough cutlery, accessories, and china to supply an orgy of eight. I also selected a bottle of white zinfandel which I tucked onto the bottom shelf of the fridge. Our table wine was stacked in the utility room. The vintage stuff was kept in a massive temperature-controlled cabinet in my father's study, protected by a combination padlock. R5-L8-R4, as well I knew.

I hopped into the Miata and, as usual, turned its nose toward the Horowitz manse. There was one little question I had to ask Lady C. It had been bedeviling me since that talk with Rogoff.

I banged the brass Bacchus on the front door, and eventually it was opened by the saucy housemaid, Clara Bodkin. She still had sleep in her eyes and looked all the more attractive for it.

"Good morning, Clara," I said.

"Hi, Mr. McNally," she said, and yawned. "The party's not till tonight."

"I know," I said, smiling, "and we'll certainly be here. Is Lady Horowitz up and about?"

"She's in the sauna."

"Oh," I said, disappointed. "I guess I better come back another time."

"You can talk to her through the intercom," Clara offered. "In the north wing just inside the terrace."

"Thank you," I said. "I'll find it."

"I love the way you smell," she said suddenly.

I remembered Simon Pettibone's observation: Life is not merely strange, it is *bee*-zar.

"It's not me, Clara," I said, "it's Royal Copenhagen. But I appreciate the thought."

Lady Cynthia had two built-in saunas, dry and wet (if you're going to do it, do it *right*), and the red light was burning over the door of the latter. The door itself was thick redwood planks and inserted at eye-level was a judas window of heavy glass. Alongside the door, fixed to the wall, was the intercom transmitter-receiver: a round knob of metal mesh.

I tried to look through the glass, but it was so fogged with steam that I could see nothing. I addressed the intercom.

"Lady Horowitz," I called, "it's Archy McNally. May I speak to you for a moment?"

A brief wait, then she replied, her voice sounding thin and tinny. "You don't have to shout," she said. "I can hear you perfectly well. How are you, lad?"

"Very well, thank you," I said, and watched as her fingers wiped away the steam from the inside of the glass, and she peered out at me.

"Care to join me?" she asked.

"Not right now," I said, laughing. "Just one short question and I'll be on my way."

She disappeared from the window, but I continued staring inside with nary a qualm. I was certain she was aware of my scrutiny and just didn't give a damn.

She moved slowly through swirling clouds of vapor like an Isadora Duncan dancer, seeming to float. She appeared to be performing a private exercise, for her knees rose high and her extended arms waved languidly. She was a white wraith; all I could see was that wondrous body pearled with steam. It made me forget age and believe in immortality.

"What's the question?" she asked.

"Did you ever examine the back of those Inverted Jenny stamps?"

Her face came close to the glass again and she stared at me. "Examine the *back*? Whatever for? Have you gone completely bonkers, lad?"

"Just wondering," I said hastily. In a moment the glass was fogged again and she was lost to view.

I drove into town wondering if Lady Cynthia had been telling me the truth. People do lie, you know. I do. Frequently.

I had been delegated by my parents to purchase an inexpensive going-away gift for Felice and Alan DuPey, to be presented that evening at the party. So I wandered Worth Avenue, viewing and regretfully rejecting all the glittering baubles that Street of Impossible Dreams has to offer.

Finally, in a tiny shop on Hibiscus Avenue, I found something for the DuPeys I thought they'd cherish: two lovely polished seashells, as a remembrance of their stay in South Florida. One was a Banded Tulip, the other a Flame Auger. In size and shape, there was a definite physical symbolism in those shells, and I thought them a fitting gift for randy newlyweds. I admit my sense of humor sometimes verges on the depraved.

I returned home and helped Ursi pack the picnic ham-

198

per, complete with a linen tablecloth and napkins. I added the chilled bottle of zinfandel (not forgetting a corkscrew) and set out for the home of Jennifer Towley across the lake.

Her reaction to the picnic hamper was all I had hoped for.

"You scoundrel!" she cried. "You told me it would be takeout food."

"So it is," I said. "From the spotless kitchen of the Chez McNally."

"How wonderful everything looks," she said, inspecting all the viands neatly packed in covered dishes. "Shall I set the dining room table?"

"Don't you dare," I said. "This is an indoor picnic. We'll eat on the floor."

And so we did, spreading the tablecloth over the worn dhurrie in her small office. We sat cross-legged, surrounded by file cabinets, books of fabric and wallpaper samples, a desk cluttered with documents, her word processor, and all the other odds and ends of a littered sanctum devoted to business.

We lunched with enthusiasm, exclaiming over the flavor of the lemon chicken, the taste of oregano in the greens, the touch of garlic in the German potato salad. We were down to the macaroons and the remainder of the wine before we collapsed against furniture and talked lazily of this and that.

Jennifer looked especially attractive that afternoon, hair piled up and tied with a mauve ribbon. Her face was free of makeup and seemed shockingly young. She wore an oversized sweatshirt with nothing printed on the front—thank God!—and pleated Bermuda shorts. Her feet were bare, and I saw once again those toes that had driven Clarence T. Frobisher mad with lust.

"Have you heard from your ex lately?" I asked casually.

"A few times," she said just as casually. "He seems to be doing wonderfully. The man he works for is thinking of opening a branch store in West Palm Beach and asked Tom if he'd like to manage it."

"Sounds like a great opportunity. Has he mentioned anything about his gambling?"

"Continually. He keeps assuring me that he's cured."

"But you've heard those assurances before, haven't you?"

"Yes," she said. "May I have another macaroon, please."

I watched her white teeth bite into the cookie, and I went through the now-familiar mental wrestle: tell or not tell. If she meant nothing to me, I would have told her at once that Thomas Bingham was up to his old tricks again. But she did mean something to me, a great deal, and so there would be a selfish motive in my revelation, and that would be base.

One day I must try to draw up a blueprint of my moral code. Then, perhaps, I might know what the hell I'm doing and why I do it.

"He wants me to have dinner with him," Jennifer said in a low voice, not looking at me. "And he wants to visit me. Here."

"Oh?" I said. "And how do you feel about that?"

"I don't know how I feel," she said, almost angrily, and

raised her eyes to look directly at me. "And I don't want to talk about it anymore."

"All right," I said equably. "Then we shan't."

"Let's talk about you," she said.

"My favorite subject."

"What do you want to do with your life, Archy?"

"I can't write, paint, sculpt, compose, or play the piccolo. So I want to make my life a creation. I want to elevate artificiality into a fine art."

She laughed. "You're putting me on."

I raised a palm. "Scout's honor. And now let's talk about you. What do you want to do with your life?"

"I wish I knew," she said. "I'm betwixt and between. A crazy, mixed-up kid. May I finish the wine?"

"Of course. But there's only a drop left. I should have brought two bottles."

"Oh no," she said. "That would have pushed me over the edge. And I've got to get back to my bookkeeping; I'll need a clear head."

I nodded. "I'll pack up and be on my way."

She stared at me, and I couldn't interpret that look. Something heavy was going on behind those luminous eyes, but I didn't even guess what it might be.

"No," she said finally in a steady voice, "don't do that. Not yet."

What a delicious afternoon that turned out to be, the most paradisiacal I had ever spent in my life. Most of the credit, of course, was due to Jennifer, who seemed to be a woman bereft of her senses. But if it was within my power to award a medal for actions above and beyond the call of duty, I would have pinned a gold star and ribbon to her sweatshirt—or affixed it to her bare bosom with a Band-Aid.

I returned home so fatigued that I knew an ocean swim would risk instant immolation. So I took a nap, slept fast, and awoke in time to shower, dress, and join my parents for the ceremonial cocktail. Then we all set off for Lady Horowitz's party, my father driving the Lexus and humming something that sounded vaguely like "On the Street Where You Live."

It was a sterling night, absolutely cloudless. And if there was no full moon, there were a jillion stars spangling the sky. A cool ocean breeze caressed, and the whole world seemed to have been spritzed by Giorgio. Perfect weather for an outdoor party. That was the luck of the wealthy—right? Remember the old Yiddish joke? A guy gets splattered by a passing bird, looks up and says, "For the rich you sing."

The pool-patio area was strung with Chinese lanterns. There was a hurricane lamp with scented candle on each table, plus a bowl of fresh narcissi. As they say in New York, "Gawjus!"

A small portable bar had been set up in one corner, and service was provided by temps. Chef Jean Cuvier, wearing a high white toque, presided over the grill. All the other staff members were present as well as houseguests and about a dozen invited couples in various degrees of "informal dress," from tailored jeans to sequined mini-dresses. For the record: I wore my silver-gray Ultrasuede jacket.

Two small added notes on that night's festivities: A

three-piece combo played old show tunes amongst the palms, and a small red neon sign set atop the bar proclaimed: NO SMOKING.

Since the McNallys knew most of the other guests present, there were many air-kisses and handshakes. My mother handed our gift to Felice and Alan DuPey, and they were delighted with the shells. I could see they made a polite effort to conceal their hilarity for, being French, they immediately saw the symbolism of those shapes. I was happy they hid their mirth; mother would have been horrified if they had tried to explain why the shells were so "fonny."

I headed for the bar to get in a party mood and was waiting for the ham-handed keep to mix a vodka gimlet when my elbow was plucked. I turned to find the hostess, radiant in flowered evening pajamas and a silk turban that looked like a charlotte russe.

"Good evening, Lady Cynthia," I said. "Lovely party."

"Is it?" she said. "I hadn't noticed. Listen, lad, what was that business this morning about my looking at the back of my Inverted Jennies?"

"Oh, that was just nonsense," I said.

"Of course it was," she said. "You ninny." And she stroked my cheek with such a smarmy smile that I was certain she was lying. But for what purpose I could not fathom.

She moved away and I sampled my drink. Passable but not notable. Carrying my glass, I joined the chattering throng and greeted several friends and acquaintances. I garnered two dinner invitations. Single women (mostly widows and divorcees) outnumber single men in Palm

Beach, and hostesses are continually searching for the odd man to complete their table—and I'm as odd as they come.

I spotted Angus Wolfson standing apart, observing the scene with what I imagined he thought was amused detachment. He was wearing an embroidered guayabera shirt that hung in folds on his shrunken frame, making him look like an emaciated barber. He was holding an opened Perrier, no glass, and I wondered if he was drinking directly from the bottle. I strolled over.

"Good evening, Mr. Wolfson," I said. "How are you feeling tonight?"

He didn't exactly glare at me but he came close. "You seem to have an obsessive interest in my health, young McNally," he said.

"Not obsessive," I said, "but certainly concerned."

I thought he was about to give me the knife, but he caught himself, chuffed a small laugh, and took a swig from his bottle. "If you can't become mean, nasty and grumpy," he said, "what's the point of growing old?"

"I'll remember that," I said, laughing.

"Oh, you have a few years to go," he said, looking at me with a peculiar expression. "Spend them wisely. Don't try to set the world to right. No one can do that. Just accept it."

Either he was playing the Ancient Guru or his Perrier bottle was filled with gin. In either case, I had no desire to hear more of his homilies, so I smiled, nodded, and sauntered away. Besides, I had a bit of business to do.

When we drove through the opened gate in the Lexus, we found that Kenneth Bodin was parking guests' cars.

He was doing a fine job, too, maneuvering all those Cadillacs, Lincolns, and BMWs on the driveway until they were within inches of each other with no scraped fenders. I found him leaning against the trunk of a white Excalibur, sucking on a cigarette and simultaneously prying into one ear with a matchstick. That young man was obviously in need of a couth IV.

"Having fun, Mr. McNally?" he asked me.

"Not yet," I said, "but I plan to."

"How's the Miata doing?"

"Taking the jumps like a thoroughbred," I said, pleased at having found a reasonable segue to the question I needed to ask. "As a matter of fact, I'm thinking of taking a drive down to the Keys. Have you ever been there?"

"Never have," he said, "and don't want to go. Disney World is what I like. I was there last year and had a helluva time. Did you know you can—"

But I was saved from listening to how he shook hands with Mickey Mouse by the melodious sound of dinner chimes coming from the patio.

"Got to run," I said hastily, "while the food lasts."

"You're having ribs," he said. "My favorite. I'll get mine later."

He was correct: Jean Cuvier was grilling big racks of pork spareribs along with ears of corn in the husk. There were kabobs of onions, mushrooms, green peppers, and cherry tomatoes, a salad of romaine and escarole with an anchovy dressing, and loaves of crusty French bread heated on the grill. Also bottles of a very decent merlot.

There was just one thing wrong with that feast: my dining partners. It happened this way:

I returned to the patio and found most of the tables already occupied. I was looking about for a seat with jovial companions when Consuela Garcia grabbed my arm. She was wearing a long-sleeved, off-the-shoulder crimson cashmere sweater that ended at midthigh. Tanned thigh. She looked sensational, and I started to tell her so but she cut me short.

"Listen, Archy," she said, leaning close, "you've got to eat with Harry and Doris Smythe."

I looked at her with horror. "Why do I have to ruin a perfectly splendid evening by eating with the Smythes?"

"Because no one else will eat with them."

"No, no, and no," I said. "What am I—a second-class citizen?"

She stared at me. "You want me to tell you when the madam takes off alone in her Jag?"

I sighed. "I get the picture, Connie. You are one cruel, cruel lady. All right, where are Loeb and Leopold?"

"Who?"

"The nasties," I said. "Where are they stuffing their ravenous maws?"

And that's how I was forced to share a culinary masterpiece by Jean Cuvier. The barbecue sauce was tangy without being too spicy. I learned later that its smoothness was due to a dash or two of bourbon. I only wish my dining partners had been as mellow.

The Smythes went through that dinner like a plague of locusts, devouring everything in sight. (I craftily moved the bowl of fresh flowers beyond their reach.) And as they munched, gnawed, and gulped, they complained. Nothing pleased them. The ribs were too fatty, barbecue sauce too mild, kabobs undercooked, salad dressing too salty, bread not *quite* warm enough, the wine corky.

For most of the meal I had to listen to their litany of kvetches as an audience of one. The fourth chair at our table belonged to Connie Garcia, but she had to play the social secretary and was constantly disappearing to solve minor crises. So I was left alone to endure the Smythes' endless bitching.

After a while I began to get a glimmer of why they claimed to be so dissatisfied. Lady Horowitz had called them "professional guests," and they were that. But they had the wit to recognize it, and the only way they could hang on to shreds of their ego was to disparage the charity provided. Viewed in that light, their carping was understandable. Unpleasant, but so human it made one want to weep.

However, I had no intention of spending the remainder of the evening weeping. Dessert was served—warmed New Orleans pralines and chilled Krug—and I excused myself. I carried a handful of the buttery confections and a flute of bubbles to the table where my parents were seated alone, the couple they had dined with having risen to dance to the combo's rendition of "June Is Bustin' Out All Over"—which indeed it was.

"Did you enjoy dinner?" I asked mother.

"So good," she said, patting her tummy, "but I'm afraid I ate too much. And drank too much."

"Mother is feeling a bit faintish," my father said, looking at her anxiously. "I think perhaps we better go home."

"Are you really ill?" I asked her, taking up her hand. "Shall I call Doc Semple?"

207

"Don't be silly," she said. "I just stuffed myself, that's all. I'll have a nice cup of hot tea, and I'll be right as rain in the morning."

"You're sure?"

"Absolutely. Don't worry so, dear."

"No point in your leaving early, Archy," my father said. "Will you be able to get a lift?"

"Of course," I said. "Plenty of wheels around. I'll be along in an hour or so. Mother, have a bit of blackberry brandy with your tea. It's wonderful for the grumbles. Believe me, I know."

She reached up to stroke my cheek, and then my parents rose to seek the hostess and make their farewells. I finished my pralines, returned to the bar with my empty champagne glass, and asked for a refill. For a few moments I watched dazed couples dancing on the verge of the pool and wondered who would be the first drunk to fall in. Or jump.

I craved a cigarette but that red neon sign was staring at me. So I wandered back into the wooded section of the estate, hoping that if I got far enough away from the patio, Lady C. would be unable to sniff my transgression and call the cops.

That area of the Horowitz empire was flippantly called "the jungle" by its monarch. But it was far from that, being artfully landscaped with hundreds of tropical plants, including a few orchids if you knew where to look. Paths meandered, garden statuary was half-hidden in the thick foliage, and benches of weathered teak were placed here and there to rest the weary.

It was on one of those slatted seats that I paused to light an English Oval, sip my Krug, and wonder what more life could hold. I soon found out. I became aware of a murmur of voices coming from the direction of the lake. Once I heard a raucous laugh and once a sharp cry as if someone had suffered a sudden pain.

As you may have guessed, I am not totally innocent of nosiness. I stubbed out my cigarette butt and moved slowly toward the sound of the voices, careful to keep off the pebbled path and step only on the spongy earth.

I cautiously approached a place where old, gnarled ficus trees encircled a greensward with a concrete bird-bath in the center. Concealed in shadow, I could see the people I had indistinctly overheard. Illumined by the light of the starry sky, the scene was clear enough and startling enough: Angus Wolfson and Kenneth Bodin locked in a fierce embrace, lips pressed.

I retraced my steps as noiselessly as I could, returned to the party, and exchanged my empty flute for a snifter of Rémy Martin. I downed that in two gulps.

"Again," I said hoarsely to the bartender.

He looked at me warily, but poured another ounce.

"You driving tonight, sir?" he asked.

"Of course not," I said. "I'm the designated drinker. The people I came with are sticking to Pepsi."

I left him to puzzle that out and went to a deserted corner where I could sit, stretch out my legs, and ponder. Instead, I sat, stretched out my legs, and sipped my cognac. At the moment I was incapable of pondering.

And that's how Connie Garcia found me a half-hour

later, staring into my empty snifter and wondering if I should give up a career of discreet inquiries and learn how to flip hamburgers at McDonald's.

"So there you are," she said. "Dinner with the Smythes wasn't so bad, now was it?"

"I loved it," I said. "Just as I love root canal work. Connie, when are you leaving?"

"Very soon," she said. "Why do you ask?"

"Can you give me a lift home? My parents left early."

"Of course," she said. "Just give me a few minutes to make sure everything's under control."

I wanted to express my gratitude and bid a fond farewell to mine hostess, but Lady Cynthia had discarded her turban and was dancing an insane Charleston with a partner who appeared to be seven feet tall. I left them to their madness and walked slowly out to the deserted driveway. Connie appeared in about ten minutes and we climbed into her Subaru.

She looked at me. "You okay?" she asked.

"Tiptop," I said. "Wonderful party."

"Do you really think so?" she said eagerly. "I thought it went well."

"A joy," I assured her. "An absolute joy."

We drove home in silence. I leaned my head back and closed my eyes. Connie pulled into the McNally driveway, killed the engine, and turned to face me.

"You're uncommonly quiet tonight, Archy," she said. "Are you sure you're all right?"

"Just a bit weary," I said. "After ten thousand and forty winks I'll be ready for a fight or a frolic."

"Something I wanted to tell you . . . I think your idea about Lady Horowitz being blackmailed is all wet."

"Then where is she going on those solo jaunts?"

"I think she's got a new lover."

"Oh?" I said. "Man, woman, or cocker spaniel?"

"No, I'm serious," Connie said. "You probably think a woman's instinct is all b.s., but I definitely have the feeling that she's found someone new. She's been buying lingerie you wouldn't believe. Kinky stuff."

"So?" I said. "She's entitled. We're all entitled; the Declaration of Independence guarantees it. Life, liberty, and the pursuit of happiness—remember? Of course it doesn't guarantee you'll find it, but you can pursue the hell out of it."

Connie laughed and reached to stroke my cheek. It was certainly my night for cheek-stroking. First Lady Cynthia, then mother, now Connie.

Then she stretched to kiss me, which was a lot nicer than a pat on the mandible.

"Take care of yourself, Archy," she said lightly. "You mean a lot to me."

"And you to me, sweet," I said. "Thanks for the lift."

My father's study was darkened, so I locked up and plodded bedward. In truth I *was* weary. It had been a long, eventful day, and I didn't even want to think about it, let alone scribble an account in my journal.

I undressed and crawled between the sheets. Sleep was a mercy. I didn't even have the strength to stroke my cheek.

13

During my undergraduate days at Yale I studied Latin for two years and did quite well—with the aid of some wonderful trots. As I recall (don't quote me on this), *"Hic in spiritum sed non incorpore"* means "Here in spirit but not in body." Turn that around and you've got a clue to my mood and behavior that weekend. I was there in body all right, but where the spirit was, the deponent knoweth not.

Confusion reigned supreme, and I waltzed through those two days with a glassy smile that probably convinced my golf-, tennis-, and poker-playing companions that McNally was finally over the edge. Well, I wasn't—but I was teetering. There were just too many bits and pieces, and I couldn't see any grand design to the Case of the Inverted Jennies—if there was one.

I returned home late Sunday night after a subdued dinner with a couple of cronies at the Pelican Club. I was in such an anomic mood that, to give myself the illusion I was capable of working purposefully, I scrawled notes in my journal for almost an hour, jotting down everything that had happened since the last entry. Then I spent another hour reading over the entire record of the Inverted Jenny Case. No light bulb flashed on above my head. I groaned and went to bed.

It must have been a shallow sleep because when my phone rang I awoke almost instantly. I glanced at the bedside clock; the luminous dial showed 4:40 A.M. At that dark hour it had to be Death calling. I answered warily.

"Hello?"

"Archy? Al Rogoff. I just got a wake-up call from the Beach Patrol. They pulled a floater out of the surf near the Horowitz place. Elderly male Caucasian. He was naked, but there were clothes stacked on the sand. They tentatively ID him as Angus Wolfson."

I swallowed. "Dead?"

"Very," Rogoff said. "Want to meet me there and positively ID the body?"

I really didn't want to. "Sure," I said. "I'll get dressed."

"Take your time," the sergeant said. "It'll take me at least twenty minutes. Listen, any chance of your bringing some hot coffee along?"

"Yes, I can do that. We've got a thermos."

"Good," Al said. "No sugar or cream. Black will be fine."

I dressed as quietly as I could because my bedroom is directly above my parents'. I tiptoed down the stairs to the kitchen, switched on the light, put a kettle of water on to boil. I went into the pantry for the thermos and a stack of plastic cups. When I returned to the kitchen my father was standing there.

Was he the last man in America to wear a full pajama suit: long-sleeved jacket and drawstring pants? Under a robe of maroon silk, of course. With matching leather mules on his long feet.

"Trouble, Archy?" he asked.

I repeated what Sergeant Rogoff had told me.

Father nodded once. "Keep me informed," he said, turned, and went back to bed.

The unflappable Prescott McNally.

I was at the scene within a half-hour after Al's call. It wasn't hard to find; three police cars, a fire-rescue truck, and an ambulance were parked on Ocean Boulevard. I pulled up, and Rogoff came over before I could dismount from the Miata.

"You bring the coffee?" he asked eagerly.

I nodded.

"We better have a slug," he said. "There's a cold wind down on the beach."

He did the pouring, for which I was grateful; I didn't want him to see that I had the shakes.

"How did they happen to find him?" I asked.

"Some dentist from Lake Worth wanted to try out his new ATV, a three-wheeler. He figured he could get away with driving on the beach at four in the morning. He spotted the body bobbing around in the shallows and decided to be a good citizen. He had a cellular phone with him and called 911. Good coffee, Archy."

"Thanks. Was it suicide?"

"Could be. But does a suicide stack his clothes neatly on

215

the sand under a palm tree before he takes the long walk?"

"I don't believe suicides are thinking rationally in their last few minutes."

"You may be right. But there are some other things."

"What things?"

"You'll see. Finished your coffee? Let's go."

We walked down that same flight of wooden stairs I had taken to stroll the beach with Angus Wolfson. He had looked like a rakish boulevardier then. I tried not to imagine what he looked like now.

The body lay on the sand, covered with a blue blanket. There was a group of officers nearby, smoking cigarettes, conversing, occasionally laughing. Rogoff had been right; it was chilly down near the water. The wind was kicking up whitecaps, and clouds were moving swiftly across the night sky.

"Can I get some light here?" Rogoff called.

A woman from the fire-rescue truck came over with a big lantern. She turned the beam onto the blanketed corpse. The sergeant leaned down and uncovered the naked body to the waist.

The face was remarkably peaceful. Almost serene. A few wet strands of thin, grayish hair were plastered to his cheeks. He was so pale, so pale. But I had the irreverent notion that he looked younger in death than he had in life.

"Yes," I said steadily, "this is the body of a man I knew as Angus Wolfson. He was a houseguest at the home of Lady Cynthia Horowitz."

The sergeant turned to the woman holding the lantern. "You hear that?" he demanded.

She nodded.

"Al," I said, "what are those blotches on his neck and chest?"

"The things I mentioned to you—bruises. Could have been caused by the body banging around in the surf. But look at this."

He beckoned, and we both squatted alongside the remains. "What do you make of that?" Rogoff asked, pointing.

Four faint parallel scratches ran down the torso from clavicle to navel.

I peered closely. "Looks like fingernails did that," I said.

The sergeant grunted. "Could be," he said. "Made by himself in the final moment when he was gasping for air. Or made by someone else. Or made by shells on the bottom of the sea. We'll let the ME figure it out. Let's go finish that coffee."

I started back to the stairway.

"Take him away," Al called to the waiting officers and followed me up to the corniche.

We sat in the Miata and sipped coffee. It was lukewarm now, but we drank it.

"What I've got to do now," Rogoff said, "is go to the Horowitz place, wake up the dear Lady, and tell her what happened. Care to come with me?"

"No, thanks," I said.

He laughed. "Didn't think you would. What I want to do is see if he left a suicide note. Not that it means a helluva lot. Sometimes they do, sometimes they don't."

"So you think it *was* a suicide."

"I didn't say that. But you told me he was ill."

"That was my idea. He didn't tell me, and I don't have a medical degree."

"How old did you say he was?" the sergeant asked.

"I didn't say because I don't know," I said, a trifle peevishly I admit. "I'd guess about seventy-five. Around there."

Al turned to stare at me. "That's amazing."

"Being seventy-five? What's so amazing about that?"

"Because when we were going through that neat stack of his clothes on the beach, in the hip pocket of his slacks we found a condom."

"Oh lord," I said.

"Unused," Rogoff added. "Still in a sealed packet."

I drew a deep breath. "I better tell you something, Al," I said. "On Friday night my parents and I went to a party at Lady Cynthia's. After dinner . . ."

I described the scene I had witnessed between Angus Wolfson and Kenneth Bodin deep within "the jungle" of the Horowitz property. The sergeant listened intently without interrupting. When I finished, he drained his last few drops of coffee and tossed the plastic cup onto the roadside.

"You're littering," I pointed out.

"I know," he said. "Listen, what I want you to do right now, even before you go home, is drive to the palace and dictate a statement. I'll radio ahead and set it up. I want you to include what you just told me about Wolfson, and also everything you told me at the Pelican Club about Bodin, his girlfriend Sylvia, and that Fort Lauderdale stamp dealer—what's her name?"

"Hilda Lantern."

218

"Well, make sure you describe your dealings with her: what you said and what she said. Go into detail. Even the stuff you don't think is important. I want everything."

"Al, that'll take hours!"

"Sure it will," he said. "But you're pulling down a nice buck, aren't you? Now earn it."

But despite his instructions, I did go home first—to shower, shave, change my clothes, and have an early morning breakfast with the Olsons at the kitchen table.

I was leaving for the palace to dictate my statement when I encountered my father coming downstairs for *his* breakfast. He saluted me by elevating one bushy eyebrow, and I gave him a precis of what had happened at the scene of Wolfson's death.

"Dreadful business," he said in magisterial tones. Then, dryly: "I expect I shall hear from Lady Horowitz this morning."

"I think you probably will, sir," I said. "If I learn anything more from Sergeant Rogoff, I'll get word to you."

"Yes, do that," he said. "Thank you, Archy."

As I drove into town through the June afterdawn, I rehearsed in my mind what I would reveal in my statement. It seemed to me that up to this point I had been reasonably straight with Al Rogoff. I had given him all the facts as I knew them, with the exception of any mention of Thomas Bingham. And his implication in the crimes was iffy.

What I hadn't told the sergeant, of course, were my personal feelings about the people involved, my no doubt prejudicial reactions to their personalities, and certain wild ideas I entertained that had absolutely no hard evidence to sustain them. I was sure Al had as many private fancies. And there was little point in either of us going public with them until we had some solid facts to quote. You can't convict on opinions, except those of judge or jury.

I was correct about spending hours providing that statement. After I finished dictating, I waited for the transcription. Then I read the eight-page manuscript carefully, making some minor changes, deletions, and additions. I was signing all eight pages when Rogoff came in and plopped down wearily in the wooden armchair behind his desk.

"Not even noon," he said, "and already my ass is dragging."

"You spoke to Lady Horowitz?"

He nodded. "You know what spooked her the most? Not the death of an old friend. But she was upset at how this 'unpleasantness'—her word—might affect a reception she's giving tomorrow afternoon for a visiting Italian tenor. Can you believe it?"

"Lady Cynthia," I said carefully, "is a rather self-centered woman."

"No kidding?" Rogoff said. "And all this time I thought she was a selfish bitch. Anyway, I didn't find a suicide note. But like I told you, that means zilch."

"Who is next of kin?"

"A sister in Boston. Horowitz phoned your father while I was there, and he agreed to notify the sister. Thank him for me. Informing the next of kin of victims is not my favorite pastime. You finished here?"

"All done," I said, and slid the signed statement across the desk to him. "That's everything."

He stared at me. "You sure?"

"Absolutely. Except for my hat size, which is seven and three-eighths. Al, have you contacted all the local stamp dealers?"

"We're working on it. But some are out to lunch, some are on vacation, some are retired. It's a miserable job. But we should have it finished in a day or two."

"Good," I said. "I still think you'll pick up Kenneth Bodin or Sylvia or both."

Rogoff looked at me thoughtfully. "You think Wolfson might have been in on it?"

"The possibility had occurred to me," I admitted. "Wolfson steals the stamps and gives them to Bodin to sell. Then they split the take. There's only one thing wrong with that scenario."

"What?"

"Wolfson wasn't a thief. I didn't particularly cotton to him, but he was trying hard to be a gentleman. He just wouldn't steal."

Al stared at me. "Would he kill?"

"Anyone can murder if the time and circumstances are right. You've told me that yourself, many times."

"So I have," the sergeant said, sighing. "Thank you for your keen perceptions, Hercule Poirot. I wish with all my heart that we may soon meet again."

"I pray we shall, Inspector Maigret," I said, and departed.

I drove to the McNally Building, intending to ask my

father to fill me in on his conversation with Lady C. But the lobby receptionist handed me a message: Consuela Garcia had phoned and wanted me to call her immediately.

"She said it was important," the receptionist told me. "She repeated three times: Urgent! Urgent! Urgent!"

"Probably heard a new Polish joke," I said.

I called Connie from my office. She sounded harried.

"Archy," she said breathlessly, "did you hear about Angus Wolfson?"

"Yes," I said, "I heard."

"And on top of that," she went on, "the caterer called and said he can't get any fresh pineapples for the reception tomorrow. What a morning!"

"And that's why you called?" I asked. "To tell me about the pineapples?"

"Oh, don't be such a schnook," she said. "I called to tell you the madam is taking off about one o'clock. She said she'd be gone a few hours. She didn't tell me where she was going, and I didn't ask."

"Thank you, Connie," I said gratefully.

"If you follow her, will you tell me later where she went?"

"No."

"I didn't think you would," she said. "You still seeing that Jennifer Towley?"

"Occasionally."

"Well, my guy gave me the brush."

"Why would the idiot do that?"

"He found some tootsie with mucho dinero. Her father owns a used-car lot."

I laughed. "I'm looking for a nymphomaniac whose father owns a liquor store."

Connie giggled. "Well, if you break up with the Towley woman, put me back in your little black book."

"You've never been out," I assured her.

I glanced at my watch, saw it was a bit past twelve-thirty, and decided to put my talk with father on hold. I went down to the garage, waved to Herb, and crawled into my rented Ford Escort. I headed for Ocean Boulevard, hoping Lady Cynthia hadn't decided to leave early. If she had, I was snookered.

As I drove I wondered how I was going to handle this. I don't claim to be an expert at shadowing, but I had read enough espionage novels to know how it's done—or how the novelists *think* it's done. You hang back, occasionally let a car or two get between you and your quarry, and you might even speed up and tail from in front of your target. It all seemed so simple I was certain I'd bollix it up.

I drove past the Horowitz mansion. The gate was open but I saw no activity within. I went northward a few hundred yards, made an illegal U-turn, and passed the house again, going southward. I repeated this maneuver twice more with no results.

Finally, on my fourth drive south, I observed the bronze Jaguar convertible pull out of the Horowitz driveway, turn, and also proceed southward. I distinctly saw Lady Cynthia driving, her hair bound with a periwinkle scarf.

"Thank you, God," I said aloud.

She headed down the coast and surprised me by staying within the speed limit. I was several car lengths behind her, and there seemed no need for tricky tactics; she never once turned her head to look back and gave no indication whatsoever that she sensed a nose was on her trail.

The Jag went on and on and on, and I was beginning to wonder if our destination was Miami. But then we came to a stretch of the corniche south of Manalapan Beach. This area of the island, between the Atlantic Ocean and Lake Worth, is so narrow that a long-ball hitter (say Mickey Mantle) might stand on the beach and swat one into the lake.

Lady Horowitz slowed, and I slowed right along with her. Then she signaled a right and turned into a driveway, through opened gates. I drove past at a crawl and took a good peep.

It was a frumpy place, a mansion gone to seed. The wrought-iron gates were rusted, grass sprouted from the brick driveway, and several red tiles were missing from the roof. The house, designed in a vaguely Spanish style, had a sad, sheepish look about it, as if its dilapidation was its own fault and not that of the neglectful owner.

The Jaguar was nowhere in sight when I drove past. From this, Monsieur Poirot deduced that the driveway led down to the rear of the house, facing Lake Worth. Perhaps a garage was there. Certainly a turnaround. And probably a lawn, patio, or terrace giving a loverly view of the lake. I imagined a dock, rotting now, that was large enough to accommodate a thirty-five-foot cabin cruiser.

I made a U-turn again and headed northward. This time, on a slow pass, I noted the untrimmed shrubbery, a broken window, paint peeling from the portico columns. Even more perplexing was no sign of habitation; the entire place was silent, deserted, and so melancholy it could have been a set for *The Exorcist XII.*

I also made certain to memorize the house number, painted on a weathered shingle dangling by a single nail from one of the stained stucco entrance pillars.

I drove home sedately, ruminating on my next move. I wasn't about to hang around Manalapan until Lady Cynthia emerged from the Castle of Otranto, and then follow her back to Palm Beach. What was the point of that? I even considered the possibility of renting a boat with the intention of approaching from the lake side, on her next visit, and observing any activities taking place in the rear of the house. But even with an advance alert from Connie, I could never arrive in time.

What on earth was the wealthy Lady Horowitz doing in such a ruin? Could my original wild scam turn out to be correct? Was she really meeting blackmailers to make a payment? The whole idea was absurd, but I could conjure no other explanation, except that possibly she had flipped her wig, joined a coven of witches, and drove to that shabby house to engage in satanic rites.

The truth turned out to be even more unbelievable.

14

I returned to the McNally Building, parked the Escort in the underground garage, and waved to the security guard. Then I rode the elevator to the second floor, occupied by our real estate department. We didn't hawk homes and condos, of course, but represented our clients at closings, advised on leases and, when requested, suggested investments in raw land and commercial properties.

The woman I sought, Mrs. Evelyn Sharif, was chief of the department. She was married to a Lebanese who sold Oriental rugs from a very elegant shop on Worth Avenue. At the moment, Evelyn was obviously, almost embarrassingly, pregnant.

"Archy," she said, "if you ask me if I've swallowed a watermelon, I'll never speak to you again as long as I live."

"I'd never be guilty of such gross humor," I said. "A cantaloupe?"

She laughed and punched my arm. It hurt. Evelyn was a jovial lady but very physical. When she slapped you lightly on the back, your knees sagged.

"When is the Little One due?" I asked her.

"In about six weeks," she said. "Did you drop by to hear details of my morning sickness?"

"Thank you, no," I said. "A small favor is all I ask."

I explained that I had the number of a property on Ocean Boulevard down near Manalapan and wanted to find out who owned the place. With Evelyn's contacts in Palm Beach County real estate circles, that should be duck soup.

"Why do you want to know?" she asked.

"Discreet inquiries," I said. "Cloak-and-dagger stuff. Absolutely, positively top secret."

She smirked. I knew what she was thinking: that I had seen a centerfold entering the house and wanted her name. Ridiculous! I had done that only once before.

She was silent a moment, and I could see she was debating whether or not to grant my request. But after all, I was Prescott McNally's son, and she didn't want to endanger her paid maternity leave.

"All right, Archy," she said, sighing, "give me the number and I'll see what I can do. Maybe I'll have something for you tomorrow."

"Thank you, dear," I said. "And may your Blessed Event be twice blessed."

"It is," she said, grinning. "The doc says twins."

"Mazeltov!" I cried.

I went up to my very own cul-de-sac and phoned my father's office. But Mrs. Trelawney said he was at a protracted lunch with a client. So I headed down to the garage and waved at Herb for the third time that day. I drove the Miata toward the beach, brooding about Lady Cynthia's motives for traveling miles to spend a sunny afternoon in the House of Usher.

I learned a long time ago that in any investigation it was goofy to devise a theory early on and then try to fit the facts to your hypothesis. You find yourself disregarding important evidence simply because you can't cram it into your harebrained idea. The best method, by far, is to collect as many facts as possible, even the most trivial, and let them form their own pattern. Logic beats conjecture every time.

I was still in the fact-collecting phase when I turned into the Horowitz driveway. The place appeared to be abandoned; not a soul in sight and no sounds of human presence. Great security. Jesse James could have waltzed in there and carted off the patio furniture.

No one answered my knocks at the front door, so I wandered around to the swimming pool. Gina Stanescu was seated at one of the umbrella tables. She was wearing another of her voluminous gowns, and a floppy brimmed panama hid her eyes. But she looked up when I approached, and I was glad to see she wasn't weeping.

"Ma'am," I said, "I'm sorry about Mr. Wolfson. I'm sure you and everyone else are devastated by what happened."

She nodded without speaking and motioned for me to sit down. I pulled up a canvas director's chair and moved it so that I was facing her.

"Life is sad, Mr. McNally," she said. "Is it not?"

"Frequently," I said. "I don't wish to add to your sorrow, but it seemed to me that in the short time you had known Mr. Wolfson, you and he had established a special rapport."

"Yes, yes," she said eagerly. "He was a dear man, very gentle. He liked to act the bugbear, but he was really kind and understanding. He was ill—did you know?"

"I thought he was," I said, thinking that sadness had softened her sharp features.

"He refused to speak of it, but I saw several times that he was in pain. But he was a gallant." Her smile was faint. "An aged gallant."

"That was my impression," I said. "That in spite of his problems, he was determined to face the world with a fresh flower in his lapel."

She knew immediately what I meant and looked at me with approval. But I wanted to get away from Wolfson eulogies and asked if she would care for something to drink; I would bring it from the kitchen. She declined, which disappointed me. At the moment I could have endured a stiff wallop of 80-proof.

"The last time we spoke," I said, "in the game room, you mentioned the possibility of a miracle rescuing your orphanage. I hope it has occurred."

Whatever animation she had shown a moment ago disappeared, and her face became stony and set.

"No," she said, "that miracle dissolved when Angus died. *Pouf!*"

"I don't understand."

She tried to smile. A miserable failure. "I spoke to Angus of my problems at the orphanage. He said he could help. A relative had recently died, and Angus would inherit a great deal of money. He said he had no need for it and would be happy to donate it to the orphans of Rouen. Wasn't that magnificent of him?"

"Very," I said. "Did he happen to mention how much his inheritance might amount to?"

"Much," Stanescu said. "Perhaps a half-million American dollars. That would have been my salvation."

"Yes," I said. "Now I understand."

"Mr. McNally, you are an attorney, are you not?"

"Not, I'm afraid. But my father is, and I work for him. And I have studied law. Why do you ask?"

"The promise Angus made to contribute his inheritance to the orphanage, is that a legal agreement? May I claim his inheritance?"

"Did Mr. Wolfson state his intentions in writing?"

"No."

I pulled a face. "Then his inheritance becomes part of his estate, to be distributed according to the terms of his last will and testament."

"Yes," she said, "I thought that might be so." She attempted a brave smile again, and again it didn't work. "Then I must find another miracle for my children."

I wasn't thinking of the orphans of Rouen at that moment; something was stirring in that moist mass of Roquefort I call my brain.

"Ma'am," I said, "remember the day you and the others were to go on a yacht cruise but it was canceled because of high seas?"

"Yes," she said, looking at me curiously, "of course I remember."

"Mr. Wolfson told me that you and he left the party early, went window-shopping on Worth Avenue, and then later met at the Cafe L'Europe."

"Yes," she said, still puzzled, "that is correct."

"Could you tell me what shape Mr. Wolfson was in when you met for a drink?"

"Oh, he was in a dreadful condition. It was an extremely hot day. He was exhausted, obviously in pain, and I had to hold his arm while we waited for Kenneth to come get us. Why do you ask?"

"He was upset?" I persisted. "Disturbed? Unusually so?"

She considered a moment. "Yes, I would say so. Pale and trembling. I remember suggesting he might wish to see a doctor immediately, but he'd have none of that. Again, why do you ask?"

I shook my head. "I really don't know. We're still trying to solve the theft of your mother's stamps, and this may possibly have something to do with it. Miss Stanescu, I thank you for speaking to me so openly. I hope I may see you again under happier circumstances."

She smiled—and this time it was the McCoy. "I hope so, too, Mr. McNally," she said. "I enjoy your company. You are so pleasant."

"Thank you," I said, and left her.

Do you recall my telling you that on the previous night,

Sunday, I had reviewed my notes on the Inverted Jenny Case and no light bulb had suddenly flashed above my head? Well, now the bulb was there. It wasn't burning brightly, but it was glowing dimly and flickering.

I remounted the Miata and was heading out when the bronze Jaguar pulled in. I stopped, and Lady Horowitz braked the Jag next to me. I was mortified: a shlump in a rubber dinghy moored alongside the USS *Iowa*.

"Hello, lad," she called. "What are you doing here—still snooping around?"

I was offended. "I came to express my condolences," I said. "On the death of Angus Wolfson."

"Well, people do die, you know," she said blithely. "One way or another."

She seemed in a radiant mood. The periwinkle scarf was gone, and her white hair, wind-whipped, formed a springy halo as if she had stuck her big toe in an electric outlet.

"Something I'd like to ask . . ." I said. "Did you know Wolfson was ill?"

"Was he?" she said. "Well, I can believe it. The idiot just didn't take care of himself. I once saw him swallow a live goldfish. He was drunk, of course—Angus, not the goldfish—but that's no excuse. I'm going to live forever; I'm too mean to die."

I thought her levity in poor taste, but I knew it was foolish to expect delicate sensibility from that woman. Might as well expect a curtsy from King Kong.

"Lady Cynthia," I said, "what was Wolfson doing down here? A vacation?"

"Of course," she said quickly. "A holiday. The poor man

couldn't afford Antibes so he grabbed at the chance to spend a few weeks on the Gold Coast."

"Couldn't afford?" I asked. "I thought you told me he was well-off."

"Did I?" she said. "I don't think so. I probably said he wasn't hurting. Meaning he wasn't rooting through garbage cans or anything like that. But he did have to count his nickels and dimes. Why this sudden interest in his finances?"

"I was just wondering if he was on his uppers. And if he was, if he pinched your stamps."

She shrugged. "I wouldn't put it past him. He liked the lush life but just couldn't buy it. Fortunately I can. But I've paid my dues. My life would make a book."

"I can imagine," I said.

"No, you can't," she said. "Ta-ta, lad. I've got to grab a bath."

I drove home. The light bulb was still glowing. But the flickering had ceased.

I had plenty of time for a swim before the family cocktail hour. And the ocean was calm and brilliant under the westering sun. So why did I feel such a disinclination for plunging into those warm waters? Because, I realized, I was unnerved by the persistent image of the pale corpse pulled from that same sea.

But if I didn't conquer that fear, I might never dare the ocean again, and that would be shameful. So I resolutely changed, went down to the beach, and doggedly completed my two miles. I can't say I enjoyed it, and when I emerged, the image of the dead Angus Wolfson had not been banished. Never would be, I acknowledged.

It was a strange dinner that night. My father and I were in a rather subdued mood, but mother was almost hyper, laughing and yakking on and on about a flower show she had attended that afternoon. She had served as one of three judges, and apparently a contestant (an also-ran) had thrown a snit and loudly accused the judges of racial prejudice against African violets.

The guv and I listened to this account with small smiles. I think we were both happy to have mother monopolize the conversation. If it hadn't been for her, it would have been a dinner of grunts and mumbles, and Mrs. Olson might have wondered if we were dissatisfied with her poached salmon and dill sauce. Far from it.

After coffee and a dessert of fresh strawberries marinated in white crème de menthe, my father drew me aside.

"Are you planning to go out tonight, Archy?" he asked.

"No, sir. I'm staying in."

"Good. I brought some work home, but I should be finished by ten o'clock. Could you stop down? There are a few matters to discuss."

"I'll be there," I promised.

I went upstairs and worked on my journal awhile in a desultory fashion. Then I took off my reading specs and stared at the far wall. Not much inspiration there, but I didn't expect any. One thing bothering me was that Lady Cynthia had been so quick to agree that Angus Wolfson might have stolen her stamps. She had identified him as an "old friend." Surely she knew as well as I that the man was incapable of the crime. He may have been many

235

things, not all of them noble, but I was convinced he was not a thief.

And I kept recalling that unlocked jewel box close to the rifled wall safe. Surely any crook, man or woman, would have paused long enough to lift the lid and grab up a handful of gems.

There was a third puzzle I had not yet brought to the attention of Sgt. Al Rogoff. It concerned the murderous assault on Bela Rubik. Kenneth Rodin was a likely suspect, since apparently the purloined Inverted Jennies were now in his possession, or girlfriend Sylvia's.

But as I well knew, the stamp dealer kept his door locked and carefully inspected visitors before allowing them entrance. Would he have unlocked for Bodin, who even in his chauffeur's uniform looked like an 800-pound gorilla in a purple Nehru jacket?

But even those three questions, important though they might be, paled before an enigma that had troubled me since I had uttered, "Yes, this is the body of a man I knew as Angus Wolfson." To wit: Did he really commit suicide, or did his nakedness, neatly stacked clothing, and the unused condom all indicate a sex scene that had gone awry, ending in murder instead of rapture?

But I was not such a beginner at criminal investigation as to believe that *all* riddles can be solved, *all* snarls untangled, *all* questions answered. Ask any law enforcement officer and he or she will tell you that some mysteries remain so forever—mysteries. I went downstairs a few minutes after ten. I found the lord of the manor seated behind the desk in his study. He looked weary but, as usual, he was dressed as if he expected a visit from a

Supreme Court justice at any moment. As I entered, he was replacing files in his Mark Cross calfskin briefcase.

"Perfect timing, Archy," he said with a pinched smile. "I've done all I can do tonight. Interesting case. It concerns the estate of the late Peter Richardson. Did you know him?"

"No, sir. But I know Eddie Richardson. I think he's the youngest of three sons."

Father nodded. "Three sons and two daughters. All are contesting Peter Richardson's bequest of approximately two million dollars to a California organization that allegedly freezes the recently deceased in liquid nitrogen with the claim that they may be thawed and restored to sentient life at some future date. The children are denouncing the claim as fraudulent and petitioning that the bequest be ruled invalid."

"What is your opinion, sir?"

"Oh, we've just started," he said. "This will require extensive research." He smiled coolly. "And many hours of billing. I think I deserve a glass of port. Will you do the honors, Archy. And help yourself, of course."

A few moments later I was seated in a leather armchair alongside his desk. We raised glasses to each other, then sipped. I thought the port was a bit musty but made no comment.

"As we anticipated," my father began, "I received a phone call from Lady Horowitz early this morning. She informed me of the death of her houseguest, Angus Wolfson. I already knew it, of course, from your report, but didn't feel it necessary to tell her that. She gave me the name, address, and telephone number of the next of kin

237

and requested that McNally and Son handle all the 'grue-some details.' Those are her words."

"She just can't be bothered," I said.

"I suspect you're correct. In any event, the next of kin is an unmarried sister, Roberta Wolfson, who shared an apartment with her brother in Boston. She is flying down to identify the body, claim the personal effects, and make funeral arrangements."

"And you want me to squire the lady about?"

"Very perspicacious of you, Archy. Yes, that is exactly what I wish. Lady Horowitz volunteered to pay all expenses, including burial costs."

"That was decent of her."

"Yes," he said. "In some ways she is a very generous woman. Mrs. Trelawney has arranged a round-trip airline ticket for Miss Wolfson. I understand she is an elderly lady, a year older than her brother. I know you will offer what sympathetic assistance you can."

"Yes, sir. When is she arriving?"

"Around noon tomorrow. Mrs. Trelawney will give you the details."

"Will she be staying with Lady Cynthia?"

He was silent a moment. "No," he said finally. "Apparently Miss Wolfson met Lady Horowitz once and was not favorably impressed. She prefers to stay elsewhere. Mrs. Trelawney has taken a comfortable suite at The Breakers for her use."

"Seems to me Mrs. Trelawney has been doing most of the donkeywork," I said. "What about the undertaker? Won't Angus have to be iced and boxed for shipment?"

Father sighed. "Not the terminology I would have

used. Miss Wolfson insists on cremation. She says that was her late brother's wish and is so stated in his will. She will carry his ashes back to Boston."

"How did she sound, father? Tearful? Hysterical?"

"No, she seemed remarkably self-possessed. As if she had been expecting a phone call like mine for some time. Very cool, very formal. A proper Bostonian. She treated me with what I can only describe as condescension."

"It figures," I said, nodding. "Proper Bostonians believe anyone who lives beyond Beacon Hill is a peasant. All right, I shall meet and escort Miss Wolfson. How long does she plan to stay?"

"As briefly as possible. She hopes to return to Boston on Wednesday."

I was dubious. "I'm not certain the police will release the body that quickly. I'll check with Rogoff in the morning."

"That would be wise. Now then, the other matter I wanted to discuss with you is the theft of Lady Horowitz's stamps and the murder of Bela Rubik. How is that investigation coming along?"

I told him about Kenneth Bodin and Sylvia, Hilda Lantern, and the attempt to sell Inverted Jennies to a Palm Aire dealer who stated they were forgeries.

Mein papa seemed stunned. When he spoke, his voice was not quite steady. "I think we could use another glass, Archy," he said.

While I poured, he rose and went over to the sideboard. He began to pack a pipe, his favorite James Upshall. His back was to me.

239

"Have you told Lady Horowitz that her stamps are counterfeit?"

"No, sir."

"Why not?" he said sharply.

"Because I don't know for certain that they *are* counterfeit. All I have is hearsay. When the Inverted Jennies are recovered, an independent examination can be made by experts."

He came back to his chair and flamed his pipe. I took that as a signal that I could light up an English Oval, and did.

"But what if the stamps are not recovered?" he asked.

"I think they will be, sir," I said, and explained how Sgt. Al Rogoff was alerting all the dealers along the Gold Coast.

"I hope he'll be successful," father said, calming down as he puffed. "The reason I am so concerned is that Lady Horowitz has become insistent on filing an insurance claim. She mentioned it again this morning. But if the stamps are counterfeit, obviously no legitimate claim for a half-million dollars can be made."

"Can you stall her awhile? If the stamps are recovered and prove to be forgeries, she'll have no claim. And if they are recovered and prove to be genuine, she'll still have no claim since they'll be returned to her."

"Yes, that's true," he said slowly. "I'll try to convince her to hold off filing, but she is a very strong-minded woman."

"As well I know," I said. "Something else about this case is troubling me, father, and I'd like your opinion."

He nodded.

I described the passionate embrace between Angus Wolfson and Kenneth Bodin I had witnessed the night of Lady Cynthia's party. Then I related how Wolfson had been found: naked, clothes neatly stacked, unused condom in pocket. These were details I had not previously told my father, and he listened intently.

"Are you suggesting," he said when I concluded, "that the chauffeur murdered Angus Wolfson?"

"I'm suggesting it's a possibility."

"Have you informed Sergeant Rogoff?"

"Yes, sir."

"And what was his reaction?"

"Nothing immediate. Knowing Al, I'm sure he'll dig into it. But unless he can find a witness or Bodin confesses—both highly unlikely—I doubt if the sergeant will be able to make a homicide case. Then he'll label it suicide and close the file."

The master went into one of his reflective trances, and I waited patiently. I thought he would be offended by the story of Wolfson's predilection, but when he spoke it was more in sadness than distaste.

"I hope Rogoff does close the file," he said. "What possible good could it do to make public that poor man's past? He is dead now; I would not care to see details of his life exploited in the tabloids."

He surprised me. "And let a murderer escape?" I asked.

"If he *was* murdered. You are not certain and, from what you say, the police will not be able to prove a homicide."

"They might," I argued. "If the Medical Examiner's

report indicates an assault or a struggle, or Rogoff finds additional evidence to prove the presence of a killer."

He looked at me somberly. "Archy, don't let your desire for justice overcome your good sense. It seems to me this is a matter to be quietly swept under the rug. We are all guilty of actions in our lives which, while not illegal, may be morally reprehensible and which we would certainly not wish to be made public."

I was shocked. My father is usually the most logical and coldly judicial of men when forming and expressing his opinions. Now it seemed to me his reasoning was confused and his pronouncements perilously close to blather. I could not understand this crumbling of his Olympian standards.

"Homicide is illegal," I reminded him.

"I am quite aware of that," he said. "I am merely pointing out that sometimes the law must yield to decency and the protection of human dignity. It is a fine line, I admit, but there is a gray area where the rights of society conflict with the rights of the individual. Try not to be too rigorous in the defense of society. The day may come, Archy, when you will plead for mercy for yourself rather than justice."

I grinned. "One never knows, do one?"

"And that's another thing," he said testily. "I do wish you would stop saying that. Not only is it ungrammatical, but it is a superficial observation on the uncertainties of existence."

"I'll try not to use it again in your presence, father," I said gravely, wondering if there had ever been such a stodgy man.

I returned to my quarters, smiling at the final go-around with the pater. I don't know why I derived such pleasure from stirring him up occasionally. Perhaps I fancied I was saving him from priggery. Or it may have been a very small declaration of independence. I was well aware that only my father's largess enabled me to drive a snazzy sports car, dine young ladies, and wear silk briefs emblazoned with images of *Tyrannosaurus rex*. But even the lowliest of serfs must assert himself now and then. (But not too often and not too loudly.)

I phoned Jennifer Towley, and to my horror I woke her up.

"I'm sorry," I said. "I really am. Please go back to sleep and I'll call you tomorrow."

"No, no," she said. "I'm awake now, and I haven't spoken to you in ages."

"I know," I said. "Last Friday."

"Well, it *seems* like ages. That was a fabulous indoor picnic."

"The best," I agreed. "How about dinner tomorrow night?"

Pause. Then: "Oh, I can't, Archy. I'm so sorry, but I promised a client she could come over and we'd select a fabric for her Louis Something-or-other love seat."

"What a shame," I said. "May I call you late tomorrow? Maybe you'll feel like dashing out to the Pelican Club for some light refreshment."

"Well . . ." she said doubtfully, "all right. I should be finished around nine o'clock."

"I'll call," I promised. "Sleep well, dear."

"You, too," she said. This time she didn't add "darling."

She hung up, and I sat there with the dead phone in my hand, the green-eyed monster gnawing away like a mastiff. But after a while I convinced myself she really was going to spend the evening with a client discussing the upholstering of a love seat.

Did you say you had a bridge in Brooklyn for sale?

15

After my father departed for work on Tuesday morning, I moved into his study and sat in his swivel chair behind the big, leather-topped desk, feeling like a pretender to the throne.

My first phone call was to Mrs. Trelawney. She gave me the number and time of arrival of Miss Roberta Wolfson's flight from Boston. Also the number of the suite at The Breakers that had been reserved for her use.

"Those charges will be billed directly to the company," Mrs. T. explained. "If there are any other expenses, pay with your plastic and add them to your next swindle sheet, Mr. Dillinger."

"Bless you," I said. "I'll call you from Saint-Tropez."

I then phoned The Breakers and arranged for fresh flowers to be placed in the suite reserved for Miss Roberta Wolfson. I figured if Lady Horowitz was picking up the tab, there was no point in scrimping.

My third call was to Sgt. Al Rogoff, who sounded a mite churlish. From this I deduced he had not yet had his fourth cup of black coffee that morning.

"Anything new on Wolfson?" I asked.

"Some," he admitted. "The doc says he drowned all right, but he was also full of painkillers. Heavy stuff. You told me you thought he was sick. So maybe he went for a midnight swim and couldn't fight the undertow. The doc says that stuff he was taking could have weakened him."

"It didn't happen that way, Al," I said. "Wolfson couldn't swim; the DuPeys told me that. He'd never take a dip, especially in the ocean at night."

"Then it was definitely suicide," he said.

"Don't be so sure," I said. "What about those bruises?"

"The ME says they could have been made in the surf, the body banging around on the bottom."

"And those scratches that looked as if they had been made by fingernails?"

"There was stuff under Wolfson's nails indicating he might have scratched himself, clawing at his chest in that last minute."

"Did you search the beach?"

"Of course we searched the beach," he said crossly. "A mile north and a mile south. Nothing. By the way, Wolfson had a surgical scar on his abdomen. The doc estimates the operation was done about a year ago. He couldn't say positively what it was for."

"But Wolfson did drown?"

"Sure he did."

"Al, he could have been dragged underwater."

"What's with you, Archy?" he demanded. "You're really trying to pin a killing on the chauffeur, aren't you? What have you got against the guy?"

"He carries a cigarette behind his ear."

Al roared. "And if he used a salad fork on steak, you'd want me to charge him with rape—right?"

"Bodin's a nogoodnik; I just know it."

"Beautiful. I go to my boss and tell him I'm arresting Bodin for first-degree murder because Archibald McNally says he's a nogoodnik. Will you please, for God's sake, talk sense."

"I guess you're right," I said, sighing. "Maybe I'm just trying to inject a little drama into this."

"You're trying to complex things up is what you're doing. As usual."

I told him the next of kin, a sister, Miss Roberta Wolfson, would be arriving at the Palm Beach International Airport a few minutes after noon. I would meet her and drive her to The Breakers. After she was settled, I would deliver her to police headquarters.

"She wants to claim the body and personal effects," I said. "All right?"

"I guess so," Rogoff said slowly. "What time do you figure to be here?"

"Around two o'clock or so."

"Well, if I'm not here I'll have a policewoman standing by to help her with the paperwork."

"And you'll release the body?"

"I'll have to get the okay of the brass on that, but I don't think they'll have any objections. I still think it was a suicide, and that's the way I'm going to sell it."

"Al, it's just the ambiguities that bother me."

"Ambiguities?" he said. "The story of my life. If you can't live with them, you really should be in another line of business."

My final phone call was to the airline Roberta Wolfson was flying. They reported her flight was on time. I had heard that fairy tale before but thought it better to hie myself out to the airport in case they were correct this time.

I had dressed as conservatively as my wardrobe allowed: navy tropical worsted suit, white shirt, maroon tie, black penny loafers. I even tucked a chaste white handkerchief into the breast pocket of my jacket. My sartorially retarded father would have been proud.

I thought the screaming-red Miata might be a bit too animated for the occasion, so I drove to the office garage and switched to the black Ford Escort, a sober and more suitable vehicle. I needn't have bothered. Roberta Wolfson turned out to be such a self-possessed woman I think she would have been at ease if I had shown up in a two-horse chariot.

I arrived at the airport in time to see her plane taxi up to the gate. I waited for the passengers to disembark, and hoped it would not be necessary to have her paged. It wasn't. All the others were wearing T-shirts and Bermuda shorts, and then appeared this tall, stately lady, confident and aloof.

I recognized immediately the image she called to mind: the Gibson Girl. She had that forthright, don't-give-a-damn air about her, and I could see her in an ankle-length middy dress, wearing a boater, or, in the evening, a wine-dark velvet gown by Worth. Her posture was splendid, her features pleasantly horsey. She was carrying an enormous tapestry portmanteau with bone handles.

I approached her. "Miss Roberta Wolfson?" I inquired.

She looked down at me from what seemed a tremendous height. "I am," she said in a deep, resonant voice. "And who might you be, young man?"

"Archibald McNally," I said. "I believe you spoke to my father yesterday." I proffered a business card.

She was wearing a lightweight tweed suit (with sensible brogues), and beneath the jacket was a frilly jabot with a high neckband of lace. Pearls, of course. Dangling from her wishbone was a pince-nez framed in gold wire. It was attached to a fine chain released from a spring-loaded disk pinned to her bodice. I had never seen a gadget like that before.

She used the small spectacles to examine my card. "McNally and Son, Attorney-at-Law," she read aloud. She caught it at once. "Two individuals, one attorney. Which one?"

"My father," I said. She requested no further explanation, for which I was grateful. "Miss Wolfson, may I express the condolences of my father and myself on the passing of your brother."

"Thank you," she said. "I appreciate your solicitude. May we go now?"

I attempted to relieve her of that huge bag she was schlepping but she would not relinquish it. So we marched out to the Escort. She made no comment on the heat, which was a welcome surprise. Usually, arriving visitors say, "Oof!"

As we drove eastward she looked about with interest. "Is this Palm Beach?"

"West Palm Beach, ma'am."

"Oh? Tell me something about the geography of this region."

"We are in Palm Beach County. This is the City of West Palm Beach on the mainland. We are going to the island of Palm Beach, which is separated from the United States by Lake Worth, crossed by bridges. There is also North Palm Beach and South Palm Beach."

"But no East Palm Beach?"

"No, ma'am. Only the Atlantic Ocean."

"And what is the population of Palm Beach?"

"At this time of year, the off-season? About fifteen thousand."

"And during the season?"

"Zillions," I said, and she laughed for the first time, a nice, throaty sound.

We didn't speak again until we arrived at The Breakers, that glorious remembrance of things past. I left the car with the parking valet and accompanied Miss Wolfson to the desk, where she registered.

"Ma'am," I said, "would you care for lunch before I drive you to make arrangements?"

"Thank you," she said, "but I had breakfast on the plane."

"Surely not very satisfying," I commented.

She looked at me as if I were demented. "Naturally I brought my own food," she said. "Yogurt, a cucumber sandwich, and herbal tea which the attendant was kind enough to heat for me. What I would enjoy, after I freshen up, is a glass of sherry."

"Of course," I said. "Suppose you meet me at the Alcazar Lounge. Any of the hotel employees will be happy to direct you there."

"I shan't be long," she said and left, still lugging that huge satchel, which she refused to yield to the bellhop.

I headed for the Alcazar and took a seat at the bar. I ordered a vodka-tonic with lime from a comely barmaid who provided a bowl of salted nuts to keep my thirst at a fever pitch. I had scarcely finished half my drink when Miss Wolfson appeared. I hopped from the barstool and asked if she'd care to sit at a table.

"No, this is fine," she said and swung aboard the stool next to mine with a practiced movement that made me think barstools were not an unfamiliar perch.

She ordered a glass of Harvey's Bristol Cream, took a small sip when it was served, and nodded approvingly. She gazed out the picture windows at the sea but said nothing about the beauty of the scene. After all, she was from Boston and had seen the Atlantic Ocean before—but not framed in palm trees.

"Miss Wolfson," I said, "are your accommodations satisfactory?"

"Perfectly," she said, then turned to gaze at me. "The flowers are lovely. Were they your idea?"

I nodded.

"You are a very *nice* young man," she said, and took another sip of sherry.

"Thank you," I said, happy this proper Bostonian didn't

251

think me a rube. "Ma'am, I'd like to ask you a question about your brother, but if speaking of him will distress you, I'll say nothing more."

"It won't distress me, I assure you. You knew Angus?"

"Briefly. I found much to admire in him."

She gave me a look of wry amusement. "And much *not* to admire, I'm sure. My brother was a difficult man to know, Mr. McNally. He would be the last to deny it. What did you wish to ask?"

"Was he ill?"

"Mortally. A year ago he was operated on for prostatic cancer. They were unable to remove the entire malignancy because of possible damage to other organs. But the doctors felt that with radiation and chemotherapy his life could be extended. But Angus refused treatment."

I was aghast. "Why on earth did he do that?"

"He said it would be undignified. He said he had enjoyed a good life, and it would be humiliating to attempt to prolong it for a few miserable years by intrusive medical means. He was told that without treatment he would probably be dead within a year. He accepted that."

I finished my drink in two gulps and ordered another, and a second sherry for Miss Wolfson. She made no demur.

"Yes," I said, "that sounds like him. He was a brave man."

"Was he?" his sister said. "Possibly. He was certainly a foolish man because he had discounted the pain, although the doctors had warned him. The pain became fierce. Drugs lost their effectiveness until I believe he was constantly in agony."

"It must have been difficult for you," I offered.

She made the tiniest of shrugs. "I nursed both parents through lingering illnesses. I have become inured to suffering."

I didn't believe her for a minute. Here was a woman, I thought, hanging on to sanity with a slippery grasp. And perhaps a bottle of sherry.

"So his suicide really didn't come as a shock?" I asked.

"Not at all," she said, and now she was sipping her wine at a faster pace. "I was surprised it hadn't come sooner. He spoke of it frequently. I didn't attempt to dissuade him. He would have considered it effrontery on my part. As he said, who can feel another's pain?"

"Who indeed," I said. "Miss Wolfson, I think we better finish up and be on our way. I took the liberty of telling the authorities we'd meet them at about two o'clock."

"Of course," she said, draining her glass. "Mustn't be late for a funeral. Correct, young man?"

She was absolutely steady on her feet, her speech was still crisp and well-articulated, she gave no evidence whatsoever of having downed two glasses of sherry in a short time. We drove to police headquarters slowly while I pointed out places of interest and she asked lucid and intelligent questions. I hoped that when I was her age I might hold my schnapps as well as she did her wine.

"By the way," I mentioned as casually as I could, "Lady Horowitz has volunteered to pay the expenses of your trip to Palm Beach as well as all funeral costs."

I saw her expression change ever so slightly, and I had the feeling this news had come as a great relief. But the only words she uttered were a murmured, "Dreadful woman."

Sgt. Rogoff was not there to greet us, but we were met by a policewoman I knew, Tweeny Alvarez. (That really was her name.) Like Consuela Garcia, she was a Marielito, but about ten years older and fifty pounds heavier than Connie. Al couldn't have picked a better woman to assist Roberta Wolfson, for Tweeny was soft-spoken and *muy simpática.*

"You're in good hands," I assured Miss Wolfson. "We call Officer Alvarez 'Mother Tweeny.'"

"Oh you!" the policewoman said.

"I'm going back to my office now," I said. "Please call when you're ready to return to the hotel or if you need transportation elsewhere. I'm at your service."

"You're very kind," Miss Wolfson said faintly.

To tell you the truth, I was relieved to be absent while she viewed the remains and made arrangements for her brother to be cremated. This line of duty was not my cup of tea at all. I shine at games of darts and an occasional chugalug contest. But funeral stuff is not exactly a bowl of cherries, is it?

When I arrived back at my office, I found a note taped to my telephone handset. Printed on the top was the legend: *From the desk of Evelyn Sharif.* Notepaper like that sends me right up the wall. I mean, desks can't communicate. People, not furniture, write notes. I once contemplated having a notepad printed up that read: *From the bed of Archy McNally.* I didn't do it, of course. The senior would have taken a very dim view.

But the message itself raised my spirits. It stated: "Got an answer to your inquiry. Stop by. Evelyn."

I clattered down the back stairwell to the real estate department where I found Mrs. Sharif performing some sort of esoteric exercise.

"It strengthens the abdominal muscles," she informed me.

"Keep it up," I said, "and you're liable to drop the twins on your fax machine. What did you find out about that property down at Manalapan?"

"Interesting story," she said. She moved behind her desk and began flipping through a sheaf of notes. "A retired couple came down from Michigan in the late fifties. They had plenty of loot. He had made a fortune manufacturing portable johns, those white closets you see at construction sites. They bought the raw land between the ocean and the lake and had a house built. They called it Hillcrest."

"Love it," I said. "There isn't a hill worth the name within five hundred miles."

"Well, that's what they called it," Evelyn went on. "The man died in the seventies, and the widow died about three years ago. They had two grown children who inherited a bundle. But the house and acreage were left to the woman's alma mater, a small college in Ohio. The children are contesting the bequest. They want that house as a place to vacation with *their* children. So the whole question of ownership has been tied up in litigation for almost three years, and since no one was living there, the place went to rack and ruin. But about a year ago, all the litigants agreed that until the court case is decided, the house could be rented on a month-to-month basis. And that's the way things stand now."

"What's the monthly rental?" I asked.

"Five thousand."

"Cheap enough for that location," I said, "even though the place looks like a slum. Who's renting it now—did you find out?"

She consulted her notes again. "A single woman," she reported. "Clara Bodkin. Does the name mean anything to you?"

"Negative," I lied smoothly. "Never heard it before. Thank you, Evelyn; you did your usual bang-up job."

"Be sure and tell daddy," she said, only half-joking.

"I will," I promised.

I didn't laugh until I returned to my office. Clara Bodkin indeed! Lady Cynthia's maid could no more afford five thousand a month than I could. It seemed obvious to me that Horowitz herself had rented the empty house under her maid's name. A silly deception—but then she hadn't expected a Nosy Parker like me to come sniffing around.

It was at least ninety minutes before Roberta Wolfson phoned. I spent the time recalling everything she had told me of her brother's illness and mental state. I came to the regretful conclusion that I had been wrong and Al Rogoff right. Angus Wolfson did take that determined hike into the sea voluntarily. And, under the circumstances, it was difficult to blame him. People usually say of suicides, "He (or she) had so much to live for." That could hardly be said of Angus Wolfson.

After his sister phoned, I drove back to police headquarters. But this time, knowing the lady's temperament,
I took the Miata. Miss Wolfson was waiting for me on the
sidewalk and looked at my racing sloop with some amaze-
ment.

"Do you own two cars, Mr. McNally?" she asked.

"No, ma'am," I said, "the black Escort is a company car.
This one is mine."

"Very nice," she said, and slid into the bucket seat with
no trouble. She was an agile spinster.

On the trip back to The Breakers, I said, "I hope things
went as well as could be expected."

"Oh yes," she replied. "Everyone was most cooperative. And you were quite right about Officer Alvarez.
That woman is a treasure. She insisted on driving me to
a funeral home. In a police car—can you imagine!" Unexpectedly she laughed. "I must tell my friends in Boston
that I arrived at a mortuary in a police car! They'll be
much amused."

"Yes," I said.

"In any event," she continued, "everything has been
settled. Angus will be cremated tonight, and his ashes will
be delivered to me at the hotel tomorrow."

She said this as matter-of-factly as if she was expecting a
package from Saks. It has been my experience that women
are much more capable of coping with illness and death
than men. But I must say Roberta Wolfson's attitude approached a sangfroid I found somewhat off-putting.

We pulled up in front of the hotel.

"Ma'am," I said, "would you care to have dinner with
me this evening?"

"Oh no," she said. "Thank you but no. It's been a long, tiring day, and I believe I shall have dinner brought to my suite, write a few letters, and then go to bed."

"As you wish," I said. "Suppose I come by at one o'clock tomorrow to drive you to the airport."

"One o'clock?" she said. "But my plane leaves at two."

"An hour will be plenty of time to get to the airport."

"I prefer to leave nothing to chance," she said severely. "I suggest we leave at noon."

"All right," I agreed. "No problem. I'll be here at noon."

She put a soft hand on my arm. "I do appreciate all you're doing for me, young man."

"I'm happy to be of help. Sleep well."

"I intend to," she said firmly, and I had no doubt she would.

I drove home, had my swim, and after dinner that night I delivered a condensed report of my day's activities to father. He listened closely and then went into a study— not *his* study but a brown study.

Finally he asked, "Then you are satisfied that Angus Wolfson committed suicide?"

"Yes, sir."

"I'm glad to hear you say that, Archy. There has been quite enough gossip and rumormongering as it is. How is Miss Wolfson taking all this?"

"Remarkably well," I said. "A very staunch lady."

"Yes," he said. "I phoned a friend in Boston to inquire about her family. She comes of good stock. Blood will tell."

And he was absolutely serious. Can you believe it? This from a man whose own father was Ready Freddy McNally, the most roguish second banana on the Minsky burlesque circuit!

I went to my aerie to scribble in my journal for an hour until it came time to call Jennifer Towley. The events of the day had been wearing, no doubt about it, and I was sorely in need of a spot of R&R. I had a vision of a delightfully mellow evening with Jennifer.

But it was not to be. She came on the phone distraught and close to tears.

"What's wrong?" I asked.

"Nothing," she said. "Or everything. I don't think I better see you tonight, Archy."

"I think you should," I told her. "I listen very well."

She didn't speak for a beat or two, then said, "Yes, I need a sympathetic ear. Will you come soon?"

"On my way," I said.

I sped to her home wondering at the cause of her distress. Something to do with her ex-husband, I had no doubt. The realization was growing that she was as hooked as he—but on different habits, of course.

I knew at once she had been weeping: eyes swollen, tissues crumpled in one fist. We sat in her shadowed living room, leaning toward each other. She offered no refreshment, and I wanted none. I was unsettled by her mood and appearance. I had always thought of her as a marmoreal woman, and learning a statue could suffer and cry was a stun.

"I lied to you," she said at once. "I didn't spend the

259

evening with a client. I had dinner with Tom and then we came back here for a talk. Just a talk. He left only a few minutes before you called."

"He wants you to take him back?"

"Yes," she said. "Archy, he cried, he actually cried. He sat where you're sitting right now and sobbed his heart out."

"And you did, too," I pointed out. "A weepy meeting."

"I didn't cry until he left," she said. "I was proud of keeping control while he was here. But then, after he was gone, I lost it. Dear God, I don't know what to do."

"Jennifer, I can't tell you. No one can. It's your decision to make; you know that. Did he say anything about his gambling?"

"He said he hadn't made a bet since he was released. He was so forceful about it, so anxious that I believe him."

"And do you?" I asked, realizing that Thomas Bingham was indeed a demon salesman.

"I don't know what to believe. My mind is going like a Cuisinart. Everything is all chopped up. Archy, help me."

I reached forward to take her hand. I knew then I was in a no-win situation. If I told her that her ex was gambling as heavily as ever, she'd probably ditch him—but I don't believe she'd ever forgive me. She'd think I had acted out of jealousy (a reasonable assumption) and that I had robbed her of possible happiness. For what had I to offer?

And if I didn't tell her that Bingham was still a compulsive gambler, she would probably take him back and her nightmare would begin again.

If I had drawn up that blueprint of my moral code, as

I intended to do but hadn't, I doubt if it would have given me any clues on how to resolve this dilemma.

It had been a gloom-and-doom kind of day, and I was stressed-out, physically and emotionally.

"Jennifer," I said finally, "I can't help you. I wish I could, but I can't. It's a heavy, heavy decision. It's your life and you must decide how you want to live it."

She tried to smile. "Yes," she said, "of course. I'm acting like a simpleton. It's my responsibility, isn't it?"

"It surely is," I said. "And you must decide on the basis of what is best for you. Be completely selfish. Don't even consider the wants and needs of Thomas Bingham or Archibald McNally or anyone else. Decide what you really want—and then go for it."

She nodded dumbly and I stood up to leave.

There was just nothing more to say.

Hours later, lying awake in bed, waiting for sleep that was slow in coming, I suddenly remembered that weeks ago Lady Cynthia and Connie Garcia had warned me that Jennifer Towley would be a problem. How did they know? How do women *know*?

16

I recall those last few days of the Inverted Jenny Case as taking on a momentum of their own, whirling toward a resolution no one could have predicted, least of all me. Events governed, and neither I nor the police nor anyone else could control them. We all had to sit back, as it were, and watch with fascination as everything unraveled.

It began with a telephone call from Sgt. Al Rogoff on Wednesday morning while I was having a late breakfast in the kitchen with Jamie Olson. It was then about ten o'clock.

"Hiya, sherlock," Al said, sounding jubilant. "I think we fell in the crapper and came up with a box lunch. I just got a call from a stamp dealer up in Stuart. Early this morning, right after he opened, a bimbo breezes in and tries to sell him a block of four Inverted Jenny stamps. He described her as young, blond, pretty, with all her doo-dads in place. Sounds like our pigeon—right?"

"Right," I said. "It's got to be Sylvia."

"She's asking a half-million for the stamps. The dealer told her he'd have to see if he could raise the cash and to come back around noon. She said she would. I've got a car on the way with three heavies. I just changed to civvies, and I'm taking off. I'll play a clerk in the store, and the others will be backup. How's it sound?"

"Sounds great. Good hunting, Al, and give me a call as soon as it goes down. Or I'll call you."

"Sure thing," he said. "I've got something else to tell you, but it can wait. Keep your fingers crossed, old buddy."

He hung up, and I finished my breakfast. Rogoff was a brainy cop, and I was confident he'd grab Sylvia in the act of trying to sell stolen property. But then what? Would she talk or wouldn't she? I reckoned she had enough street smarts to cut a deal with the SA. I hoped she'd rat on Kenneth Bodin in return for a slap on the wrist.

I had time to kill before heading for The Breakers to pick up Roberta Wolfson, so I wandered out to the greenhouse, where my mother was wielding a watering can and humming contentedly.

"Good morning, Mrs. McNally," I said. "Sorry I overslept. Did you rest well?"

"Splendidly," she said, "just splendidly. Now give me a kiss."

She held up her tilted face, and I kissed a velvety cheek.

"There!" she said, beaming. "Now wasn't that nice? I always say one should start the day with a kiss. It brings good luck."

I laughed. "Who told you that?"

"No one," she said, giggling. "I made it up. Archy, are you still seeing that nice lady you told us about, the interior decorator?"

"She's really an antique dealer, and yes, I'm still seeing her."

"Oh my," mother said, going on with her sprinkling chores. "Is it serious?"

"It is with me," I said without thinking, and then suddenly realized it was the truth: I *was* serious about Jennifer. "But I'm not sure how she feels about me. She's also seeing someone else."

"Have you told her how you feel?"

"No, not really."

Mother stopped her work and turned to face me. "Oh Archy," she said sorrowfully, "if you are serious about her, you should tell her. Isn't there some saying about unspoken love?"

"Love unspoken is love denied," I said.

"Exactly," mother said, nodding. "Who said that?"

"I did," I said, "just now. You're not the only one who can make things up."

"Well, it's completely true. You simply *must* tell her how you feel."

"You really think so?"

"Absolutely," she said firmly. "If you don't, you'll lose her."

"You're probably right," I said. "I'll think about it. Thank you for the advice."

"That's what mothers are for," she called gaily after me.

I did think about it—thought of what a dunce I had been not to have realized it myself. A sincere, passionate avowal of love, followed by a marriage proposal, might very well solve Jennifer's problem and my dilemma.

There was only one thing wrong with that scenario: I wasn't sure I was up to it. I did love the woman, I really did, but I could not decide if I wanted to give up the life of a happy rake for a till-death-do-us-part intimacy with one woman. After all, I was the man whose pals had considered nominating for a Nobel Prize in philandering.

In other words, I dithered.

When I arrived at the hotel, Miss Wolfson was waiting outside, still clutching that gigantic catchall. I slung the bag into the back of the Miata, and she made a little yip of protest.

"Do be careful," she said. "Angus is in there."

"What?" I said.

"Well, I thought the urns at the funeral parlor were in dreadful taste. Angus would be horrified. I'll find something more suitable in Boston."

"I see," I said. "And what are the ashes in now?"

"A mason jar," she said. "May we go?"

She was unusually voluble on the ride to the airport. She said it was her first trip to semitropical climes, and the weather, flora, the dress of inhabitants, and the colors of homes were all new to her. I found her comments quite discerning. She even noted the pace at which pedestrians moved along the streets, so much slower than in the northeast.

We arrived at the airport in plenty of time, of course. We checked the gate number of her departing flight, then found a nearby cocktail lounge for a farewell drink. I had a vodka gimlet, and she ordered a glass of her usual.

"Thank you," she said, "and please thank your father for me. You both have been enormously supportive. I also intend to write a letter to the mayor of Palm Beach commending the diligence and sympathetic assistance of Officer Tweeny Alvarez."

"That's very kind of you," I said. "I'm sure the letter will go into her file and may help her career."

"I believe in giving credit where credit is due," she said sternly. "I also have no hesitation in voicing criticism when it is deserved."

I could believe that. I would not care to be a waiter who served lukewarm coffee to Miss Roberta Wolfson.

"I am only sorry," I said, "that we have met under such unhappy circumstances. What a shame that your brother's holiday ended as it did."

I swear that's all I said. I wasn't prying. I didn't intend to ask any questions. I was merely trying to express a conventional sentiment to an elderly lady who, despite her courage, had obviously been under a strain. But what my comment elicited was a shocker.

"Oh, Angus wasn't on a holiday," she said casually. "It was a business trip."

That was my first alert, and no way was I going to let it pass without learning more.

"A business trip?" I said, trying to be as casual as she.

"Yes," she said, sipping her wine primly. "Lady Horowitz had sent him some old stamps she owned. She wanted Angus to have an appraisal made in Boston. I believe she intended to find a private buyer or put them up for auction."

"Oh?" I said. "And did Angus have an appraisal made?"

"He didn't have to. My brother was an antiquarian and very talented in his field. He saw at once that the stamps Lady Horowitz had sent him were counterfeit."

"Goodness gracious," I said.

"Oh yes," she said, nodding. "They were forgeries and completely worthless except as a curiosity. Whatever profit that unpleasant woman expected simply went out the window."

She uttered those words with some satisfaction, and I saw that even to a proper Bostonian revenge is sweet.

"So Angus came down here to return the stamps to Lady Horowitz and give her the bad news?"

"May I have another glass of sherry?" she asked.

"Of course," I said, "and I shall keep you company."

We didn't speak until our fresh drinks were served, and then she took up her tale again. Please don't blame her for speaking so openly to a comparative stranger. She did so innocently; she had no knowledge of the theft of the Inverted Jennies and knew nothing of the roles her brother had played and I was playing.

"Yes, he came to Palm Beach to return the stamps and tell Lady Horowitz they were fakes. Poor Angus was in a funk. He knew that woman's terrible temper and feared she would blame the messenger for the news."

"Yes," I said, "I can imagine."

"However," she went on, "everything turned out well. Angus phoned me a few days after he arrived down here. He said he had already told Lady Horowitz her stamps were forgeries, and she had accepted it with little fuss. In fact, Angus said, she had invited him to stay a week or two and try to recover his strength."

"Thoughtful of her," I said. "Miss Wolfson, I believe I just heard the first call for your flight. Perhaps we should move to the boarding gate."

"Let's," she said, and polished off her second sherry like a longshoreman downing a boilermaker.

"Ma'am," I said, "I travel occasionally and may get to Boston one day. If I do, may I call you? Perhaps we might have dinner together?"

"I'd enjoy that," she said, smiling. "You are a very dear young man." And she swooped to kiss my cheek.

I watched her stalk away from me, indomitable, head high and spine straight. And still lugging that enormous bag containing Angus Wolfson in a mason jar.

I drove back to the McNally Building in a broody mood, trying to assimilate what Roberta Wolfson had told me. Vital stuff. Some of those oddly shaped pieces of a jigsaw puzzle that had frustrated me for so long were beginning to snap together with an almost audible *click*. The picture they formed was not a sweet one— not something you'd care to hang over your mantel in place of that Day-Glo portrait of Elvis Presley on black velvet.

The problem with the scenario I envisioned was that, if proved valid, it was going to leave my father with an ethical dilemma as racking as the one I faced with Jennifer Towley. The future did not promise a million laughs for the McNallys, *père et fils*.

I arrived back in my office to find a message from Al Rogoff asking that I call him immediately. That I hastily did without even removing my panama.

"Got her!" he said exultantly. "Full name: Sylvia Montgrift. And guess what? She's got a sheet. Did you know that?"

"No," I lied, remorseful that I had neglected to tell him. "What's she done?"

"She was running an unlicensed massage parlor. The West Palm Beach cops closed her down. She got off with a suspended sentence. Hey, she's a real looker."

"Not my type," I said. "I suspect she may be a closet Hegelian. Al, may I come over?"

"Sure," he said, "but don't butt in. We're waiting for her lawyer to show up. Lou Everton. You know him?"

"Of course," I said. "Six-stroke handicap. He's skunked me many times. And he's also a very smart apple."

"He is that," Al agreed, "but I've worked with him before, and he'll cut a deal. He likes fast-food justice as much as I do. He'll tell her to talk and cop a plea. If he doesn't we've got a problem. I mean what if she insists she found the stamps in the gutter. Then where are we? No way can we prove burglary."

"Well, if she talks," I said, "there's something I'd like you to ask her. I'm on my way."

The last thing in the world I wanted was a confrontation with Sylvia but, as we all know, fate delights in the unexpected rabbit punch.

I got over to headquarters and found Rogoff in the corridor chewing on a cold cigar.

"Where is she?" I asked.

"Right now? In the john. Tweeny is with her to make sure she doesn't climb out the window."

"How did the bust go?"

"Like silk," he said. "She showed up with the stamps

at the Stuart dealer a few minutes after twelve. I flashed my tin and grabbed her. That was it. No muss, no fuss."

"Did she say anything?"

"Yeah, she said, 'Shit.' "

"Where are the stamps now?"

"We've got them. Crazy little things. I've contacted a retired professor in Lantana who's supposed to be a hot-shot on questionable documents. He's going to take a look—at no cost to the county."

At that moment Sylvia came out of the loo, Tweeny clasping her by the elbow, and they walked toward us.

She took one look at me and gasped, "Dooley! What are you doing here? Have you been arrested, too?"

But Officer Alvarez escorted her firmly into the sergeant's office and closed the door.

Al looked at me. "Dooley?" he said. "What's that all about? You haven't been getting any massages lately, have you?"

"No, no," I said hurriedly. "It's just the name I used at Delray Beach."

"Dooley," Rogoff repeated, grinning. "Beautiful."

"Listen, Al," I said, "if Lou Everton lets you question her in his presence, ask her if Thomas Bingham was in on the deal."

"Who?"

"Thomas Bingham."

"Who the hell is he?"

"A friend of Bodin's. He might have been part of it."

The sergeant looked at me reproachfully. "Have you been holding out on me again?"

"Al," I said, "this Bingham is just a walk-on. He might or might not be involved. Ask Sylvia, will you?"

"All right," he said grudgingly, "I'll ask."

I saw Lou Everton coming through the front door and I went out the back, leaving the attorney and the police officer to their merry-go-round. I climbed into the Miata and headed for the Horowitz spread. I planned to do something exceedingly imprudent. If I had told Rogoff, he'd have had the pip.

Cut-rate justice, also known as plea bargaining, is as prevalent in Palm Beach as it is in Manhattan and everywhere else. Everton and the State Attorney would have disagreements, many arguments, and perhaps many drinks together. Eventually a quid pro quo would be forged: what Sylvia would deliver and the punishment she would receive.

My only problem with it, at the moment, was that it would take time. And there was always the possibility, of course, that Sylvia would refuse to peach on her muscleman. I could not believe loyalty was her strong suit, but I didn't want to chance it.

So I drove beachward, too impatient to wait for a done deal. When I banged the brass clapper on the Horowitz front door, Mrs. Marsden opened it and didn't even say hello.

"I hear the cops got the stamps back," she said immediately, "and arrested the one who took them."

"Mrs. Marsden," I said, "the grapevine in this town is astounding. NASA should latch on to it, and they'd be hearing from Jupiter in seconds."

"Then it's true?"

I nodded. "The Inverted Jennies have been recovered. Happy?"

"Very," she said, and led the way into the cavernous foyer.

I saw a set of matched luggage piled near the door. "Someone leaving?" I asked.

"Miss Stanescu," the housekeeper said. "That Ken Bodin is going to drive her to the airport."

"Then perhaps I'll see her for a moment and say good-bye, if I may."

"Sure, Mr. McNally," she said. "She's upstairs." Then she suddenly grabbed my arm tightly and looked directly into my eyes. "Is everything going to be all right?" she demanded.

"Everything is going to be fine," I assured her, wishing I was telling the truth. "Exactly the way it was before all this started."

She nodded, but I knew she didn't believe me. Things were never going to be exactly as they were before. But Mrs. Marsden had learned to endure change. I was still learning.

The door to Gina Stanescu's bedroom was ajar, and I glimpsed her packing toiletries into a small leather case. I rapped on the doorjamb. She looked up, smiled, beckoned me in.

"I understand you're departing, Miss Stanescu," I said, "and just wanted to stop by to say farewell."

"Not farewell," she said. "I prefer the German *auf Wiedersehen,* which means until we see each other again."

"Of course," I said, "and I hope we do. I wish you a safe and pleasant trip home, and Miss Stanescu—" I paused,

273

not wanting to make a promise I might not be able to fulfill.

"Yes?" she said.

"Keep believing in a miracle," I said. "Even a very small one."

"A petite miracle?" she said, her smile strained.

"Sometimes they do happen, you know."

We shook hands and parted. It was my day for good-byes. And I feared more lay ahead.

I went downstairs and out to the garage. Kenneth Bodin was wiping down the Rolls as gently as a groom might curry a derby winner. He turned around at my approach, glanced at me, went back to his task. His jacket was off, and in his form-fitting T-shirt with cutoff sleeves, he looked a proper anthropoid.

"I hear the cops got the stamps back," he said, still turned away from me.

"That's right," I said breezily, "and they nabbed the woman who was trying to sell them. Sylvia Something-or-other. They're questioning her now. They don't think she was the thief, so they want to know who gave her the stamps to sell. I understand she's singing like a bird."

I had him pegged as a rash lad with nothing but ozone in his bean. I wanted to provoke him into doing something exceptionally stupid, such as taking off as soon as possible: added evidence of his guilt. In his lavender Volkswagen Beetle, he wouldn't be hard to trace. And if I had any luck at all, he might even resist arrest. That would put the frosting on the éclair.

"How did the cops happen to catch her?" he asked in a low voice, buffing the brightwork on the Rolls.

"Oh, that was my doing," I boasted, hoping my brag-gadocio would infuriate him even more. "I told the police to alert every stamp dealer in South Florida. I figured the guy who had the Inverted Jennies was such a complete moron he'd try to convert them to cash locally as quickly as possible. And that's exactly what the imbecile did."

Then, reckoning I had pushed him as hard and as far as I could, I called cheerily, "See you around," and wandered away, well-pleased with myself.

I know it wasn't Confucius, but it may have been Charlie Chan who said, "Man who pats himself on back risks broken arm." Right on, Charlie.

I stopped at Consuela Garcia's office simply because I wanted to see her again. She always gave me a lift. If Jennifer Towley was a marmoreal woman, Connie was a warm, fuzzy type, as comforting as a teddy bear. Also, she laughed at my jokes: an admirable quality.

She was on the phone, as usual, and waved me to a chair.

"Yes, that is correct," she said in the cold, official tone she used when speaking to reporters. "We understand the police have recovered the stolen stamps. Naturally, Lady Horowitz is delighted. Yes, you may quote me on that. Thank you *so* much for calling."

She hung up and grinned at me. "All's well that ends well," she said.

"Uh-huh," I said. "Also, look before you leap versus nothing ventured, nothing gained—and where does that leave anyone? How did Lady C. *really* take the news that her stamps had been found?"

Connie frowned. "Not with wild jubilation," she said.

"In fact, I thought she was shook. She snapped, 'Who the hell cares?' A typical Horowitz performance. Listen, Archy, if the stamps are back, it's obvious she didn't use them to pay off a blackmailer. So your whole plot is demolished—right?"

"Wrong," I said. "There's still plenty of evidence that someone is leaning on her."

"And you're going to keep following her?"

"Whenever I can. It's in her own interest, Connie," I added earnestly. "She may be in danger."

She looked at me suspiciously—but what could I tell her? That I was still curious as to why Lady Horowitz wouldn't reveal her whereabouts at the time Bela Rubik was killed? If I told Connie that, she'd tell me to get lost and probably never give me another *Hola!* as long as she lived.

"Well . . ." she said hesitantly, "just one more time. And that's it. She's taking off tomorrow at one o'clock; destination unknown—to me at least."

"Thanks, Connie," I said gratefully. "I do appreciate it. You seeing anyone regularly these days?"

"Yeah," she said in a doleful voice, "my periodontist—and that's not much fun. In case you ever break up with the Towley woman, I'm footloose and fancy-free."

"I'll remember that," I said. "One more question: The DuPeys have left and Gina Stanescu is on her way; when are Doris and Harry Smythe going to brighten Florida by their absence?"

"Those dolts?" Connie said, then giggled. "Listen to this, Archy: The madam knows a retired British couple who live in Kashmir. They're both horse people, and for years they've been trying to get Lady Horowitz to sell them a Remington bronze she owns. She's refused up to now, but yesterday she phoned and said she'd sell them the bronze, but they have to invite the Smythes for a two-week stay, beginning immediately. So on Monday, Doris and Harry take off for Kashmir."

I laughed. "Lady Cynthia is a professional conniver."

"Oh sure," Connie said. "And you don't do too badly in that game yourself. You're not in her class, of course, but I'd rank you as a talented amateur."

I was wounded. If she had known what I was planning, she'd have upped my rating. Semipro, at least.

17

On Thursday morning, after breakfast, I futzed around in my nest for an hour or so. I was in a smug mood, believing I was going to set the world aright and eventually get my eternal reward in Heaven. Or, prior to that, a weekend in Paris. Surely there was *some* way I would be honored for the good deeds I intended.

I decided I would motor at a leisurely pace to the office and spend time bringing my swindle sheet up-to-date. I had tabs for all those sherries consumed by Roberta Wolfson, plus bills for money spent on gas and the rental of the Ford Escort. And, of course, a few expenses of a more creative nature.

I came out into a nothing morning, the sky as colorless as a slate pavement, the air unmoving and damp. It was bloody hot, and a nice, refreshing cloudburst would have been a blessing. But that leaden sky offered no shadows and no hope. All in all, a grayish scene—enough to depress the most chipper of do-gooders and make one ponder the value of crawling out of bed on such a blah day.

I drove into town, thinking of how I might improve my shadowing technique when, later in the day, I tailed Lady Horowitz to her rendezvous at that dump near Manalapan, if that was again her destination. I decided to transfer my zoom binoculars from the glove compartment of the Miata to that of the Escort. I do believe I had some foolish notion of doing Inspector Clouseau: skulking in the underbrush and spying like a demented birdwatcher.

I pulled into the underground garage and glanced at the glassed booth inhabited by Herb, the security guard. I waved but drew no response; he had his nose deep in a paperback book, probably *Fun with Piranha.* I stopped alongside the Escort and climbed out of the Miata. As I did, Kenneth Bodin straightened up from behind a parked car and advanced toward me with a ferocious grin.

He was wearing jeans and a black leather jacket decorated with steel studs. In this heat? I wondered. Does vanity have no bounds? But then his hands came from behind his back, and I saw he was grasping a baseball bat. It was either a Louisville Slugger or a reasonable facsimile thereof.

He stepped close to me, drew back his shillelagh, and swung. I suspect he had eyes for my kidneys.

He was large and muscular. But dreadfully slow. The bat came around no faster than one of Jennifer Towley's tennis serves. I leaned back, his cudgel whooshed past. I moved in, shifted my weight to my left leg, and kicked him briskly in the *cojones*. I am really not as effete as I may have given you reason to believe.

Bodin dropped the bat and fell to the concrete floor of the garage. He curled up into the fetal position, clutching the family jewels and making "Gaugh, gaugh, gaugh" sounds of pain and anguish I found delectable.

"Herb!" I shouted as loudly as I could, and the guard came lumbering.

He looked down at the writhing man on the floor, saw the baseball bat nearby and then, with some difficulty, drew his long-barreled Colt from a dogleg holster. He pointed his ancient weapon at Bodin.

"You okay, Mr. McNally?" he asked anxiously.

"I'm fine, thank you."

The chauffeur looked up at me accusingly. "You hurt me," he said between moans.

"That was my intention, old boy," I said. "Herb, I'm going to call the cops. You stay here and keep your howitzer trained on this vicious assassin."

"If he gives me trouble," the guard said, "where should I shoot him?"

"Oh, I don't know," I said. "I imagine the kneecaps would be satisfactory."

"Small target," Herb said doubtfully. "How about the brisket?"

Kenneth Bodin groaned.

Sgt. Al Rogoff was in, which was a relief. I explained briefly what had just happened.

"You all right?" he asked.

"A mite shook," I admitted. "But no injuries."

"Good," Al said. "You saved us a lot of trouble. We've

been looking for that guy since last night. Sylvia talked. Hang on to him; I'll be right over."

Herb and I stood alongside the recumbent assailant, observing his physical agony with some satisfaction. We discussed how he had managed to sneak into the garage. The guard decided it had probably happened while he was on one of his periodic security tours throughout the building. I didn't argue. Herb was a nice enough chap but about as alert as a stuffed sailfish.

Two police cars came rolling down the ramp, sirens dying away to a whisper. Sgt. Rogoff got out of the lead car and two stalwarts exited from the second. All three officers joined us in a circle about the fallen chauffeur, watched his contortions, and listened to his laments.

"What happened to him?" Al asked me.

"Testicular trauma," I reported. "Resulting from a sudden, sharp blow from the toe of an Allen-Edmonds cordovan kiltie, size ten-and-a-half."

The sergeant grinned at me. "Thank you, Bruce Lee," he said. "Dollars to doughnuts he sues you for causing him emotional distress." He turned to the other two cops. "Get the bum out of here. Take him in and book him."

"What's the charge?" one of the officers asked.

"Impersonating a human being," Rogoff said. "Just sit on him till I get back."

We watched as the two hauled Bodin to his feet and dragged him to their car. He was crouched over, feet dragging, and he was still whimpering.

"Thank you, Herb," I said to the guard. "You behaved splendidly."

"Happy to be of service, Mr. McNally," he said. I believe that if he had a forelock he'd have tugged it.

Al and I sat in the Miata. He lighted a cigar and I an English Oval.

"The girlfriend talked?" I asked him.

"Yep," he said, "but didn't spill much we didn't already know. She claims Bodin gave her the stamps to sell."

"Did she know they were counterfeit?"

"She didn't say, and I didn't tell her. But I think both she and Bodin thought they were the real thing. By the way, those Inverted Jennies *are* fakes, according to the expert we called in."

"Did Sylvia tell you where Bodin got the stamps?"

"She says they were given to him by an elderly man who was staying at the Horowitz place. That would be Angus Wolfson—right? The deal was that Bodin was to get ten percent of whatever he sold the stamps for."

"You're telling me Wolfson lifted the Inverted Jennies?"

Rogoff laughed. "I know what a keen student of human nature you are, Dr. Freud. You already told me it would be completely out of character for Wolfson to steal anything. But in this case I'm afraid you have more crap than a Christmas goose. Wolfson pinched them, all right."

I thought he had it wrong, but I wasn't about to tell him that.

"Speaking of Wolfson," I said, "I hereby confess I was mistaken about his death. You were right; it was suicide."

He looked at me quizzically. "What convinced you?"

I related what Roberta Wolfson had told me about her

brother's terminal illness, his refusal to undergo radiation and chemotherapy, the constant pain he suffered.

"Reason enough to shuffle off this mortal coil," I said.

"Uh-huh," the sergeant agreed. "But he had another reason."

"Oh? And what, pray, was that?"

"Guilt. While we had Wolfson's body, we took his fingerprints. They matched up pretty well with the prints we took off the glass paperweight that caved in Bela Rubik's skull."

I hadn't anticipated that, but I wasn't shocked. The stamp dealer would have unlocked his door for Angus Wolfson, but not for a bruiser like Bodin.

"You're sure, Al?" I asked. "About the prints, I mean."

"Seventy-five percent sure," he said, "and that's good enough for me. This case is officially closed as far as I'm concerned. Rubik's homicide is cleared. The killer, Wolfson, is dead. Lady Horowitz gets her fake stamps back. Maybe Bodin will do some time, but it won't be heavy. Now the PBPD can concentrate on important investigations, like who's been swiping kiwis and mangoes from the local Publix."

"Do me a favor," I urged. "Tell me how you figure the whole thing went down. From the top."

"Sure," he said genially, puffing away at his cigar. "Wolfson had a lot of medical expenses, and he wasn't a rich man to begin with. As you would say, he was getting a bit hairy about the heels. So he swiped the Inverted Jennies, figuring Lady Horowitz had zillions and could stand the loss. Then he does something stupid: he tries to peddle the stamps to a local dealer. I figure he left the

Inverted Jennies with Bela Rubik, giving him a chance to make an appraisal. Rubik already had the stamps when you first met him.

"Wolfson goes back to Rubik's shop on the afternoon the yacht cruise was canceled. Rubik tells him his stamps are forgeries. Knowing Rubik, I'd guess he got hot about it and threatened to tell the police that Wolfson was trying to sell counterfeits. Wolfson panicked and bounced the paperweight off Rubik's skull. I don't think he meant to kill him. Just knock him out, get his stamps back, and lam out of there.

"Then Wolfson reads the local papers and realizes he's a murderer. Also, he hasn't got the wheels to get around to other dealers, and he knows he's getting weaker. So he makes a deal with Kenneth Bodin, a money-hungry sleaze if ever I saw one. The chauffeur agrees to sell the stamps for a piece of the take. It's the best Wolfson can do. The rest you know. How does it sound?"

"Did Wolfson tell Bodin the stamps were forgeries?"

"No. Bodin and Sylvia thought they were handling something of genuine value. Look, maybe even Wolfson himself thought Rubik was wrong, and that he had stolen the real thing. Well?"

He had some of it right, but not all of it. But I had no desire to point out his errors; most of the mistakes were due to information I had not revealed. If Al's scenario was going to be the official version, so be it. It hurt no one. And I had other fish to fry.

"Yes," I said, "everything sounds plausible."

"No objections?"

I knew he'd be suspicious of total agreement. "A few

minor questions," I said. "Like Wolfson's relations with Kenneth Bodin. I think he really had a thing for that mug."

"Sure he did," Rogoff said, nodding. "That's why he picked him as an accomplice and offered a piece of the pie. Hoping for favors in return."

"Yes," I said, "that makes sense. Was Bela Rubik really going to turn Wolfson in?"

Al gave me a twisted smile. "Only after he examined the stamps and saw they were counterfeit. If they had been legit, Rubik would have made a deal even if he knew they were stolen property. He was that kind of guy."

I sighed. "Well, I guess that wraps it up. Sorry to have dumped this mess in your lap, sarge."

"It comes with the territory," he said shrugging. "I'm leaving it to your father to tell Lady Horowitz her stamps are forgeries. I'm taking a week of my vacation starting tomorrow. I want to be out of town when she hears that. There goes her insurance claim!"

I laughed along with him. He got out of the Miata, lifted a hand in farewell, and strutted toward his squad car, still chewing on his cigar. I had a brief pang at not revealing the whole truth, but consoled myself with the thought that it would cause no loss to him and might benefit others.

Suddenly I yelled, "Al!" I got out of the car and trotted after him. "Did you remember to ask Sylvia about Thomas Bingham?"

"I remembered," he said. "She claims Bingham is a

drinking buddy but knows nothing about the Inverted Jennies. Disappointed?"

"Yes," I admitted. "Will you ask Kenneth Bodin?"

"You never give up, do you? All right, I'll ask the master criminal."

He got in his car and backed up the ramp. I glanced at my watch, muttered a curse (mild), and hurriedly transferred my binoculars to the Ford Escort. Then I set out in pursuit of Lady Cynthia Horowitz.

I just did make it. I was heading north on Ocean Boulevard and as I passed the Horowitz gate I saw the Jaguar heading out, Lady C. at the wheel. She turned south, and I averted my head as I went by, hoping she wouldn't spot me.

I continued north for about fifty yards, made a screaming U-turn, and set off after the Jag. It wasn't difficult to keep it in view; the madam's hair was bound with a fuchsia scarf, and on that dreary day it glowed like a beacon in the fog. Traffic was light, and I thought it wise to hang back. I knew where she was going; there was no need to tailgate.

Sure enough, she eventually turned into the driveway of Hillcrest. I drove slowly past and was delighted with what I saw: The Jaguar had not been driven around to the rear of the house, facing Lake Worth, but was parked in front on the brick driveway. Lady Cynthia was out of the car and just entering the front door as I went by.

I drove back and forth a few times, considering my options. Not many. My notion of lurking in the underbrush with my binocs was nutsy. The homes north and

287

south of Hillcrest were occupied, and if I was seen slink-
ing furtively about, the gendarmes would have been sum-
moned for sure.

I finally decided my original fear of looking like a demented bird-watcher wasn't such a bad idea after all. So
I drove north to a small area that provided parking space
for beachgoers. I locked the car and hiked back to Hillcrest, the binoculars hanging from a strap around my
neck. Occasionally I paused to use the glasses, scanning all
the foliage in sight and sometimes peering eastward, pre-
tending I was looking for seabirds. What a performance!
Stanislavsky would have been proud of me.

I came to Hillcrest and casually examined the surrounding trees. In the process, of course, I took a good look at
the house itself. The Jaguar was still parked in front, but
I could discern no action, no one moving behind any of
the windows.

I continued my impersonation of a birder, parading
north and south, using my binoculars until my eyes began
to ache. I wondered how long I would have to maintain
this charade—an hour? Two? Three? It turned out to be
exactly one hour and forty-three minutes. I knew; I
looked at my watch often enough.

I was then south of the house, standing on the eastern
verge of the corniche, partially concealed by a row of
big-leafed sea grapes. I was watching the house when the
front door opened and Lady Cynthia came out. Her hair
was unbound; she was carrying the fuchsia scarf. She
paused on the portico, turned around, and spoke animat-
edly through the opened door to someone within.

I used the zoom lever and adjusted the focus to bring

her into closer and sharper view. She was laughing, shaking her head prettily, and once she pouted and stamped her foot. I saw her reach out to the person within.

"Come out, come out, whoever you are," I sang aloud. And then, unsure of my grammar, I sang again, "Come out, come out, whomever you are."

Out he came.

My father.

I watched, glasses trembling slightly, as the two clutched in a fervid embrace and kissed. That was no fond and friendly farewell between attorney and client; it was an impassioned grapple and the osculation seemed to go on forever.

What may amuse you (or possibly not) was that my most convulsive shock came from seeing my father tieless, vestless, and coatless. Prescott McNally in shirtsleeves at midday! I can't tell you how *lubricious* it made the scene appear to me.

Finally they drew regretfully apart. Lady Horowitz went down to the Jaguar and gave father a final wave. He waved in return, went back into the house, closed the door.

She turned northward, heading for home. I sprinted for my Escort. I figured my father had parked the Lexus behind the house and soon he too would be heading north. I wanted to be long gone before that.

I drove back to the McNally Building at an illegal speed. I couldn't seem to cease brooding on the fact that I had recently witnessed two illicit embraces: Angus Wolfson–Kenneth Bodin and Cynthia Horowitz–Prescott McNally. Sgt. Al Rogoff had claimed that things happened in threes. I had a gloomy premonition of who might be involved in the third doomed embrace.

I pulled into the garage, and Herb hustled over before I got out of the Escort.

"You feeling all right, Mr. McNally?" he inquired anxiously.

"Tiptop, thank you, Herb," I said. "Couldn't be better."

"Glad to hear it," he said. "I should have shot that no-good. He deserved it."

He went back to his booth, still muttering. I climbed into the Miata and lighted a cigarette. I was pleased to see my hands were steady. I slumped, put my head back, stared at the sprinkler pipes overhead. I found that my reactions to what I had just seen took the form of an interrogation, a personal Q-and-A.

"What amazes you most about the affair?"

"The logistics involved. The planning! They had to find a place relatively safe from public view and gossip. So she rented an old house away from Palm Beach. And he arranged his absences from the office so no one might suspect."

"Why didn't you? After all, on at least two occasions he was not available at the same time she was mysteriously gone. And he was quick to correct you when you thought her older than she really is."

"That's right, but it just never occurred to me that they might be having a thing."

"Why not? Because of their age?"

"Don't be ridiculous. You think there's a certain cutoff point in everyone's life when the dreams end? They never end. (I hope.)"

"How long do you think their liaison has been going on?"

"Oh, I don't know. Probably for months. I could find out by asking Evelyn Sharif how long Hillcrest has been rented. But what's the point of that?"

"Be honest: You really have a grudging admiration for your father, don't you?"

"I guess I do."

"Because you have inherited his propensities?"

"The turd never falls far from the bird."

"Are you going to tell him you know?"

"Good God, no! I happen to love the man, despite his faults. Maybe because of them. He and I have a very special relationship."

"What you just learned—won't that end the relationship?"

"Of course not. It may change it, but it'll remain special."

"Will you tell your mother?"

"She already knows. I realize that now, from things she's said recently. How do women *know?* But for all her nuttiness, she has a wisdom that eclipses mine. And she has love and patience. She knows he'll come back to her."

"So you're not going to tell anyone?"

"I didn't say that."

The questioning ended, and I knew what I was going to do. I derived a sour amusement from recalling the scam I had used with Connie Garcia—that someone was blackmailing Lady Horowitz. It had turned out to be true. The blackmailer was me.

I drove out into a mizzle that swaddled the world in a foggy mist the color of old pewter. It wasn't drizzling hard enough to put on the Miata's hat, but I could see moisture collecting in pearls on windshield and hood. It became thicker as I neared the coast, and when I turned into the Horowitz driveway I headed directly for the garage to get my baby under cover.

I entered the house through the back door, and in the kitchen I found chef Jean Cuvier and maid Clara Bodkin sparking up a storm. I think they were just trying to have a few laughs on a dismal day, but then again their flirting had an edge to it as if their banter might become serious at any moment.

"Ar-chay," he said, "tell this innocent she must not be frightened of life, of love, of passion, of romance."

"And you tell this whale I know all about those things," she said, "and I am very particular as to whom I bestow my favors."

I admired her syntax but held up my hands in protest. "Peace," I said. "I refuse to enlist in this war. I just stopped by to have a word with the lady of the manor. Is she receiving?"

"I don't know," Clara said doubtfully. "I think she's having a bath. Why don't you go up and knock on her door."

"So I shall," I said. "And try to be kind to each other, children. What the world needs is love, sweet love."

"Just what I've been telling her," the fat chef said.

I went out into the hallway and then up that magnificent staircase to the second floor. I rapped gently on the door of Lady Cynthia's suite.

"Who?" she called.

"Archy McNally. May I speak to you for a moment?"

"Come on in."

If it was pewter outside, her chambers were silver, steamy and scented from her bath. The windows were open, but the voile curtains were unmoving. I could hear the susurrus of a rain that was now falling steadily. There was an ambience of quiet intimacy: a secret place fragrant and isolated. What a setting for an orgy à deux! But it was not to be.

She was reclining on the chaise lounge, clad in a peignoir of some diaphanous stuff. It revealed almost as much as it concealed. One leg was extended, bare foot on the floor. Very naked, that leg.

"Pull up a seat," she said languidly. And so I did, moving a velvet-covered ottoman into a position where I could face her directly.

"What's on your mind, lad?" she asked.

"At the moment?" I said. "You. I'm sure you've heard by now that the police have recovered your counterfeit stamps."

"My *what?*" she cried, shock and horror oozing from every pore.

"Oh, cut the crap," I said as roughly as I could. "You're a great actress but not *that* great. You've known for weeks that your Inverted Jennies were fakes. Even while you were bugging my father to file an insurance claim for their loss. It's called fraud, dearie."

She didn't order me from the premises immediately. Just turned her head to stare out the window where the rain was still whispering.

"What a filthy thing to say," she said. "But it's only your mad fancy. You have no proof, of course."

"Of course I do. You sent the stamps to Boston, asking Angus Wolfson to have an appraisal made. You had read of that block of four Inverted Jennies being auctioned for a million bucks and you thought: Why not mine? But then Wolfson came to Palm Beach to return your stamps and tell you they were forgeries."

"You're just guessing," she said. "That's not proof. Go away."

"Do you take me for an idiot?" I said. "I am not an idiot. Wolfson told his sister your Inverted Jennies were fakes. Roberta Wolfson does not harbor a favorable opinion of you, m'lady. If push comes to shove, she'll be happy to testify that her brother had determined the stamps were forgeries. And further, he phoned her a few days after he arrived here and told her that he had informed you the stamps were worthless and that you had accepted the bad news calmly."

(I didn't bother mentioning that Roberta Wolfson's testimony, being hearsay, would probably be inadmissible in any litigation.)

Lady C. turned her head to face me. "He told his sister that? What a fool the man was!"

That angered me but I tried to suppress it. "I wondered why you would try to pull an insurance swindle; your net worth is hardly a secret. Then I remembered something you told me during our first conversation. You said, 'When it comes to money, enough is never enough.' Greedy, greedy, greedy."

"You know what happens to greedy people?" she

asked. "They get rich. Tell me something, lad. Suppose you discovered that a twenty-dollar bill you were trying to spend was counterfeit. Would you turn it in and take the loss as the law requires, or would you try to pass it along to someone else? Be honest."

I didn't answer that. I was afraid to. "That's twenty dollars," I blustered. "We're talking half a million."

"No difference," she said. "You'd try to pass it along; you know you would. That's all I was trying to do. Why should I take the bite? The insurance company has oodles of cash. They should; my premiums are high enough."

"But it would be outright fraud," I argued.

"Fraud-schmaud," she said, shrugging. "What's the big deal?"

Her imperturbability disconcerted me. I had expected heated denials. But she was admitting everything with a cool calmness I found maddening.

"Here's what I think happened," I said, trying to regain the initiative. "Wolfson told you the stamps were fakes. It took you perhaps three seconds to cook up the idea of a fake theft and then file an insurance claim. Wolfson didn't steal the stamps; you *gave* them to him and told him to get rid of them. Instead, he decided to try to sell them."

"I told you the man was a fool. He turned out to be greedier than I."

"Not so," I said. "He didn't want the money for himself. He wanted to assist your daughter, Gina Stanescu. She told him her orphanage was in trouble, and he hoped to help by selling the stamps to some unsuspecting dealer and turn over the proceeds to Gina. He was as larcenous as you, but from somewhat purer motives."

295

Finally, she was rattled. "Gina's orphanage needs money? Why didn't she tell me?"

"She's frightened of you."

Her eyes went wide. "Why would anyone be frightened of me?"

"Maybe because they think you're a barracuda with bucks—a scary combination. Anyway, she told Angus, and he was determined to try to help her. What did he have to lose—he knew he was dying. But the stamps were recognized as counterfeits by dealers, so Angus was never able to deliver. Now, of course, the police think he was the thief."

That naked leg slipped a little farther from its filmy covering.

"Do they?" she said. "And I suppose you're going to tell them the truth."

"Not necessarily," I said.

She was amused. "Oh-ho," she said, "it's deal-making time, is it? All right, lad, what's your proposition?"

"Two things," I said. "First of all, give Gina Stanescu enough money to save her orphanage."

"Done," she said promptly. "No problem. I can deduct it. What's the second thing?"

"Give my father the brush."

I had been wrong about her thespian talents; she *was* a great actress. The most her features revealed was a small ironic smile.

"My, my," she said, "you *do* get around, don't you?"

I nodded. "Dump him, Lady Cynthia," I urged. "You know how little it means to you; just a pleasant interlude a few afternoons a week. You'll find someone else."

"And your father?"

"He'll probably suffer awhile—he deserves to—but eventually he'll recover. Losing you will not prove a mortal wound."

"It never does," she said, the paradigmatic woman of the world. "Although there was a young man in Venice who died after I kicked him out. But he was tubercular."

Then she was quiet a moment, and I could almost hear the IBM AS/400 in her gourd go into action, circuits clicking.

"And if I don't?" she asked finally.

"If you don't," I said, "I'd feel myself duty-bound to inform my father that you were attempting grand larceny by fraud and deception."

She was absolutely expressionless. "And I suppose the word would get around."

"I'd make sure it did," I said.

"You know, lad," she said, " 'devious' isn't the word for you. You're a solid-gold sonofabitch."

"I try," I said modestly.

Then there was a long silence while she pondered the risk-benefit ratio. I wondered if she had learned mulling from Prescott McNally.

"Your father is something of a bore," she said at last.

"I know," I agreed.

"Do you?" she challenged. "Do you also know that he happens to be a very passionate lover?"

"How on earth would I know that?" I asked, reasonably enough.

She made up her mind. "Very well," she said. "I'll give your father a pink slip. And in return, you'll keep your mouth shut and go along with the police opinion that Angus was the thief?"

"Agreed."

"And that I was unaware the Inverted Jennies were fakes?"

"Again, agreed."

"Then consider the contract signed," she said. She lifted her arms above her head in a long, lazy stretch. The peignoir gaped open, a little. It could have been an accident. She looked at me thoughtfully. "Now I must find a replacement," she said.

"Not me," I said hastily.

"You have no desire to pinch-hit for your father?"

"I think not. I am not in your class, Lady Cynthia. A lightweight wouldn't go up against a heavyweight, would he?"

She grinned at me. "I don't weigh so much," she said. "I wouldn't hurt you."

"Tell it to the Marines," I jeered.

"I have," she said. "Frequently. Are we still friends, lad?"

"I devoutly hope so," I said, and meant it. "I assure you that I have the greatest respect and admiration for you."

That naked leg inched toward total revelation.

"Well, it's a start," she said, and I got out of there as fast as I could.

I drove home in the rain, not caring that both I and the Miata were getting drenched. Along the way I sang, "Yes! We Have No Bananas," never wondering why it gave me so much pleasure to finagle other people's lives.

18

But by Friday morning, my joy had evaporated, and I suffered a seizure of introspection and doubt.

For the sake of McNally family unity I had brought an end to my father's fling with Lady Horowitz. I termed it a "fling," but what if it had been the world's greatest romance since Bonnie and Clyde? In other words, I had played God—and who gave me the divine right to manipulate people? I was, I acknowledged briefly, guilty of hubris, if not chutzpah.

It was a miserable day, and I had a mood to match. Flurries of rain came boiling in from the sea, and if there was a sun up there behind that fat mattress of clouds, there was no sign of it.

After breakfast I went back to my haven and mooched around awhile. I decided there was no point in driving to the office and sitting in my cramped sepulcher creating fictions for my expense account. I came to the conclusion that to prevent a fatal onslaught of the megrims I absolutely had to see Jennifer Towley, for lunch or dinner. That wonderful woman would elevate my spirits and give me a reason to go on breathing.

I called instanter and was rewarded with a mechanical message from her answering machine, followed by that damnable *beep*. I recited a piteous statement, pleading with her to call me as soon as possible. After I hung up, I wondered where on earth she might be so early in the morning on such a venomous day.

I told myself that jealous suspicion was an unworthy emotion, perilously close to paranoia, and I would have none of it. So I resolutely set to work on my journal, completing the record of the Inverted Jenny Case. I didn't call Jennifer again for almost an hour. Then, hoping she might have returned home and neglected to replay her messages, I phoned. All I got for my effort was the machine. Derisive, that gadget. I hung up, gnashing my molars in frustration.

Finally, close to noon, my phone rang and I leaped for it.

"Hello!" I caroled as melodiously as I could.

"What the hell?" Sgt. Rogoff said. "Are you yodeling or something?"

"Hello, Al," I said sheepishly. "Just clearing my throat. What did you learn from Kenneth Bodin?"

"His story's the same as Sylvia's. He says Wolfson gave him the stamps to sell and promised him a ten percent commission."

"Did Wolfson tell him how he got the stamps?"

"He claims Wolfson said Lady Horowitz gave them to him to sell."

"Do you believe that?"

"You think I was born yesterday? Of course not. The chauffeur knew damned well that Wolfson had stolen the stamps. But he didn't care; he just wanted a piece of the action."

"Uh-huh. What are you going to do with Sylvia and Bodin?"

"Not a whole hell of a lot. You want to bring assault charges against him?"

"Good lord, no!"

"Then I think we'll just tell him to take his playmate and vamoose. If we get both of them out of the county I'll be satisfied. By the way, he says Thomas Bingham wasn't connected with the caper in any way, shape, or form. I think he's telling the truth."

"Probably," I said. "It was just a wacko idea. Thanks for checking it out. So you're closing the file?"

"You betcha. I gave the stamps to your father. He's going to return them to Lady Horowitz this afternoon and tell her they're fakes. Lucky man!"

"Yes," I said, "isn't he. When are you leaving on your vacation?"

"As soon as the rain lets up. And the way it's coming down, that might be next year."

"Where are you going?"

"Lourdes," he said. "My hemorrhoids are killing me."

It was the first laugh I had all day. "Have a jolly time,

Al," I said. "Give me a call when you get back and we'll get hammered at the Pelican Club."

"Will do," he said and hung up.

It wasn't the telephone call I wanted, but it soothed the fantods a bit. I wasn't even depressed to learn that Tom Bingham had nothing to do with the theft of the Inverted Jennies. Thinking he might be involved had been a selfish wish on my part, very unprofessional, and I was happy to have been proved wrong before I made an even bigger ass of myself.

I went down for lunch about twelve-thirty. Mother and I sat in the kitchen with the Olsons, and we all shared a big salad bowl of shrimp, crabmeat, and chunks of sautéed scallops, along with a basket of garlic toast. Mother was in a frolicsome mood and drank a glass of sauterne. No use telling her it was the wrong wine; it was right for her.

I went back upstairs, looked out the window, and saw that the rain was slackening. But the sky was still clotted with clouds, and there was grumbling eastward and an occasional flash of lightning. It was not a scene to photograph for South Florida's tourist brochures.

I resolved to call Jennifer one more time, just once, and if she wasn't in, the solution was simple: I'd just slit my wrists. Her phone rang twice, was grabbed up, and she said breathlessly, "Hello?"

"Archy," I said. "What have you been doing wandering about in this monsoon?"

"Oh dear," she said, "please let me call you back. I just got in, I'm soaked and have to change. Are you home or at the office?"

"Home."

302

"Call you back in five minutes," she said and hung up.
It was more like fifteen minutes, but I waited patiently;
I had no choice.

"Listen, Archy," she said, very businesslike, "I know it's
a rotten day, but I must talk to you. Could you come
over?"

"Now?" I said. "This minute? How about dinner tonight?"

"No," she said firmly, "no dinner. I'd like to speak to
you as soon as possible."

"Is something wrong?"

"Archy," she said, voice tight, "let's not discuss it on the
phone. Can you or can you not come over now?"

"All right," I said, wondering what the crisis was. "I'll
be there within the hour."

I pulled on a nylon golf jacket and my rainhat. I went
downstairs and found my mother and the Olsons still in
the kitchen, laughing up a storm and sharing a plate of
Ursi's sinful chocolate-chip cookies.

"Mother," I said, "I've got to go out and don't want to
waste time raising the Miata's roof. May I take the station
wagon?"

"In this weather, Archy?" she said. "Whatever for?"

"An errand of mercy," I said.

She looked at me, suddenly worried. "I hope so," she
said. "Of course, take the Ford." She paused. "I'm not
sure about the gas," she said doubtfully. "I think there's
some in the tank. You better check, dear."

"I shall," I promised, leaned to kiss her cheek, and
snaffled two of the cookies.

She was right about the gas; the dial showed less than

a quarter-tank. But the instruments on that antique vehicle had eroded over the years, and I could just as easily be starting out with Full or Empty. I took the chance, comforting myself with the old maxim that God protects fools and drunks.

Despite a few asthmatic coughs and wheezes, the old wood-bodied station wagon behaved admirably and, boasting high clearance, had no trouble navigating the flooded streets en route to Jennifer's home. It had stopped raining, but I was forced to leap a few deep puddles to reach her door. I didn't quite succeed; my Bally loafers were squishing.

Inside, with her permission, I kicked off the shoes and left them in the umbrella drip-pan of her Victorian hall-tree. Then we looked at each other with very small and very tentative smiles. Jennifer was wearing an enormous white terry robe with the crest of a Monte Carlo hotel— the same cover-up she had donned the first night we were intimate.

I wanted desperately to believe that a good omen, but her troubled appearance and agitated manner convinced me that there was to be no instant replay of our initial frolic. She led the way into her living room which, on the mournful day, seemed overdecorated with lumpish furniture and ancient tchochkes.

Before I quite knew what was happening, she had me seated and had thrust into my hand a double old-fashioned glass that appeared to contain ice cubes and a half-pint of vodka.

"What?" I said, looking at that enormous drink. "No blindfold and a final cigarette?"

"Archy," she said without preliminaries, still standing, "I can't see you anymore."

"Oh?" I said. "Ah?" Not a brilliant reply, I admit, but I felt as if I had just been examined by a doctor who then asked, "Mr. McNally, do you have a will?" I mean I was devastated. Talk about utterly; I was about as utter as one could get. "Why not?" I finally managed to croak.

"I've been seeing Tom Bingham. I was with him last night and all this morning. I promised to remarry him."

I stared at her. Suddenly I realized her distress was not caused by vacillation about her decision; she was concerned that I might be hurt. Very kind of her, of course, but at the moment the last thing in the world I wanted was her solicitude.

"Jennifer," I said as steadily as I could, "why are you going to remarry Bingham?"

She lifted her chin a trifle, once more the cool, complete woman she had been. "Because I love him," she said.

If there was an answer to that, I didn't know it. I have a smattering of several foreign languages, but love isn't one of them. When it comes to the tender passion, I am a total illiterate.

"You've given it a lot of thought?" I asked.

"Too much," she said. "It's had me in a whirl. And then I realized thought and logic can take you only so far. But if they don't make you happy, what's the point? Then it's time to trust feelings and faith. I must do what my heart tells me to do." Then, recognizing the soap-opera triteness of that final remark, she tried a timid smile.

"Jennifer, you told me that life with him was a nightmare."

"It was. But I'm willing to gamble that he's changed. He promised he has, that those years in prison have made him a different man."

"You're willing to gamble?" I said, trying not to sound bitter and not succeeding. "You're doing exactly what you divorced him for—compulsive betting."

I think she was startled, as if the idea had never occurred to her.

"I suppose you're right," she said. "But even if you are, it doesn't affect the way I *feel*. And if he begins gambling again, so be it. But this time I'll stick by him. I *must*. Don't you see that, Archy? Because life without him is simply unendurable to me. Empty and without meaning. I know that now."

Jennifer turned upside down! I listened to that brainy, self-possessed woman calmly tell me what she intended to do, and I couldn't believe it. Where was her dignity, her self-esteem, her independence, her keen, cutting intelligence? All demolished by the virus of love for which, I had heard, there was no known cure.

There were things I could have told her. I could have said that while we all may be created equal in the sight of God and the law, people have varying degrees of quality. There are such things as ambition, emotional depth, and intellectual curiosity. Some are born with these attributes, some acquire them over a lifetime, some remain deficient until they are deep-sixed. But we are *not* all equal.

Thomas Bingham, it seemed to me, was a lowlife, simply not in Jennifer's class. And if that is *snobisme,* I plead guilty. Yet here was this high-quality woman willing— nay, eager!—to sacrifice her life for a low-quality man. I swear I shall never fully comprehend the vagaries of human nature.

I didn't say all that to Jennifer, of course. Nor did I tell her that Bingham had already resumed his old habits. I realized that to her, at the moment, the truth was inconsequential. I merely put my drink aside without having tasted a sip, for which I was justly proud. I stood and in ringing tones I wished Jennifer Towley all the happiness in the world and thanked her for all the joy she had given me.

Tears came to her eyes, she rushed to hug me, kiss my lips, touch my cheek.

The third embrace.

I reclaimed my sodden shoes, golf jacket, rainhat, and exchanged a final wave with Jennifer. What brave smilers we were! Then I drove home, determinedly *not* brooding on what my dithering had cost me. But I could almost hear my mother's sorrowful, "Oh, Archy!"

I stopped on the way to fill up the Ford's tank (it had been half-full—or half-empty, depending on your philosophy) and then continued on to the McNally stage set. I garaged the station wagon and entered the house through the kitchen. Ursi was at the range stirring up a bouillabaisse in a big cast-iron pot.

"Smells sensational," I told her, "but unfortunately I'm going out for dinner tonight. If there's any left, will you put it aside for my breakfast tomorrow?"

"Sure," she said, seeing nothing unusual in someone wishing to breakfast on her fish stew.

"And also, Ursi," I added, "please tell my parents I'm feeling a bit mangy and won't be able to join them for the cocktail hour."

She stopped stirring the stew to look at me. "If you say so," she said.

I trudged up to my hideout, feeling like something the cat dragged in. After I locked the door, which I rarely do, I stripped off damp jacket and hat, kicked off soaked loafers, peeled away sodden socks. Then I lay on my bed and wished for a quick and merciful quietus. People would cluck and say, "He died of unrequited love," little knowing that I had croaked from chronic indecision.

I am, as you may have gathered, a social creature. I can endure solitude, but it is not my favorite indoor sport. I much prefer the company of others and the reassurance that they are as screwed-up as I.

But now, staring at a water stain on the ceiling that resembled a map of Iceland, I told myself there was a lot to be said for solitude. I told myself that man is not necessarily a herd animal. I told myself that self-knowledge is of utmost importance and can only be achieved through solitary rumination, a sort of mental cud-chewing.

I therefore resolved to spend a quiet, reflective evening alone, pondering my shortcomings and planning how I might become a kinder, gentler human being.

After about twenty minutes of this mawkish self-flagellation, I decided the hell with it and spake aloud Popeye's admirable dictum: "I yam what I yam." Invigorated, I rose and poured myself a very small marc. Then, in honor of Jennifer Towley, I put on a tape of Frank Sinatra singing "It Was a Very Good Year." I needed to hear it. His reading of that line ". . . and it came undone" is the perfect elegy for a lost love.

I played more Sinatra, and Billie Holiday, Bessie Smith, early Bing Crosby ("Just a Gigolo"), and Ella Fitzgerald singing Cole Porter. Then I listened to my favorite ballad-eer: Fred Astaire. Most people remember Astaire as a dancer, but no one has ever done a better vocal of "A Fine Romance."

While I listened to all this swell stuff, I took a shower, washed my hair, trimmed my toenails, and generally reconstructed my life. The cocktail hour passed, the dinner hour passed, and I dressed and was thinking vaguely of making a run to the Pelican Club when I heard a tentative knock on my door. I unlocked to find my father standing on the landing.

I was surprised to see him because he infrequently invaded my sanctum. I stared at him, wondering if his hairy eyebrows and mustache were drooping dispiritedly. They definitely were, I decided—which meant that Lady Horowitz had given him his marching papers. Not as her attorney, as her paramour.

"Ursi said you were feeling peakish," he said. "Mother asked me to stop by. May I come in?"

"Of course," I said. "I was feeling somewhat bilious, but I'm better now."

"Glad to hear it," he said, entering.

He was carrying two crystal wineglasses and an opened bottle of Cockburn's port. Considering what had happened to both of us that afternoon, it seemed a fitting brand.

He poured us full glasses, then took the chair behind

my desk. I sat on the edge of the bed. He offered no toast, nor did I.

"I saw Lady Horowitz today," he said. "I returned the Inverted Jennies and informed her they were counterfeit."

"And how did she take the news?"

"Amazingly well. Disappointed, naturally, but willing to accept the loss. We discussed whether the grantor— her first husband, Max Kirschner—had gulled her or if he himself was swindled when he purchased the stamps in Trieste."

"Perhaps both," I suggested.

Father smiled, stroking his mustache with a knuckle. "That's quite possible, but it's a moot point. I explained to Lady Horowitz that the insurance company will have to be notified, and the forgeries deleted from the list of her insured properties. She asked if that would result in lowered premiums. I advised her not to count on it."

I laughed. "She's wonderful," I said. "Always working the angles."

"Yes," father said. "Archy, I had a very brief conversation with Sergeant Rogoff this morning. Apparently he's leaving on a vacation and was in a hurry to get away. He told me the official police investigation has been terminated and the case closed. Could you fill me in on the details of the affair?"

I recited the police version of what had happened: Angus Wolfson had stolen the Inverted Jennies and had attempted to sell them to Bela Rubik. The dealer had recognized them as forgeries and threatened to call the police. Panicking, Wolfson had struck him down with the paperweight, reclaimed the stamps, and fled.

Realizing he was physically incapable of fencing the stamps himself, Wolfson had recruited Kenneth Bodin, promising the chauffeur ten percent of the sale price. In turn, Bodin had enlisted his girlfriend, Sylvia, to sell the stamps. She had failed in her first attempt in Fort Lauderdale and on her second, in Stuart, she had been arrested.

Meanwhile, in agony from his cancer and suffering from guilt because he had caused the death of Rubik, Wolfson had committed suicide.

"That's how the police have reconstructed it, sir," I finished.

My father looked at me narrowly. "But you don't entirely agree?"

I knew he would never accept my total agreement. "A few things bother me," I admitted. "What was Wolfson's motive for the theft? After all, Lady Cynthia was an old friend. The police say that because of medical expenses he was badly in need of money and didn't want to saddle his sister with debts. I suppose that's possible."

"Of course it is," father said decisively. "It makes perfect sense to me. What else bothers you?"

"The circumstances of Wolfson's suicide. The police ascribe it to his worsening physical condition and remorse for his assault on the stamp dealer. I'm sure those factors were important, but I think there was another reason. I believe he had made a date with Kenneth Bodin for that late hour on the deserted beach, anticipating a sex scene. I think Bodin showed up all right but laughed at the old

311

man and told him that he, Bodin, intended to keep the entire amount of whatever the Inverted Jennies were sold for. And there was nothing Angus could do about it. If he went to the cops, Bodin would name him as the original thief. So Wolfson was left with nothing, his dreams of love shattered, knowing he would soon die, knowing he had killed a man, however inadvertently. So he walked naked into the sea."

Father sipped his wine. "Very imaginative," he pronounced. "But farfetched, don't you think? You have no evidence that what you believe happened between Wolfson and Bodin actually occurred."

"No evidence," I agreed. "It's pure conjecture." My father smiled wanly as he always did when I attempted to use legalese. "But it's not totally improbable," I went on. "It's based on what I know of the personalities and weaknesses of the men involved."

He shook his head doubtfully. "It seems rather odd behavior to me."

I might have pointed out that his shenanigans with Lady Cynthia seemed rather odd behavior to *me*. I didn't, of course, or he'd have had my gizzard.

"But even if you're correct," he continued, "it doesn't affect the final result, does it? The stamps have been recovered, the thief identified, the case officially closed. Perhaps the police solution is not as tidy as you might wish, but these things always have loose ends."

"Yes, sir."

He finished his wine and sat a moment somberly regarding his empty glass. "A messy affair," he said finally. "I find the whole thing distasteful. I've been wondering if it might not be wise to end the relationship of McNally and Son with Lady Horowitz and advise her to seek legal counsel elsewhere. What is your opinion, Archy?"

What a shock that was! I could count on one finger the times he had asked for my opinion on matters affecting the family business.

"Oh, I wouldn't do that, sir," I said. "Admittedly she can be troublesome at times, but so can most of our clients. That's part of our job, is it not, to endure vexations and the sometimes wacky conduct of the people we represent. If they were all rational, intelligent, upright human beings, you and I would probably be chasing ambulances from a one-room office above a delicatessen."

He gave me a wry smile and stood up. "I suspect you're right. Very well, we'll keep Lady Horowitz on our roster of valued and honored clients." He appeared to notice for the first time how I was dressed. "You seem to be dandyish this evening, Archy," he observed. "Planning to visit your young lady?"

"No, sir," I said. "That's ended."

"Oh," he said, somewhat disconcerted, "sorry to hear it. Well, those things happen. But you're going out?"

"I thought I'd stop by the Pelican Club and see if there's any action."

He looked at me closely and said something that touched me: "Yes, I think that would do you good."

Did I catch an echo of envy in his voice? No matter; I felt closer to him at that moment than I had in a long time. Twin losers—right? He took his bottle of port with him when he departed, probably reckoning (correctly) that he needed it more than I.

I spent a few moments inspecting myself in the dresser mirror, wondering if I really did look dandyish. Actually, I decided, I was dressed conservatively. I was doing my silver-white-black bit, quiet but elegant: Ultrasuede jacket, white polo shirt, black silk trousers. I felt perhaps a spot of color would not be amiss so I carefully adjusted my new straw boater. It had a band of cerise silk shantung I thought rather swank.

I went downstairs. On the way, I passed the second-floor sitting room, heard the sound of the television set, and peeked in. My mother and father were seated on the couch watching a rerun of *Mrs. Miniver.* They were holding hands. Domestic bliss? Let's hear a chorus of "Silver Threads Among the Gold."

See what a devious lad with atrophied scruples can accomplish?

The night sky was not entirely clear but the cloud cover was breaking up, and as I tooled the Miata across the Royal Palm Bridge I was happy to see a few pale stars timidly peeping out. Best of all, the air had freshened; a cool sea breeze was blowing at about five knots and boded well for a golf-and-tennis weekend.

It was still relatively early but the Pelican Club was already jumping. It was the TGIF crowd of working stiffs, eager to relax after a week of strenuous labor in banks, boardrooms, and insurance offices. When I entered, heads swiveled in my direction, and my straw sailor with the cerise silk band inspired general hilarity, verging on hysteria. I accepted my friends' derisive gibes with my usual aplomb and headed directly for the bar.

"Good evening, Mr. McNally," Simon Pettibone said. "Nice hat."

"Thank you," I said. "You are a man of refined taste. What do these peasants know of casual elegance? Mr. Pettibone, tonight I yearn for something a bit more exotic than vodka, something that will clutch my palate with both fists and never let go. What do you suggest?"

"A margarita?" he asked.

"Excellent! Heavy on the salt, please."

I removed my hat and placed it on the barstool next to mine. A moment later it was whisked away and I turned to see Consuela Garcia with the boater atop her head, cocked rakishly. She looked charming.

"Archy," she said, "I simply *must* have this hat. What do you want for it?"

"Your innocence."

"Sorry," she said, "I'm broke. As you well know."

"Then have a drink with me," I said, "and the hat's yours."

"That's easy," she said and swung aboard the stool next to me. Just then Mr. Pettibone served my margarita. Connie picked it up immediately and sipped. "Divine," she said. "What are *you* drinking?"

Sighing, I ordered another margarita and turned my attention to Connie. She looked positively ripping. Her long black hair was down, splaying over a crocheted turtleneck of white wool. Her stone-washed jeans were so tight that they may not have been jeans at all but rather a hip-to-ankle tattoo. My new hat was the perfect complement to that costume. What a delicious crumpet she was!

315

"Are you baching it tonight?" I asked her.

"Yes, dammit," she said. "And on top of that, I had to take a cab here. My car's in the garage."

"What's wrong?"

"Faulty alternator."

I looked at her haughtily. "I'm not sure I want to associate with a woman who has a faulty alternator."

"Oh, shut up. Why aren't you squiring Jennifer Towley tonight?"

Just then my margarita arrived. Plenty of salt. I sampled it. Exactly right.

"Jennifer?" I said. "That's over."

"It is?" Connie said. "Want to talk about it?"

"No."

"Okay," she said equably, "we won't. But *please* tell me about Lady Horowitz. You followed her twice. Where did she go?"

"Oh, that was a false alarm. She wasn't being black-mailed."

"I *knew* she wasn't. But what was she up to?"

"You may find this hard to believe, Connie, but she's been doing volunteer work at a shelter for the homeless."

"You're kidding!"

"Scout's honor. That's where she's been going a few times a week. She passes out cheese sandwiches to the hungry and helps make soup."

"What about those regular withdrawals you told me she was making from her bank account?"

"Contributions to the shelter."

"I can't believe it," Connie marveled. "Why didn't she say something about it? It's nothing to be ashamed of."

I shrugged. "I guess she prefers to keep her charity private. Maybe she enjoys her reputation and doesn't want people to know just how sympathetic and generous she is."

"Amazing," Connie said. "And all this time she's been ministering to the needs of the deprived."

"Precisely," I said.

"She really has a heart of gold. I'll bet she's done a lot of good deeds no one knows about."

"I wouldn't be a bit surprised."

We sipped our margaritas thoughtfully. The club was filling up, with more noise, more laughter, a few voices raised in ribald song.

"Archy," Connie said, "I'm hungry. Can we have a hamburger here at the bar?"

"I have a better idea," I said. "It's clearing and there's a nice, fresh breeze. Let's take a drive down the coast. We'll stop at the first interesting place we come to and have dinner, a few drinks, a few giggles. How does that sound?"

"Sensational," she said. "Let's go."

We finished our margaritas. I signed the tab and we went outside, Connie wearing my new hat. It galled me, a little, that it looked better on her than it did on me.

I opened the door of the Miata for her, but she paused and gripped my arm. She looked into my eyes.

She said, "Do you think we might get back together again?"

I said, "One never knows, do one?"